In memory of Mary Castles
A wonderful sister and an irreplaceable friend

THE PLAYERS

In London:

Luke Glass – Head of London's most powerful crime family
Nina Glass – Luke's sister and managing partner of Glass Houses and Construction
Charley Glass – Luke's sister, the face of Lucky Bastards Club
George Ritchie – Luke's right-hand man running the family's business interests south of the river
Felix Corrigan – Gang boss in east London and George Ritchie's second in command
Calum Bishop – Nephew of Kenny Bishop, who runs north London
Stevie D – Ambitious drug dealer
Jocelyn Church – Right-wing political figure and establishment hack
Rupert Neville – Officially known as Lord Holland, an influential political insider

In New Orleans:

Madeline Giordano – Matriarch of the Giordano crime family
Beppe Giordano – Madeline's son
Antoine [Tony] Giordano – Madeline's grandson
Bruno Mura – Tony's lieutenant
Roberta Romano – Paid assassin, also known as La Réponse

PROLOGUE

GARDEN DISTRICT, NEW ORLEANS – LOUISIANA

Martha wasn't a Katrina, but she was still a bitch.

She'd roared off the Gulf like an angry drunk spoiling for trouble and determined to find it, lashing Louisiana with torrential rain leaving lives lost and businesses destroyed in her wake. But in the mansion on St Charles Avenue the naked couple on the bed ignored the 100 mph winds whipping the branches of the live oaks lining the street; they were making their own noise.

The woman straddled the man's broad thighs, throwing her long hair over her shoulders in a show of pleasure that was entirely fake. His lips parted in a satisfied grin as swollen fingers searched for her breasts. She stared into the bloated face beneath her, bit back her disgust and started to ride him in time with the banging of a shutter that had broken free of its mooring somewhere in the house. He believed *he* was dominating *her*. She'd let him: a necessary deception with a monster who'd sanctioned the killing of more people than even he could remember and would send her to the same fate without a moment's hesitation.

In his youth, Beppe Giordano had been slim and athletic. A life of hard partying had thickened his features and left him obese and unrecognisable.

His partner's name was Charlene, younger than him by two and a half decades, and by any standards a beauty. On the wall, her silhouette juddered like an old-time movie coming to the end of the reel as she quickened the pace and he moaned deep in his throat. Egyptian cotton sheets and antique stained-glass lamps were inadequate compensation for sex with this grotesque slug. Yet, it wasn't the worst thing she'd done in her thirty-three years on earth.

The gangster's motive was lust. Hers was survival.

* * *

Giordano's eyes traced the smooth line of Charlene's bare back all the way to her rump, silently congratulating himself. He reached for the scarlet robe on the chair, pulled it round him and lurched unsteadily across the floor.

Other men had vices. Beppe Giordano had habits. He'd been smoking since he was eight years old. Lighting a San Cristobal Habana was a reflex, the first thing he did every morning. He poured from a crystal decanter, watching the caramel-coloured liquid fill the glass, and glanced again at the woman. Six months she'd lasted. Longer than most. There was a reason: she was different from the Creole pieces he was used to, so thin he could break them in two like dried sticks – this one had meat on her bones. And she was better. Prime.

The best.

Giordano had more enemies than he could count and zero friends. But as long as he had Cuban smokes, fine cognac, and ladies with alabaster skin in his bed, he'd take it.

The wind howled down the length of a deserted St Charles,

where the city's oldest streetcar line ran from South Carrollton and South Claiborne Avenues to Canal Street, ruffling the tiles on the roofs like a gambler cutting a new deck. Beppe poured a drink for himself but didn't offer one to her. A reminder of the terms of their relationship.

She lifted her dress and dropped it over her head; the gangster's gravel voice admonished her. 'What the hell're you doing? Did I tell you to put your clothes on?'

'I thought—'

'*You thought? You fucking thought?*' He stabbed the air with his cigar. 'Next time somebody says, "a penny for them", do yourself a favour, girl. Sell!' Giordano laughed loudly at his own joke.

Sex mellowed most people. Beppe wasn't one of them; his temper was as legendary as his appetites. He leaned a heavy elbow on the mahogany desk at the other side of the room and got down on one knee in front of the safe his father had built into the wall when Beppe was still a child. The modest exertion left him breathing hard. He felt a sudden sensation in his left arm and ignored it, spinning the tumbler clockwise twice followed by one turn anticlockwise. The lock disengaged and the door sprang open. A wave of nausea washed through him; the robe fell away exposing his massive frame; an invisible vice squeezed his chest under the amber pendant on the gold chain. Beppe realised what was happening and struggled to his feet, one flabby arm flailing wildly before he collapsed on the carpet.

Charlene smoothed her silk stockings over her legs and didn't raise her head. When she was ready, she walked unhurriedly to the desk. Giordano was on the floor behind it, his face the colour of wallpaper paste, his lips already tinged with blue mouthing words that refused to form. She hunkered down close enough to smell the cigar smoke on him and see the sweat gathered like tears in the corners of his eyes. Slowly, deliberately, she raked a painted nail over the folds of flesh at his neck through the tangle of tight grey hair to his belly.

Charlene tapped his clammy temple with her finger. "'A penny for them' yourself, you fat bastard.'

Out in the street, the storm relentlessly bludgeoned the city; glass shattered; a dog barked, somewhere another replied, and inside the mansion the lights flickered and failed, plunging the room into darkness. When they came on again, Beppe Giordano was dead.

Charlene stepped over his body and bent to examine the safe she'd witnessed the gangster check every day since she'd known him, making sure whatever treasure it held was still there. She'd imagined the dull glow of gold bars reflected in his bloodshot eyes, or the diamond sparkle of a stolen necklace once owned by the wife of Nicholas II, last Czar of the Romanovs – too hot for the street and likely to stay that way for another fifty years. At the very least, there had to be a fortune in high-denomination bank notes to explain his concern.

The disappointment when she peered inside was like a blow, and for a moment, Charlene was too stunned to take in what she was seeing: it was almost empty.

She thrust her hand into the metal box and brought out a wad of money secured by a mustard bill strap signifying $10,000. Towards the back, another dozen like it were divided into neat piles. To a man like Beppe it was scatter cash he'd lose at blackjack in an evening; it didn't make sense.

Charlene wanted to cry.

Her eyes darted anxiously to the door, listening for the armed guards on the other side. If one of them came to check on his boss he'd see Beppe lifeless on the floor, shoot first and ask questions later. Even if he didn't, Giordano was gone. And what was she but a whore in a city full of them? His mother, Madeline, was a wizened old witch – eighty if she was a day – who'd made her distaste for her son's tart obvious and had never spoken to her. She'd relish throwing her onto the sidewalk with nothing but the clothes on her back.

Charlene was smart, yet men – certainly the ones she'd met – were more interested in her tits than her brains. She wasn't complaining, her impressive breasts had served her well, except her looks wouldn't last forever – ten years at most, then...

The decision was easy. She stuffed the money into her purse and zipped it shut. The guards were stocky, crew-cut dullards, who thought with their dicks and lusted after the foxy chick at their corpulent boss's side. They were used to seeing her arrive and leave – getting past them shouldn't be a problem. After that, Charlene had no idea where she'd go but her time in the Big Easy was finished.

The lights dimmed and flickered again: Martha wasn't close to being done. Another outage might bring Beppe's two-legged Rottweilers. She had to get clear before that happened. With luck, they wouldn't find him until morning. By then, if the highway wasn't washed out, she'd be miles away.

Charlene towered over her former lover remembering the countless humiliations the animal had made her suffer for his amusement. His rough features were smooth and unlined; death had made him younger. The temptation to spit on him was strong. She resisted and was closing the door on the safe that had promised so much and delivered so little when she noticed the envelope on the bottom with a small black diary secured by a metal buckle next to it.

Her heartbeat quickened. Beppe had checked and rechecked the safe. Not gold bars. Not stolen diamonds.

More. Much more.

He'd been making certain the source of the Giordano family's influence was still there.

The photographs were standard 8 x 10 black-and-whites, shots of grinning suits shaking hands in a hotel lobby like old friends. Charlene recognised Beppe's twenty-eight-year-old son, Tony, his dark hair slicked and combed back, beside a hollow-cheeked third-generation Sardinian called Bruno Mura, laughing with two people from the governor's office. As she flicked through the pictures, monochrome became colour and the location moved from the hotel to a yacht on a blue sea and males dressed in T-shirts and shorts, toasting each other with the sun slipping over the horizon behind them. Tony and Mura were in every picture: mine hosts, topping up glasses, encouraging their guests to relax and enjoy themselves.

To all intents, just buds having a good time.

No foul no harm.

Except, that wasn't the reality. The faces Charlene was seeing belonged to politicians and judges, prominent people familiar because of how often their well-fed mugs showed up on the TV news. Add naked young girls to the scene – some of them *very* young – and what was going down was obvious. Towards the end of the stack the images were raw: men with women who were obviously hookers, men with men, and men with boys and girls: children.

Charlene turned away, fighting down the urge to be sick.

The envelope wasn't empty. A finger-sized memory stick tipped into her upturned palm, no doubt home to yet more perversion. By comparison, the little black book, dog-eared with age, seemed an innocuous collection of phone numbers and email addresses. Not true: it was a list of Giordano's blackmail victims and a who's who of the great and supposed good in Louisiana.

The lights that had been threatening to quit, dipped and finally died, leaving her rooted to the spot with the relentless drumbeat of rain hammering the house. In the darkness, her thoughts raced over the possibilities; none of them reassured her. If she couldn't get out of New Orleans, for certain, they'd find her.

Suddenly, a cold hand grabbed her ankle. Charlene covered her mouth, forcing herself not to scream. It wasn't happening! She'd seen him – with her own eyes she'd seen him. He couldn't still be alive. Please God, he couldn't be!

The next twenty seconds were the longest she'd ever known. When the power came on, she slumped, trembling and exhausted, across the desk. A last desperate attempt to cling to life must have momentarily sparked in the gangster because, on the floor at her feet exactly where he'd been, Beppe Giordano was as dead as it was possible to be.

Charlene freed her ankle and took a deep breath, opened the bedroom door and smiled at the sullen sentinels with just one job – to protect their boss from the many who would do him harm. She held up a finger and slowly let it droop. They got the joke and grinned. Giordano was a sour bastard with a hot temper; the thugs didn't have to like him because he paid their wages.

She went down the impressive staircase under the chandelier, wanting to run, expecting them to come after her. At the front door, Charlene ignored the last of the guards and stepped outside. By the time she'd raced the short distance to the car, she was soaked. She fired the ignition and gunned the Accord Sport into the night.

* * *

The wind had stopped though it was still raining hard. From the bay window Tony Giordano saw the dark-blue Mercedes sweep up the drive and braced for what was to come. When the car slowed to a halt, a guard rushed forward with an umbrella; he needn't have bothered. The old woman in the back seat irritably waved it away and went through the front door leaning heavily on a cane. Madeline Giordano was tiny – less than five feet tall – a force of nature who rarely smiled and was as mean and unpredictable as any tropical storm, and not for the first time her grandson wondered what life must've been like for Beppe growing up with her as a mother. His own mother had died when he was young, a victim of depression, the black dog, and Beppe had been no great shakes as a father. Tony's upbringing had scarred him, yet he'd choose it any day over the old crone he was about to meet.

At the top of the staircase the soldiers who'd worked for the dead gangster backed off to let her pass. She wore the traditional Karabela dress of her native island, an off-the-shoulder top, a full-length skirt and a headscarf. All black, a statement that had nothing to do with mourning and everything to do with dominance.

Tony didn't turn to greet her. She registered the disrespect and spoke sharply, her lips pressed in a thin line under the sunglasses Madeline was never seen in public without – a trick she'd borrowed from the Haitian dictator 'Papa Doc' Duvalier.

'Why are these people here? Get rid of them, Antoine.'

Everybody else called him Tony.

He said, 'All of you fuck off. Except Bruno. I want him to stay.'

'No, this is family business.'

'As far as I'm concerned, he is family.'

Bruno Mura watched the battle of wills play out in silence: Beppe wasn't even in the ground and already it had begun. Only one could lead; who, might be decided before they left this room. Mura was a student of history who understood that through the ages the secret of power struggles was to be on the winning side at the end. Madeline was ancient; time was against her. Tony didn't have her character or her strength – nowhere near it – but he was young; he valued Bruno. Despite that, Mura's money was on the old woman: at this stage the trick was to convince each of them he was in their camp.

He went to the door, closed it and stood back to acknowledge Madeline's wishes. She ignored the body on the floor and pointed to the safe. 'Open it!'

Tony shot a look of disgust at Bruno. 'Your son is dead and your only concern is—'

Behind the shades her eyes burned with contempt. 'Open the fucking safe.'

Tony did as he was told. And just like that, he'd lost. The tumblers clicked, the final metal rod released and his grandmother heard him gasp. Fired by his error in giving ground, he spun on Mura. 'You said it was a fucking heart attack.'

'It was. Everything with the whore looked the same.'

Tony slammed his fist against the safe. 'What does it look like now, idiot?'

Bruno stared at the carpet and didn't answer.

'What time did she leave?'

'Around midnight.'

'Nine fucking hours ago in the middle of the storm. And nobody thought that was strange?'

Mura regretted not leaving when Madeline had wanted him to. 'I don't know.'

The veins in Giordano's neck tightened under the skin. '*You don't know? You don't know?*' he screamed. 'Find her! Wherever she is, find her and bring her here!'

The old woman stood in the window, a dark figure against the morning light. Outside, New Orleans was picking up the pieces after yet another mauling, the St Charles Streetcar line in the middle of the avenue buried under broken branches and sodden drifts of autumn leaves that would have already started to decay. Of course, it would recover, but in the long run, it didn't matter. The city was sinking; in thirty years it would be underwater.

She said, 'Have you any idea what this whore has done to us?'

He snarled his reply. 'Of course I fucking do. Who do you think I am?'

Madeline could've told him. On another day she would have.

'Inconvenient though it may be, what she's taken will be replaced. Our business will go on. What can't be replaced is the family's reputation. If a glorified hooker can steal from the Giordanos and get away with it, sooner or later others will try to do the same. It's an insult that cannot be allowed to stand. No matter where she goes or how long it takes, track her down.' She paused. 'And when you kill her, make sure it isn't quick.'

His grandmother was a sly dog, seizing the reins, while deftly shifting responsibility to him. Tony saw failure staring him in the face. 'It's been hours and she's a smart one. What if we can't?'

'Then, I suggest you do what your mother did and kill yourself.'

PART I

1

NINETEEN MONTHS LATER

South London

George Ritchie tilted his head and spoke without drama or irony, as though what he was suggesting was merely common courtesy. 'When we're done, one of the boys will take you to Casualty.'

Behind him in the back of the white BMW X3, blindfolded and sandwiched between two men, Sonny Cole shivered with fear. In his teenage years he'd been addicted to heroin and still carried the scars on his arms and much of his body. Under the black hood his jaw hung slack. His lips were dry and his legs wouldn't stop shaking. He wanted to tell Ritchie he had it wrong, spin him a Jackanory like he'd done with the people he'd mugged off all his days. Instinctively, he sensed that would be a mistake. A very serious mistake. Because George Ritchie wasn't 'people' and he didn't have it wrong. Sonny had been a silly boy. He'd taken what hadn't belonged to him and kept taking until they'd caught him.

Now, it was payback time.

Cole had been on the end of a few rinsings. When it happened he'd accepted it and let the bruising heal. This was different. Ritchie wasn't some two-bob villain you could mess with. Sonny had heard whispers about an abandoned factory and prayed they weren't taking him there. His voice cracked; he was close to tears, realising his life might be about to end. 'You know me, George. Known me for years. Luke understands what it's like on the streets. I never meant to hurt him. Whatever you think... whatever you've been told...'

Ritchie stared out of the window. 'It's better if you don't talk, Sonny. Do yourself a favour and shut it.'

'I can explain.'

'No, you can't.'

'I—'

A punch to the kidneys from the guy next to him cut the sentence short and they travelled on in silence. Near the river the driver turned off the ignition and they sat listening to the engine cool. The hood was dragged from the terrified man's head. Sonny saw the lights of Central London blinking across the river. Landmarks since his childhood, bathed in neon blues, reds and greens; the familiarity brought him no comfort.

Ritchie leaned between the seats so he was facing him and shook his head; he had better things to do than chastise idiots. The thief's hair was matted with sweat; air rattled in his chest. The Sonny Coles of the world never learned. On the dodge was all they understood. Ritchie wasn't a sadist; he took no pleasure in this. If he had any reaction it was resentment about having to waste breath on a loser who thought he was smarter than everybody else and for a moment the old George – the Newcastle street fighter – flared behind his eyes. That George Ritchie would've let his fists do the talking, beaten Cole to a pulp and left him bleeding in the road.

'You had a good thing going. Why fuck it up?'

'It wasn't like that.'

'No? Tell me what it was like. I'm curious.'

Sonny chose the lie from the selection he kept for tight situations and went with an old favourite. 'It's my mother.'

'What about her?'

'She needs an operation.'

'I'm sorry to hear that, Sonny. A hardworking woman who kept herself to herself and didn't deserve to have you as a son. Yeah, a nice lady. Or at least she was until she died. You tapped two hundred off me to help pay for the funeral. Don't you remember? Any chance of getting it back? No? That's what I thought.'

Sonny's pale skin faded a couple of shades. 'George... That was stupid. I'm sorry. I did a wrong thing, a stupid thing, and I'm scared. I can pay the money back.'

'What money are we talking about, the two-ton the funeral director's still waiting for, or the money you've been stealing from Luke?'

Sonny stammered. 'Both... I mean all of it.'

'That'll be interesting since you haven't got a job. And how much do you think we're on about?'

'I... I...'

'Go on, Sonny, take a guess.'

'Not much. A few thou.'

Ritchie laughed mirthlessly. 'Yeah, and the rest. Get out of the car.'

'No. No. Please...'

Cole tried to delay the inevitable and failed. Ritchie rolled the window down and stayed in the passenger seat. 'You've heard the expression an eye for an eye?'

'Please, please, George.'

'It's from the bible. Exodus, if I remember my Sunday school. Any idea what it means? Pretty straightforward, really.'

Sonny fell to his knees, pleading. 'George. George. Don't do this.'

Ritchie ignored him. 'All right, I'll tell you. Ever heard of the principle of reciprocal justice?' He paused. 'Too complicated for you? What about an eye for an eye? That too complicated for you too? Christ, Sonny, I can't make it any simpler. Okay, it's saying if you hurt somebody, you should be hurt equally in return. Get it now?'

'Ahhh! Ahhh! George. Geor...'

Sonny started to cry. Ritchie stared at him, unmoved. 'Sounds about right, doesn't it? Sounds fair, the old eye for an eye malarkey. The problem is that because of people like you everybody ends up blind. You're washed, mate. Done. Accept it.' He opened the car and spoke to the two men. 'Bring him over.'

Cole retched and vomited on his shoes: it didn't change anything. It was too late.

'Which hand did you use to steal from the family?'

Cole didn't answer; he couldn't. He screamed, 'No, no, no, oh, no!'

Ritchie's order was free of emotion; he was completely calm. 'Put his fingers in the door and keep them there. Right or left, doesn't matter. Push the whole hand in if you have to.' He grabbed the thief's shirt through the window and twisted it. 'This is nothing. Next time, it'll be Fulton Street.'

The door slammed on the ruined flesh, again and again; bone shattered, blood splattered and streaked the white chassis like an abstract work of art.

Sonny Cole stopped screaming.

2

LORD HOLLAND'S ESTATE, YORKSHIRE

This is what I know: when a member of the aristocracy asks a south London boy brought up on a council estate to spend a shooting weekend at his country pile, it isn't his brilliant conversation he's after: he wants something. On another day, I would've turned Rupert Neville down, but the truth was I had nothing better on and seeing how the other half lived in their natural habitat was too hard to resist. Politically, Peter Rupert Neville was to the right of Attila the Hun. His views on everything from climate change to fox hunting were common knowledge; if he'd done his homework, he couldn't possibly believe we were on the same page. So, why the invite? Was having a gangster under his roof a treat for the females in the family, or did His Lordship have something else in mind? Driving through England's green and pleasant land, I looked forward to discovering what it was.

Three days of clipped vowels was more than I could stomach so I told him I'd join the party late on the Saturday afternoon. Best I could do. Pressure of business and all that. Over the phone, Rupert had hidden any disappointment he might have felt and given me directions.

Four and a half hours after leaving London, I found the entrance to the estate on a B road, partially concealed by the branches of ash trees, and followed the gravel path for what seemed like miles. He was at the end of a long drive, wearing a wax jacket, dark-green wellington boots and a soft hat; when he saw me, he waved. If he'd ever been handsome, he wasn't now. His face had the ruddy look of a man who took bracing early morning walks in the fresh air to drink in the natural beauty of the dales and spent the rest of the day indoors hammering the bottle of Glenfiddich at his elbow. There was a crudeness to His Lordship's jawline that even an accent as well modulated as his couldn't soften.

Whether he knew it or not life had been good to him. While he was inheriting the family fortune, the estate, and the title that came with it, I was inheriting my older brother's shoes, my station in the world symbolised by a pair of worn-at-the heel brogues tied with two different shades of brown laces.

Rupert – he preferred to be addressed by his middle name – was an interesting guy, one of the first platinum card members at LBC, my club in Margaret Street. A couple of nights a week he indulged his taste for expensive champagne and even more expensive women and paid his bill without checking it. To suddenly be invited to his home had been unexpected.

I got out of the car and we shook hands.

'Made it, I see. Any problems on the way up? Those roadworks near Sheffield are a bloody nuisance. Keep meaning to raise it with the Secretary of State for Transport. You missed an excellent day with the guns. Only hope tomorrow's as good.' He took my arm and led me towards the house. 'Oh, by the way, we usually eat at seven. Did I mention to bring a dinner suit? Don't worry if you haven't. It's all very informal.'

* * *

No, he hadn't and no, it wasn't.

At six-thirty when I came downstairs, eighteen people – I counted them – were standing around, talking and drinking wine, dressed as though they were on their way to the Cannes Film Festival: His Lordship's little joke at my expense. The club gave me plenty of opportunities to wear a tuxedo. I had one with me. Rupert would forget he'd tried to embarrass me, but I wouldn't.

In her day, Emma Neville had been a fine-looking woman; the young Rupert had landed on his feet. She saw me through the crowd and came forward. 'You look very handsome, Mr Glass.'

'Luke.'

'Of course. My husband spends an awful lot of time in that club of yours. What on earth does he get up to?' She gently touched my cheek. 'Don't tell me, I can guess.'

'This is a beautiful house.'

She sighed. 'Is it? I don't know any more. All I see is the crippling expense of running the damned thing. The bloody place is falling down. Not a surprise when you consider it's been the Neville family home for three-hundred years. You would've imagined somebody might have got round to fixing the roof.'

'Surely...'

'Put it this way. We haven't any Rembrandts but if we had, we'd have sold them.' She changed the subject. 'You missed a good day, today.'

'So I'm told.'

'Are you a decent shot? I expect you are.'

'Decent enough. How about you?'

'Actually, I am. Even if I say so myself. Been doing it since I was a girl.'

She pronounced it gell.

'Then you'll be out tomorrow morning?'

She snorted at the ridiculousness of the question. 'Wouldn't miss it for world. It's what living in the country's about. London's ghastly nowadays. Overrun by bloody foreigners. Can't move for them.'

'I like it.'

Her expression froze, as though I'd just suggested abolishing the monarchy.

'You can't be serious. How can anybody *like* London?'

It had taken her a whole minute to make her mind up about me. Now she had, she couldn't wait to palm me off to somebody else. Emma Neville struggled to hide her irritation and didn't succeed. She said, 'Let me introduce you to the others, they're all dying to meet you.'

We set off on a whirlwind tour of nonentities who were anything but dying to meet me. A few hesitated when they heard the name Glass. Most threw out a distracted half-smile and went back to whatever they'd been discussing. There were exceptions: Guy Arnott, a TV interviewer known for his aggressive style and the bias the BBC had become famous for in recent years, was one of them. He broke away from the company he was in and crushed my fingers in a sweaty grip that wasn't about being friendly. Arnott was already the worse for wear. His cheeks were hot and flushed. He stared hard into my face from behind horn-rimmed spectacles – the tactic he used to intimidate his political victims – and addressed me with his trademark bullishness.

'Who the hell let you in?'

His brusque approach was applauded by those who saw him as a straight shooter cutting through the crap. I wasn't one of them and didn't appreciate him trying his shtick with me.

'Come again.'

'What the fuck are you doing here?'

'Rupert invited me. Shall I tell him you don't approve?'

He took the spectacles off and put them back on again. 'In that case he's a bloody idiot. There are people here whose reputations would be trashed if it got out they'd been in the same room as Luke Glass.'

'Then, don't tell. It can be our secret.'

'Why *are* you here?'

The pompous arse was beginning to annoy me. Even if I'd known I wouldn't have shared the information with him. 'I told you. Rupert invited me.'

He spluttered. 'The poor bastard must have finally gone round the bend. Do him a favour. Eat your dinner, drink his champagne, amuse the ladies, and fuck off first thing in the morning.'

I moved closer. 'Listen... Guy... The cameras aren't running so you can drop the act. I'll leave when I feel like leaving. Not before. And speaking of secrets: are you still seeing that young boy you used to spend so much time with when your wife visited her parents in France? The Dordogne if I remember correctly.' His face went from whisky-red to the colour of the Dead Sea Scrolls. I said, 'Now tootle back to your friends before I rip your fucking head off,' and watched him re-join his sycophantic friends. I felt their eyes on me as Guy told them how he'd put a gangster in his place.

A balding PR guru, who'd helped the government convince the public that the terrible news they were seeing on the television every day was, in fact, not terrible at all but very, very good, recognised me but stayed where he was and I was left alone underneath a portrait of one of Rupert's ancestors.

A female voice at my shoulder said, 'I can guess what you're thinking.'

Its owner was a blonde in her early twenties, by a mile the youngest person in the room. She tossed her hair back and waited for me to respond, staring at me with clear blue eyes.

'All right. I'll go for it. What am I thinking?'

'You're asking how in God's name can this shower of misfits be running the country?'

'Harsh.'

'But true. Admit it.'

'Let's just say it had crossed my mind.'

She grinned. 'Honesty. I like that. Especially since I'm one of them.' She held out her hand. 'Allegra, Rupert and Emma's daughter. They wanted a son. Unfortunately, they got me and have never got over it.' She pointed to a tall weedy boy on the other side of the throng.

'That's my fiancé, James. He's jealous because I'm talking to you.'

James had his hands in his pockets. He lowered his tousled head and scowled in our direction like a schoolboy on the end of a parental lecture. His tie hung loose, an insignificant rebellion that went unnoticed by his peers.

I said, 'He's a lucky man.'

'Actually, he's a bloody bore but his father owns most of Cumbria. Or, at least, the best bits, so we're getting married.'

'Congratulations.'

She seemed not to hear me and ploughed on. 'The wedding is all my mother thinks about. She's obsessed. I've switched off.'

'Do you love him?'

Allegra's expression twisted the way Emma Neville's had at the idea anyone could like London: a mix of horror and disbelief. 'Love him? You aren't serious. How could I? He's terrible in bed. I've told him I'll have lovers so not to expect me to be faithful or anything silly like that.'

'And James is all right with that, is he?'

'No, not really. If he wants me he'll put up with it.'

'Does your mother know how you feel?'

'Of course.' She shook her head at my innocence. 'Love? What on earth does that have to do with anything?'

* * *

Rupert sat at the head of the table, a knife in one hand, a fork in the other, like Henry VIII. I'd been saddled with his sister, Daphne, a busty forty-something who'd been married to a racehorse trainer in Newmarket until he ditched her for a teenage stable girl. She had a high-pitched screechy voice and a habit of telling me what I already knew. Mr Daphne had done a runner. It was easy to understand why. She said, 'So you're up from London to see my brother. Strange, he hasn't mentioned you. You own a club, I hear. That must keep you busy.'

'It does. I'm run off my feet.'

The concept of doing work confused her. She sniffed and moved away a little. 'Don't you have... people?'

'One or two, though I find things go better when I'm involved.'

'Is it doing well?'

If I'd told her how well she would've spilled her soup.

'I have to say it is.'

'One hears of so many businesses that are in trouble. What's your secret, Mr Glass?'

'We try to—'

I was learning that asking a question didn't mean she was interested in hearing the answer.

'I used to love going to clubs, staying out late, sleeping all day. Don't have the energy now. Maybe I'm getting old.'

I laid it on with a big spoon. 'Nonsense. I'd put my money on you any time.'

She laughed a hollow laugh. 'You'd lose. An early bed suits me better.'

'An early bed and a good book?'

Daphne ran a pink tongue over her bottom lip and let the mask of vacuous conviviality fall; it had served its purpose. Behind it an entitled predator hid in its shadow. Her hand found my thigh and stroked it. 'I haven't opened a book in years. Not much of a reader, I'm afraid. All those words. Are you?'

'Not much.'

I took her hand away and put it back where it belonged; it didn't stop her. She said, 'There are so many other things I'd rather do.'

Apparently, I was one of them.

When the meal was over the ladies left the gentlemen to their port and brandy. Old-school bollocks – for sure, some of them would be smarter than their partners. Rupert signalled me to follow him into the library and put an avuncular arm round my shoulder. 'Sorry about landing you with Daphne. Love her to bits and all that, of course, though I can't deny my sister is an acquired taste. Quite a looker when she was younger. Had them queuing round the corner. Admittedly, that wasn't yesterday. The divorce has taken it out of her. No confidence. None at all. Emma has a theory that she's retreated into her shell. Did you find that?'

Was His Lordship having a laugh?

'No, can't say I did. She's an interesting woman.'

'Mmm, glad you think so. But I haven't hauled you all the way up here to mingle with that lot. Christ, no. Can't stand most of 'em for more than two minutes.' He opened the door and closed it behind us. 'There's someone I want you to meet.'

The man on the sofa turned his head, a grin I'd seen more times than I could remember spreading across his face. And why I'd been invited into this bastion of privilege became more confusing than ever. Jocelyn Church was the new rising star in right-wing politics, on the same page as Rupert and his ilk. He cultivated a man-of-the-people style, wore off-the-peg suits, and was frequently pictured with a pint of ale in one hand and a lit cigarette in the other – the kind of bloke you'd run into in any pub on a Friday night and warm to because he squared his shoulders, stood for the national anthem, and bought his round without having to have his arm broken: a straight shooter; a guy you could trust. And it was working. When he spoke at a rally people flocked to hear him: a fringe player with influence in the shires, tapped into the growing dissatisfaction with mainstream politicians. On TV, Church was charming and articulate and difficult to dislike. Until you heard the poison he was peddling: tales of a mythical England and the dark forces destroying it from without and within; incitement to violence masquerading as patriotism against a constant cry for law and order to quell the reaction his reckless rhetoric had inspired.

I wouldn't have trusted him to park my car, let alone get behind the wheel.

He'd been to LBC as somebody's guest and shared a bottle of bubbles in the corner of the bar, earnestly discussing whatever people like him discussed. Our critics – and we weren't short of them – said we'd let anybody in if they had the money. Jocelyn Church proved their point.

Rupert shepherded me towards him. 'This is the chap I was telling you about, the one who can help with our problem. Jocelyn, meet Luke Glass.'

* * *

The mattress was old and sagged in the middle. One more annoyance in a long line. Outside, it was raining. I lay listening to it drum against the window, angry with myself for having ignored my instincts and come to the back of beyond and the strange assembly of nobs and nobesses. I'd mixed with some pretty rum people – still did – yet I preferred them to the chinless wonders educated at Winchester and the like, who worked for Goldman Sachs, Deutsche Bank, or some other collection of thieves with an office. Maybe it was the realisation that a monied toad like Rupert Neville could blithely assume I was for sale, I didn't know, but I wouldn't be joining the shooting party – no fucking chance – and by the time the beaters were driving the first birds towards the guns I'd be in a greasy spoon in Peckham with a full English in front of me.

I was considering leaving when the door opened: whatever she was wearing rustled as it dropped to the floor. She slipped under the covers, wrapped her arms round me and whispered, 'I don't do this for just anybody. Consider yourself lucky.'

Yeah, she did. Her error was to assume I was the same as her. Without trying, Daphne had compounded her brother's insult. I removed her probing fingers. 'Please leave.'

In the darkness she was smiling; it was in her voice. 'Don't worry. I'll be gentle with you.'

I threw the bedclothes aside. 'Get out before I drag you out by the hair.'

It took a second for the shock of rejection to register. 'You mean it... you actually mean it. Don't you care that you're humiliating me?'

'I'm not humiliating anybody, you're humiliating yourself. Now, go.'

I'd had a chequered history with the opposite sex. With the exception of Shani, the lady from Cairo, every relationship had ended in disappointment for the women who'd made the mistake of getting involved with me. My work always came ahead of them. At least, that was how they saw it. Sometimes, I'd hear about exes who'd stayed friends after the break-up, meeting for coffee, promising to be 'there for each other': the brother or sister they'd never had.

I didn't get it. It wasn't my style and never would be.

Men were men and women were women. They were different. That was the point, wasn't it? Or had I missed something? Kicking a woman – any woman – out of my bed was a never-to-be-repeated first. I was making an exception for Rupert Neville's sister. She didn't appreciate it and berated me in extremely unladylike language, casting aspersions on my sexual orientation and my parents' marital status.

After Daphne had gone, I went downstairs to find a light on in the lounge and Allegra slouched in an armchair playing with her iPad. She spoke without taking her eyes from the screen. 'I've been researching you.'

'Have you? And am I fascinating?'

'Yes. Your family is quite famous, though not in a good way.' She looked up at me with the same frank rebelliousness I'd noticed the last time we'd spoken. No offence intended, just telling it as she saw it. Then she strayed where she shouldn't have and realised it immediately.

'Did my aunt come to your room? Don't answer that, it's none of my business.'

'I wasn't going to.'

'Which means she did. You're not the first guest to get her midnight-creeper treatment, so don't flatter yourself.'

'The thought hadn't occurred to me. I'm leaving, by the way.'

'What? Now?'

'As soon as I pack.'

'Why? Are we too good for you or not good enough?'

I laughed. 'You're a clever girl, give you that.'

Allegra slid off the sofa, came towards me and put her arms round my neck. 'It seems a pity to go so soon. Couldn't you stay just a little longer?'

'No.'

Her lips were soft and warm on mine. 'Not even for me? Not even if I asked nicely?'

'What would your fiancé say?'

'I couldn't care less.'

'Where is James?'

'Where every little boy should be at this time of night. In bed fast asleep. Shall I wake him up and ask him?'

Like all children, Allegra imagined she was different from her parents, a new breed of convention-trashing trailblazers. I admired her spirit, and her acerbic disdain for the world she lived in made me laugh, yet, under the skin, she was her father's daughter: the younger version of her horny aunt, determined to have whatever she wanted; in this case, me.

She stood on her tiptoes and kissed my forehead. 'You'll regret it if you don't, you know you will. Halfway to London you'll realise what you've turned down and wish you'd said yes.'

Allegra wasn't wrong. But my answer was still no.

* * *

I edged the car through the cold rain and down the drive as quietly as possible so as not to wake the house. Through the trees the sky was clearing and foraging rabbits making an early start scampered in the wet grass. In my rear-view, Rupert Neville's crumbling ancestral residence got smaller and smaller until it faded and disappeared. I wouldn't be back. Next weekend or the weekend after the Neville women would sneak into somebody else's bed and be guaranteed a better welcome than they'd got from me.

The roadworks north of Sheffield weren't a problem; at two in the morning I was the only one there. I opened the window and waited for the red light to go green, listening to the engine purr, enjoying the solidness of the steering wheel in my hands. The Met had a file three-inches thick with my name on it. Every now and then when they ran out of suspects, an unflattering black-and-white photograph of me got pinned to a corkboard. As a career criminal, par for the course. But the notion that because your great-great-great-great-great-grandfather had picked the winning side five hundred years ago and been given half the fucking county as a reward it somehow meant you were superior to the rest of us made me angry.

They'd been wide-boys then and they were wide-boys now.

Daphne, by her own admission, wasn't much of a reader. Neither was I, though the epigraph at the beginning of *The Godfather*, attributed to Balzac, had stuck in my brain.

'Behind every great fortune there is a crime.'

Too straight, Balz.

Jocelyn Church, so smooth he might've been rubbed down with sandpaper, was clearly convinced he had the measure of a south London gangster and I had the feeling I'd been auditioning for a part I hadn't applied for.

On my way to the door he'd said, 'Thanks for coming, Mr Glass. We appreciate you're a busy man. I'll give it a day or two, then make contact.'

At Swiss Cottage, uncollected rubbish overflowed on every corner and an epidemic of homeless people slept rough on the pavement. London was a magnet for rogues and thieves. Always had been and always would be – a city that gobbled up the unwary and spat them out when they'd served their purpose, as Jocelyn Church would do with me if I was foolish enough to give him the chance. 'Ghastly,' Lady Holland had called it.

A toff's word. And she wasn't wrong. Though I preferred it to where I'd just been.

3

LBC, MARGARET STREET, LONDON

The wine in my hand wasn't one of the ridiculously expensive bottles we kept temperature controlled and under lock and key in the darkest corner of the cellar, the kind pissed-up trust-fund managers put on their expenses when they'd scored big in the market and were celebrating. If they could get away with it, I didn't blame them. The sozzled bastards had stumbled on the universal truth that somebody else's money was a lot more fun to spend than their own and made a drunken decision to go for it. Of course, it wouldn't end well. Greed rarely did. As soon as they stopped bringing in the figures, a conversation between the accounts department and their boss would see them kicked out on their avaricious arses.

Tonight, another bunch of free spenders were in and LBC was buzzing. *Smashing It* magazine was footing the bill for a party and the club was a PR man's wet dream, awash with celebrities, some so famous even I'd heard of them. Charley had done a deal with the organisers. They got what they needed and so did we; the margin she'd negotiated would sit nicely at the bottom of an already healthy balance sheet. Good girl.

The last few months had seen more drama than a season at The Old Vic, but things were finally settling down. We had enemies and always would – jealous people who saw what the Glass family had and wanted to take it away from us.

They were welcome to try. For the moment, at least, nobody had managed it.

I was at the bar star-spotting while a slow number guaranteed to have the dance-floor crowded drifted up from downstairs.

More to herself than me Nina said, 'I hate that fucking tune.'

A throwaway comment. Except it wasn't. On the surface Nina was a successful businesswoman in her own right, a tough lady able to hold her own against anybody. It was a front. Behind it was an insecure child in constant need of reassurance. Without being certain, I guessed she'd danced with Mark Douglas to that music and was remembering.

At times our relationship had been rocky. Now, it wasn't even that. I hadn't seen her much in the last months and when I called, though she was friendly enough, it was clear she'd rather not talk to me and cut the conversation short. Coming here had taken an act of will – perhaps, even courage – I couldn't begin to understand. Yet, here she was, stunning in a dark blue sleeveless midi-length dress. The strain of the recent past showed: she'd lost weight; her face was thinner than it had been, and I caught a look in her eyes that told me her mind was somewhere else.

I said, 'Want to dance?'

She shook her head. 'Dancing with my brother? What would people say?'

'Since when did Nina Glass give a damn what people said? If you change your mind...'

She didn't answer. I let it go and we watched Charley work the room, moving between tables, blowing a kiss to a guy in a booth surrounded by leggy females – hookers hand-picked for the occasion – knowing he'd gladly trade all of them for a night with her. Both my sisters were complex women – was there any other kind? Strong characters with hidden depths I couldn't begin to fathom and was better off not trying.

Nina nodded at Charley, the beginning of a smile on her lips. Or maybe it was pride.

'She's done well, hasn't she? I mean, really well. She's a natural.'

I agreed. 'Yeah, she is.'

'I couldn't do it. I don't like people enough.'

'It isn't your thing, Nina. Charley thrives on the razzmatazz and ballyhoo, you don't. Putting up with phonies doesn't bother her. It's a game; she loves it. Secretly, she detests the lot of them but keeps it to herself. You'd tell them what you thought and that would be that. In a week, the club would be empty. In eight weeks, the administrator would be figuring out how much he could get for the chandeliers.'

She laughed, not something I'd heard her do much lately. 'You're right. I couldn't stop myself. I hated working here. Property's a better fit.'

To an outsider, the Glass family – me, Nina and Charley – had it all going on. A fair assessment. But, like the hookers in the booth, our success didn't come cheap. Along the way we'd paid our dues, none more than Nina. She'd loved a man who'd broken her heart – the saddest part was that he'd loved her, too. Her affair with Mark Douglas had been the real deal: Douglas had been her rock. Until he'd showed himself in his true colours. The reveal had devastated her; she still hadn't recovered, maybe she never would.

She read my mind and only just managed to keep annoyance out of her voice. 'For Christ's sake stop worrying about me. I'm okay.'

My good days were the ones when I thought about somebody

other than myself. With a sister like Nina I was guaranteed a lot of good days.

'Are you?'

'No. But I will be.' She changed the subject. 'The market's gone crazy. Glass Houses is doing record business – that keeps me busy. Which reminds me. Have you thought of trading up?'

'I'm happy where I am, Nina. Why?'

She shrugged. 'No reason, except the right time to buy is always now, and you can afford to. Also, moving into a new place would give you a focus.'

I reacted exactly as she knew I would. 'What're you talking about? I've got a focus.'

Nina disagreed. 'You *had* a focus, I'll give you that. Opening this place, starting Glass Construction, and putting the family back together after the mayhem and madness Danny created. Absolutely.'

'So?'

'They say Alexander wept because there were no more worlds for him to conquer.'

'And in your half-baked analogy I'm Alexander?'

She lifted her untouched champagne and sipped it. 'In your dreams. I'm making a point not a comparison. Though tell the truth. Charley's managing the club. It made sense to merge Glass Houses with Glass Construction and I've got that.' Nina was on a roll. 'George Ritchie has everything that moves south of the Thames. What does that leave for you? See where I'm coming from?'

I did see. Persuading George Ritchie to come on board had been the smartest thing I'd done. No question. Officially, as Nina rightly said, he worked for me running the streets south side. In reality, George didn't work for anybody but himself and never had, no matter who paid his wages. He'd started breaking bones for

Albert Anderson's crew when I was still in school. I'd hear his
name whispered by people who were afraid of him – which turned
out to be everybody except me and my brother, Danny. Occasionally – very occasionally, in his case, because he was a man of few
words – he'd remind me how he'd told Albert to do something
permanent about the two young rascals noising up the local shop-
keepers Anderson was supposed to be protecting and had offered
to take care of it.

Luckily for us, his advice had gone unheeded.

Nina pressed her point. 'All I'm saying is there are some
stonking places that would suit an upwardly-mobile man like yourself. We'd do the sale off the books and split the commission.'

'That's the best offer I've had this week.'

She eyed me up and down and slid off the bar stool. 'Then
you're in more trouble than I thought, brother.'

* * *

Nina locked the toilet door and took the folded paper from her bag,
opening it carefully so as not to spill the white powder inside. With
her brother about, a full hit wasn't on. All she needed was enough
to get through the next couple of hours. Nina was aware how far
she'd fallen and didn't care. It didn't matter; nothing mattered now.
Spending any real time with Luke would mean he'd notice how
much she'd changed and try to save her like he'd done before. But
she couldn't avoid him forever. Tonight had been a conscious decision to stage a performance, for his benefit, create a distraction to
convince him she was coping. Laughable, if it hadn't been so sad.
And impossible because she was beyond saving: the Nina Glass
he'd known had died in an abandoned factory in Fulton Street
south of the river; she didn't exist. This Nina lived with the echo of
the gun in her head and the flapping of startled birds in the rafters.

A naïve young doctor had been sold a fairy tale about the pressure of working at Glass Houses, of difficult clients, long hours and stress. She'd watched him scrawl a prescription for the sleeping pills she'd ditched three days later, choosing pain over the disassociated zombie they made her.

Depression was inevitable. The black dog was there until she went to bed and was waiting to greet her like a faithful pet in the morning. Nina sought relief from an old friend: in the circumstances, cocaine had been an easy decision. Luke believed those days were behind her. The challenge was keeping her return to it from him. George Ritchie was the problem. Little happened without his knowledge. The answer was to score in another part of the city from a dealer with no idea who she was.

* * *

Stevie D from Islington was a twenty-six-year veteran of the north London drug scene. Calum Bishop had forced him out but Stevie still knew how to get what she needed. From their brief phone conversation he'd sensed the female on the other end of the line was no ordinary junkie and offered to deliver. When she'd declined and suggested a pub in York Way, he'd known he was right.

The meeting had lasted less than a minute. She'd left. He'd followed and got her car reg. An hour later, he'd known her identity and done a little dance. It hadn't been Christmas. Not even winter. But it had been a gift.

Stevie had shouted to no one. 'Santa Claus settings, people!'

Calum Bishop would have to see his worth now.

* * *

Charley stood off to the side surveying the scene: the party was going well. Considering how much money had been thrown at it, not a surprise. A-list celebrities had turned out in force and a small army of paparazzi waited on the pavement in Margaret Street for them to leave. The events organiser from *Smashing It* was doing the rounds, basking in the congratulations she didn't deserve. 'Organiser' was a misnomer; her strong suit was schmoozing. Charley had met her before – a waste of space, more concerned with name-dropping than answering her emails, who took three-hour lunch breaks and spent them on her mobile wittering to her friends. Her name was Sophie and in a room full of luvvies, she was the biggest. Across the club she kissed a woman in a dress that, from a distance, seemed to be made out of toilet paper and gave her the look of a resurrected Egyptian mummy.

Charley was on her way to check in on the kitchen when she heard an Irish accent behind her and instinctively knew its owner was addressing her. 'For years the bastards have told us alcohol was killing our brain cells. Millions of them every bloody session. Now, they're sayin' it doesn't. I'm not sure I believe them.'

Eamon Brannagan had the dark, smouldering looks of a Jane Austen leading man, the tall, broad-shouldered darling of the gossip columns who breathlessly followed his many affairs more keenly than the on-screen performances that had won him two BAFTAs. His first love had been rugby, abandoned in favour of the stage. Unfortunately, the actor from Connemara was almost as well known for his drunken scrapes with authority. His last escapade had splashed across the front pages of the tabloids when he was escorted from a BA flight from Heathrow to Shannon after an altercation with the cabin crew over his refusal to turn off his mobile and end the chat he was having with a woman as the plane pulled away from the stand.

He'd been drunk then and he was drunk now, and the images

of him wild-eyed and snarling between two airport security guards hadn't been pretty. The star's management had privately and publicly urged him to seek help and booked him into the Priory. On the second day, he'd signed himself out and walked to the nearest pub. Seven hours later the landlord had poured him into a taxi back to London. It worked if you wanted it to work. Clearly, Eamon Brannagan wasn't ready to live sober. A familiar story. Almost a tradition: the guy had talent, yet he was in danger of pissing away a glittering career.

Charley was tired; it had been a long day and it wasn't over. She said, 'I think you've had too much to drink, Mr Brannagan.'

He gave an exaggerated unsteady bow. 'How very perspicacious of you. Any more observations or is that it?'

'Listen, and please don't take this the wrong way. I've been here since eight o'clock this morning; my feet are killing me. All I want to do is fall into bed and go to sleep. No offence.'

Brannagan leaned against the wall, smiling. 'Playin' hard to get, are we?'

'I'm not playing at anything. I'm dead beat. The last thing I need is somebody who thinks he's God's gift coming on to me.'

He blocked her path. 'You're turnin' me down? You can't be serious.'

'I'm asking you nicely to let me get on with my job. So if you don't mind...'

'What if I do mind?'

He was seconds away from losing his front teeth. Over his shoulder Luke and Nina were talking at the bar. All she had to do was shout and this tosser would be history, except Charley preferred to do her own dirty work. She edged closer to him and whispered in an exaggerated drawl, 'Move out of my way, you Irish wanker, before I break your fucking arm. That clear enough?'

He took a step back, blinking as though he'd been asleep and suddenly come awake.

'I'm sorry. I apologise.'

'Accepted. Maybe you should go home.'

'I'll go if you come with me.'

'That isn't happening.'

'What's your name?'

'Quit while you're behind, Brannagan.'

The smile that had worked for him so often in the past missed the mark. He said, 'All right. Let me call my driver and you can see me off the premises before I make a fool of myself with somebody who isn't as understandin'.'

* * *

Outside, photographers shared cigarettes, flasks of coffee and war stories. The *Smashing It* party had swelled tonight's number to more than a dozen, determined to catch a celebrity out of their skull falling on their famous face in the wee small hours. Once in a while the celeb fought back and a Nikon or Leica got broken in the scrum – a minor story on its own – the excuse for an angry exchange between the snapper and the star's PR representatives that usually ended in less-than-adequate compensation and no apology.

Charley led Brannagan through the crowd of paparazzi, ignoring their aggressive demands as they struggled through the throng. He said, 'Drink doesn't agree with me.'

'Then why do it?'

'Because life's too fuckin' dull.'

His reply left her unimpressed. 'Oh, spare me the sob story. You're rich, famous, talented. One of the lucky bastards this club's named after. My advice would be to stop killing yourself and grow up.'

He grinned. 'Fancy savin' me, do you? You wouldn't be the first. Who knows, it might work. The love of a good woman and all that bollocks.'

Charley smiled at his cheek. '"All that bollocks". I'll pass, if it's okay with you.'

Brannagan lost his footing and dropped to one knee. He raised his head and looked up at her. 'You don't know what you're missin', lovely girl.'

Charley stretched out her hand and helped him to his feet. 'As a matter of fact, I do.'

Photographers surged forward, flashlights going off like lightning, calling to get Brannagan's attention. The car drew level, he dragged the door open and fell inside.

'You still haven't told me your name.'

Charley tossed her red hair back. 'Tomorrow, even if you could remember, I'd be just another available female in a long line.'

'You misjudge me.'

'No, no, I don't. I've met your kind before.'

'Can I call you?'

She said, 'Take care of yourself, Mr Brannagan,' and closed the door.

4

The morning after the night before was never pretty, especially if I'd been drinking champagne. This one was downright ugly. I opened my eyes, the day rushed in, and I realised I wasn't ready to face it. Owning a club meant there tended to be bubbles about. A lot of bubbles. Every time I turned round some well-intentioned punter had sent a bottle over to my table. I could've said no and resolutely stuck to mineral water, but white-knuckle sobriety didn't have much appeal and, so far, I hadn't quite managed to get there.

Nina turning up at the party had been unexpected. She'd gone to support Charley. Given where she was in her own life, she'd made a decent stab at pretending to enjoy herself. Around two in the morning I'd put her in a taxi and got another lecture for my trouble. She'd squeezed my hand in a very un-Nina way. 'Think about what I said, Luke.'

'What, buy a villa in Portugal and take up golf? I'd be dead in a year.'

'That's not what I mean. Besides, you'd throw your toys out of the pram when you didn't win. You've achieved what you wanted to achieve and you're drifting.'

In the last months she hadn't seen me more than three or four times.

My sisters had been talking.

'Isn't it me who's supposed to be worried about you?'

'You don't need money – you've got plenty.'

'We all have.'

'It isn't a motivation any more.'

'Oh, I don't know. I kind of thought it was.'

'Then you thought wrong, brother. The streets south of the river, the club, Glass Houses and Glass Construction were all about putting distance between you and the past. Now you have there's no need to run. It's the future you have to take care of.' She stopped. 'Rich coming from your messed-up little sister, right?'

'Wrong. I'm lucky to have you.'

Nina looked away, embarrassed by the compliment, and came back when she was ready.

'Enjoy it while it lasts. Seriously, you're too young to rest on your laurels. You need a fresh challenge. Something to get your juices firing. As for me, I'll be fine.'

'Promise?'

'Of course. Us Glass girls are made of strong stuff. Let's get together for lunch next week. You have my permission to bring a girlfriend, if you can persuade some unsuspecting female to have anything to do with you. I won't bite.'

I remembered Nina's history and wasn't sure I believed her. She said, 'The word on the vine is there hasn't been much on that front, either. What happened with the Egyptian lady?'

'She preferred the desert. And the vine should mind its own business. As for the rest, I'll take it under advisement and get back to you, how's that?'

She made a face. 'Better than nothing.'

Lying under the bedclothes with a guy sawing concrete in my

head, I knew she'd hit the nail on the proverbial. Given time, Nina would get over the awful thing with Mark Douglas and be stronger, albeit she'd never completely trust another human being again. Her sisterly concern had given me hope she was actually on the mend. The rest wasn't easy to take on board. Though she was right. I couldn't say when it had started but I was 'drifting' – driving to meet a bunch of upper-class alley cats in darkest Yorkshire was a clue. The old Luke wouldn't have considered it.

I made coffee – strong, sweet and black – tossed a couple of paracetamol down my neck and went through to the lounge, feeling like death warmed up. Outside, there were people on the street living their lives. The world was turning.

It would have to wait for me to catch up; I wasn't going anywhere for a while.

The online front page of *The Sun* was split between two photographs: to the right, Jocelyn Church wore a suit remarkably like the one I'd seen him in up in Yorkshire, though it almost certainly wasn't – he probably had a dozen exactly like it – underneath a typically provocative headline that read: 'Those F——g Frogs Are At It Again!' I guessed Church was giving our friends across the Channel a good kicking. Popular stuff in some circles. To the left and further down, a man had stumbled getting into a car and was being helped to his feet by a woman. The shot did him no favours; there was a lost look in his eyes I remembered from my alcoholic father and every drunk I'd come across since. The woman in the picture was Charley.

Facebook wasn't my thing but whoever handled the *Smashing It* marketing was a fan. Images of the party were everywhere. The 'celebrities' might be household names for all I knew. I hadn't heard of most of them. Which said something about me. Eamon Brannagan was one of the few I recognised; his broth-of-a-boy mug had been posted and reposted. I'd seen him on the red carpet at the

Odeon, Leicester Square, accompanied by his short-haired female co-star, a waif in a dress with so little to recommend it, it had to have cost a fortune. That night he was lean and tanned and sober. In LBC he'd been none of those things.

Yesterday had been a long one for Sister No 2. At the end of the month she'd find a nice chunk of extra cash in her bank account – a show of appreciation for the great job she was doing. When the club opened I'd put Nina in charge; an amateur error – she'd railed against the idea and wasn't a good fit. In fact, she was a fucking awful fit. Charley, on the other hand, was perfect. For a start, she looked the part – more like a movie star than the movie stars we got in. Day or night, I hadn't seen her less than spectacular. She had a big heart, was liked by the members and the working girls, and steered the ship on a course that more than justified our investment. In the beginning, I'd used LBC to wash dodgy money and still did – plenty of it – but if the Serious Crime Squad raided us they wouldn't find it on the premises: there was a lot to be said for creative accounting and offshore banking.

Charley answered on the second ring. I said, 'Hope I didn't wake you.'

'No problem. I'm off today, thank God.'

'Any plans?'

'You mean apart from going back to bed?'

'You're front-page news.'

'Am I? For doing what exactly?'

'There's a picture of you with Eamon Brannagan on the Internet. Fancies himself as a bit of a hard case, I hear. An "Irish hellraiser". Zero out of ten for originality. They don't make them any other way over there.'

She got it and laughed. 'My good deed for the day. And for your information, he slipped.'

'When I'm shit-faced I slip, too. Everybody does. A coincidence. Nothing to do with the booze.'

'Is that what you're on to say?'

'No. It's time you were told what a fantastic job you're doing.'

I heard pleasure in her voice. 'Cheers, brother. It's a good gig so long as you can handle being surrounded by massive egos and don't mind being on first-name terms with the milkman.'

'It seems you can.'

She laughed again. 'Don't believe everything you read. Brannagan's just a country boy taking his wealth and fame out on the world. Tough at the top and all that.'

'He should try it back at the bottom, see how he likes it.'

'He's a pussycat.'

'Sounds as if "Danny Boy" made an impression.'

'You're fishing.'

'Is there anything to catch?'

'Mind your own business.'

'Did you talk to Nina?'

My question changed the mood. Charley's hesitation was almost imperceptible but I noticed it. She said, 'No. How was she?'

'Pretty good, all things considered.' She didn't comment and a worm of anxiety crawled in my stomach. 'What aren't you saying, Charley?'

'You didn't notice anything about her?'

'Like?'

'Like she's different.'

'Most people would be if they'd been through what she's been through. Except, that's not what you mean, is it? What am I missing? Tell me, I want to know.'

She backtracked. 'Forget it, I'm just tired. Last night must've taken more out of me than I realised. If you say she's fine, she's fine.'

And now I really was concerned.

My second phone conversation didn't improve the day. I'd forgotten Jocelyn Church had said he'd call me. Unfortunately, he hadn't. His voice had the same forced mateyness I remembered from Yorkshire; the godawful flannel he turned on like a tap wouldn't be far behind. Better judges than me had credited him with correctly gauging the mood in the country beyond the Westminster bubble. Maybe they were right. But his Everyman act had a tinny ring.

'You left before the fun began. Quite right. I've never seen the point of killing things that are doing no harm. Foxes are an exception. They have no natural predators and, as any farmer will tell you, left to their own devices they cause enormous damage to the countryside.'

He was waffling. I said, 'What can I do for you, Mr Church?' and heard him exhale on the other end of the line.

'I thought we might continue the chat we had up at Rupert's place, maybe over lunch. On me, of course.'

'I don't think that's a good idea.'

'But you haven't heard what I have to say.'

'Whatever it is—'

'At least give a chap a chance.'

'All right, when?'

'If you haven't got anything urgent on, how about today?'

5

I strolled with the sun warm on my face and excited tourists around me snapping everything that moved, enjoying the sights and sounds of the city familiarity had blinded me to. London was buzzing. In Berwick Street, a market trader with Rasta curls sold vegetables from a stall and danced to the music playing in his headphones. Behind him a young guy in jeans and a T-shirt saw me and drew into a doorway. Taking up Church's lunch invitation was out of character; on another day I would've told him where to stick it. I hadn't, which said Nina's assessment might be closer to correct than I wanted to admit. Some guys played golf or met their mates every other Saturday and went along to Stamford Bridge. I didn't have 'mates'. For as far back as I could remember all my energy had gone into what we now had. Either building it or protecting it.

Rupert Neville and his horny females weren't the kind of people I'd spend time with, but there was something in the wind and I was keen to know what it was: Jocelyn Church was going to tell me.

The restaurant in Parliament Square was his suggestion and

expensive. Not my problem; he was paying. A maître d' with a foreign accent showed me to the table. Church was already seated and got up when he saw me. 'We meet again, Mr Glass.' He glanced round the room and back. 'I hope this isn't too stuffy for you. I like it. Have you been here before?'

'As a matter of fact, I haven't.'

He sat down and unfolded his napkin. 'Then I assure you, you're in for a treat. Whatever else you order, I recommend finishing with the lemon tart. Exquisite. Where do you usually go?'

'Le Gavroche.'

He dabbed at his mouth to cover his surprise. 'Le Gavroche, really? I haven't been there in years. Still good, is it?'

'First rate.'

'I can never get a table. What's your secret?'

'I call them and ask for one.'

His face gave nothing away, though I had a fair idea what he was thinking: Le Gavroche was a gastronomic institution with a three-month waiting list for a reservation. Apparently, like LBC, they'd let anybody in if they behaved themselves and could pay the bill at the end of the night. I could do both.

Church said, 'What would you like to drink?'

'Water's fine.'

'I can't tempt you with anything stronger? A bottle of something chilled and dry, perhaps?'

'Just water.'

He didn't press me on the booze and launched into a potted history of himself and his political views, casually disavowing some of the more extreme positions he'd been accused of taking to persuade me he was a guy I could do business with.

I'd say this for old Jocelyn – he could talk.

I switched off and let him drone on. The lunchtime demographic in the room seemed to be balding middle-aged men on expense accounts, with the occasional female whose job was to look nice, nod her head at the right time, and sleep with her manager if she had any hope of promotion. Looking at the men, they'd need to be super-ambitious to take on any of these characters. The exception was a woman, thirty-something with dark shoulder-length hair and red lips, reading from a Manila folder in front of her. The body language of her male colleagues told me she was their boss.

Church spread his arms wide, unaware I hadn't been listening. 'So you see, Mr Glass, I'm not the monster the left-wing media paints me out to be. I'm a believer in small government and make no apology for it. That doesn't mean socialist ideas don't have merit. A few of them do.'

'Which ones?'

He saw the trap and avoided it.

'It's how they're applied that concerns me.'

I got the gist; he was recasting himself for my benefit. The question was why. In Yorkshire, he'd run the rule over me and approved of what he'd seen, otherwise why push to have lunch? Whatever the test had been, the boy from the council estate had passed it.

'Okay, you're misunderstood. Now, tell me why I'm here.'

He smiled. 'I'd expected you to be sharp and you are.'

The flattery bounced off; coming from him it meant nothing. 'Why am I here, Mr Church?'

'Why? Because the people I represent need a man with your talents.'

'My talents?'

'Indeed. They see you as very much part of their plans.' He saw my confusion. 'Without meaning to be overly dramatic, Mr Glass, London is headed for disaster.' Church searched my face for a reaction. When he didn't find it, he carried on. 'If I asked what you disliked most about this city, what would you say?'

I shrugged. 'Seeing so many homeless people when so many properties are owned by wealthy people who don't live in them. Finding somewhere to park. The usual stuff.'

The politician in him seized on the bit that helped his case. 'Exactly, it's overcrowded. In twenty years the population will be almost ten million. Not the largest city on earth, yet the sheer weight of those numbers will bring it to a standstill.'

He sat back in his chair, warming to his subject. 'Of course, we assume, as we always do, that good old technology will save us. The eggheads will come up with the answers.' Church laughed into his hand. 'For some of our challenges, no doubt they will. But one fundamental difficulty can't be fixed by a computer.'

He waited for me to ask the obvious question. I obliged. 'Which one would that be?'

'"*Lebensraum*", Hitler called it. Living space. There isn't enough and they're not making any more.'

He'd lost me. I said, 'And you have the solution?'

'Me personally, no. And *the* solution? Nobody's claiming that. Part of it – absolutely. What do you know about MTS?'

I didn't have a clue what he was on about. He enlightened me. 'Mass Transit Systems. You may have heard it called the Skytrain. Ring any bells?'

'Yes.'

A smile flitted across his lips. 'A proposal exists for the building of a monorail to ease congestion in the centre. A cost/benefit analysis commissioned on behalf of the people I represent gives it the green light. On all fronts. Overhead trains running down Regent Street are long overdue. London has been trying to get the idea going since the sixties, can you believe? Other places have had them for years – Bangkok, Vancouver, Kuala Lumpur – and they work. We've been left behind.'

'Are you looking for investment?'

'No, that's in place.'

I sensed a bullet coming my way. 'So what has this to do with me?'

He leaned forward, eyes darting left and right to make sure no one was listening. 'We—'

'Who's we?'

'I'm not at liberty to divulge that information. Suffice to say they're all top-level operators. Big dogs.'

He spoke the last part in a hushed voice like a cold-war spy in East Berlin selling out his country and I felt my patience slip.

'Again, Mr Church, what has this to do with me?'

A barely concealed smirk confirmed my bullet theory. 'We've hit a major obstacle. Despite the massive advantages, a few remain unconvinced of the project's merits. One in particular.' His eyes narrowed. 'We need him removed. We need you to remove him.'

I felt my face flush. I'd joked to myself about Yorkshire being a test. But I'd been closer to the truth than I'd realised. Church wasn't interested in my business nous or even my money. My usefulness to him was much more basic: he thought I was a thug he could hire by the hour to break legs.

He lifted a triangle of brown bread and buttered it, oblivious to the change in me.

'One figure in particular is opposed to the concept. A man with considerable influence in both chambers. We need him out of the way, otherwise the whole thing will be dead in the water, yet again.'

A waiter arrived and saved him from being dragged head-first across the table. Church turned, morphing seamlessly into bon-viveur mode, and ordered a dozen oysters on the half-shell without consulting me. He clapped his hands. 'Jolly good. You'll like these. Supposed to be good for the old... you know what.'

'Can't say I've noticed.'

'Of course not, a virile young fella like you. Some people

prefer them tarted up with caviar and cream and all sorts of bloody nonsense. I like them *au naturel*. We'll split them, how about that?'

'Not interested.'

'Don't you like oysters?'

'Oysters are fine.'

'Oh, I see. You mean coming on board with us? Thought it would be right up your street, if I'm honest.'

'Did you?'

'Actually, yes, I did. You're a businessman; this is business. I'll be frank with you, Mr Glass. You weren't our first choice.'

'Really?'

'Yes, really. My associates would rather I had this conversation with your brother. Unfortunately, he's gone to Spain or some other godawful place. Since we can't track him down, they've asked me to speak to you.'

Dragging Danny's name in was another mistake. Church sensed he'd strayed onto thin ice and tried to skate away from it. 'We aren't expecting you to do the deed yourself. I'm sure you have chaps who take care of that.'

'And exactly what "deed" would my "chaps" take care of?'

The arrogant fool didn't realise the ice had already cracked beneath him and he was about to go under. He lifted another wholemeal triangle and inspected it. 'Kill him, of course.'

I pushed my chair back. Fuck him and his lunch. He reached across to prevent me from leaving. 'Hear me out, please.'

The smug look had been replaced by desperation: for all his over-confident, urbane persona, Church was no more than a go-between, a message boy who hadn't done his job until he'd delivered the result his masters demanded.

I glanced at my watch. 'You've got two minutes.'

He lowered his voice and toyed with his napkin. 'I had hoped you'd see it our way, but I'm afraid I haven't made myself clear, Mr Glass.'

Yes, he had. In a posh restaurant a stone's throw from Parliament I was being asked to murder a stranger. Church waited for the waiter to place the shellfish in the centre of the table before he went on. 'For your own good, Luke, have the sense to listen.'

Hearing him say my name as though we had some kind of relationship made me want to break his face. His blinkered sense of entitlement meant he had no notion how close he was to more pain than he could imagine in his worst nightmare.

'That sounds like a threat.'

Denial was unnecessary; we both knew the truth.

'The people I represent are accustomed to getting what they want. No isn't a word they understand. And what they want is you.'

'Well, whoever they are, tell them they can fuck right off.'

He sighed, frustrated at his inability to get through. 'Let's start again, shall we, Luke?'

'Let's not bother, Jocelyn.'

Church pushed the oysters away, untouched; suddenly, he'd lost his appetite. 'You and I are from very different backgrounds.'

'I'm surprised you noticed. Well done.'

'You don't like me, I accept that, but this isn't about me.'

'Apart from cold-blooded murder, what is it about?'

The stark description shook him, as though the reality of what he'd proposed had only just occurred to him. 'What these things are always about: money, a decent slice of it going into your pocket.' His voice swelled, encouraging me to see the upside. 'In fact, you can name your price. So don't be too quick to dismiss it.'

'I have money. I don't need more.'

Church stopped his disbelief on the edge of a sneer. 'Really? Really, Mr Glass? Then you're fortunate, indeed. How about friends in high places? Got many of those?'

'Enough. And I prefer to choose my friends.'

Saturday night at Lord Holland's estate, his wife's haughty disdain and his sister's fingers creeping up my thigh, felt like a lifetime ago. Rupert Neville's little get-together in Yorkshire *had* been an audition. This was the show: Jocelyn Church's show. Only it hadn't turned out to be the triumph he'd hoped for. Church had heard about the gangster from south of the river and misjudged his mark. The consequences of his failure terrified him; I saw it in his eyes. The unnamed 'people' he was fronting for would hold him responsible.

He said, 'For your own good I urge you to reconsider. Anything else is a mistake, Mr Glass. A serious mistake.'

And there it was. Out in the open. What the invitation to Yorkshire and this fancy malarkey had been about. Except, Church wasn't asking me – he was *telling* me. I dropped my napkin on the table and stood. 'Take this message back to your masters. Luke Glass isn't interested. If he ever was interested, he'd insist on dealing with the organ grinder, not the monkey.'

I took a taxi back to the club, angry for wasting time on Church and Rupert Neville again. It was their world; they made the rules. Then again, rules were made to be broken. Nobody knew that better than me. At this moment all over London people were breaking them on my behalf.

But this is what I know and I'd known it all my life: whatever my failings – and a fair number of disappointed women would swear to them – I wasn't like Church and his well-heeled ilk and never would be. Shooting at things that couldn't shoot back wasn't for me. Neither was bedding females I didn't much care for. Without meaning to, Jocelyn had reminded me of a question I asked myself on nights when the club was raking in cash faster than I could spend it.

Why were people with money so often useless tossers?

6

Bruno Mura took a seat under the green-and-white awning of Café Du Monde at 800 Decatur and checked if the cute little part-time waitress from Delaware studying business management at Tulane was on duty. She wasn't. Too bad. They'd only spoken a couple of times but it was obvious she was attracted to him; he looked forward to nailing it.

Mura slept badly and often got here early enough to see the sanitation department's guys hosing down Jackson Square, cleansing it of the previous night's excesses. He began every morning with the speciality of the house – café au lait and a plate of sugar-dusted beignets – a habit from his teenage years, hanging out near the tourist-magnet French Quarter ready to pick the pocket of some unsuspecting visitor. His widowed mother had visited his father's grave twice a week, knelt on the grass, pressed her palms together and asked God to save her son.

The Almighty hadn't been listening.

To please her, Bruno had worked one hot summer in the Café Du Monde's kitchen and enjoyed the experience, though not enough to squander the precious days of his life earning honest money.

A girl he didn't recognise barely glanced at him when she took his order; she had a nice face. Mura thought again of the uni student's slim legs and small breasts and wished she were here.

He waited for the coffee to arrive, toying with his iPhone, pushing it around the wooden table, expecting it to ring and Tony to launch into his latest tirade about Madeline. The grandmother and her grandson's relationship was toxic. They blamed each other, although it was the unmourned Beppe who'd been the cause of their woes: his mother had crumbled when her husband, Silvestro, the rock her life was built on, had died and she'd allowed their son to pick up the reins, hoping it would be the making of him.

But the lazy drunken bastard had taken the easy route. Happy to settle for the cream, he'd let the streets go, opening the gates to rival gangs who'd fallen like jackals on the opportunity, fighting among themselves, swelling the city's crime stats to the worst in the country until every ward was polluted by them: the 39ers in the 9th; the D-Block Boys in the 15th; the Taliban Gang, in Pigeon Town, and the murderous Byrd Gang across the Crescent Bridge in Algiers. Not a good look for the family.

The police had turned a blind eye when, on Madeline's orders, Mura restored the balance; nobody was interested in punks dropping other punks over a dispute about a few blocks of the Lower Ninth Ward.

Strange days. But once again, the Giordanos were the undisputed kings of New Orleans. That position, unassailable for decades before Beppe presided over its decline, hadn't been threatened when the thief disappeared into the hurricane. Bruno had spilled blood, broken bones, and turned wives into widows to put Tony and his grandmother's fears to rest.

Yet, it wasn't enough. Their obsession with the Giordano name meant they couldn't accept a whore had bested them. And so the search continued.

The coffee was strong, made bitter by the addition of chicory to the blend, a perfect complement to the sweetness of the pastry. Mura assessed the new waitress – late teens, slim and aloof, certain she was destined for better than this. Unlike the uni student, she'd pencilled his order in her little notebook without gushing the standard chit-chat and hadn't bothered to make eye contact. Bruno saw her indifference as a challenge to be overcome: a week from now they'd be on first-name terms; in a month she'd lie in his arms confiding her silly hopes and dreams. He would pretend to care, say, 'Go for it, honey!', then send a text dumping her and turn his attention to the next one.

He opened his phone to check the news, a glance enough to remind him that the world was still crazy: a shoot-out in broad daylight on Magazine Street had left two bangers dead and another three mortally wounded. Mura shook his head at the latest madness, whispering to himself in French. *'Plus ça change, plus c'est la même chose.'*

The more things changed, the more they stayed the same.

Yeah, it was Beppe's fault; a loser, no doubt about it. But he'd had an excellent eye for horse flesh. Charlene wasn't just another woman, she'd been special. Mura couldn't say for sure, though he suspected Tony had moved on her at some point and been rejected. A slight he wouldn't forget. Bruno had been with him the first time they'd seen the voluptuous beauty, fabulous in a black satin dress highlighting the flame hair cascading to her breasts. A smile played on the fat man's thick lips as he introduced them to his new mistress in the lobby of Maison de la Luz, on Carondelet Street. Beppe had been pleased with himself with good reason – the couple were on their way upstairs to the bedrooms. The conversation had been brief and unmemorable, no more than an exchange of pleasantries, but Tony's eyes hadn't left Charlene, his lust undisguised; the son had wanted his father's woman.

Mura trawled the online newspapers for the match reports and football scores. The Saints had beaten the Buccaneers 36:27 out at the Superdome – a great game by the sounds of it. He ordered a second cup of Joe from the waitress, picturing her writhing under him, biting his shoulder, calling his name over and over. With every female there was a word, a touch, a trigger that made them spark and explode; the fun was in discovering it. With this one, he'd soon know.

The temperature was already in the mid-twenties. In the bayou, the gators would be waiting for tourists to feed them marshmallows from the safety of their tour boats, while the humid air hummed with the whir of flying insects.

A showbiz gossip headline caught his attention.

IRISH ACTOR'S FALL FROM GRACE

The photographer had been in exactly the right place to capture the confusion in the eyes of the guy on the ground. From the throng, a hand stretched to help him up. Bruno followed the arm all the way to the shoulder and gasped, instantly realising what he was seeing was a game changer – for the Giordano family and for him.

On a London street, Beppe's whore was more beautiful than ever. No wonder they hadn't found her. Months of trawling state after state. Wasted time they'd never get back.

And the memories rushed in.

* * *

Nine miles from the Canadian border with the wheels sliding and losing traction, they stopped. They'd left New Orleans two days after Martha hit with one objective: to find the thief and bring her back. Now, it was winter and, this far north, bitterly cold. The ploughs hadn't cleared the track, the snow was deep. The men reluctantly got out, beating their arms against themselves to stay warm. Under the white carpet, pine needles cracked and snapped like matchsticks. In five months they'd criss-crossed the country chasing down every fruitless lead, leaving a trail of violent death in their wake, but always returning empty-handed to be met by Madeline's wrath.

Above them, a long-eared owl traded one branch for another and the ice-blue sky turned an ominous grey, a sign the weather was closing in. A flock of birds, startled by the strangers' arrival, soared then swooped and flew in formation towards the horizon. Bruno Mura lit two Marlboro and passed one to Giordano. He took it, his expression taut, his breath condensing in the freezing air; the Atlantic City boardwalk was seven hours and twenty-five minutes in the rear-view and he looked tired. Mura understood that was the least of it: Tony was burning with resentment from the last conversation with his grandmother, still hearing her curses echo down the line.

His fool of a father had got them into this mess and he hated him for it. But he hated Madeline more.

Mura spoke like a friend. 'Don't let her get to you, Tony. The old bitch can't live forever. You'll get your rightful place. As for the thief, if she's here, we'll find her.'

Giordano's expression was as hard as the ground beneath him. The empathy wasn't appreciated; his features tightened in irritation, his voice had a dangerous edge. 'That's what you told me in New Orleans, Bruno. And Nashville. Do me a favour, if there's nothing to say, say nothing.'

Mura accepted the admonishment. Tony was right. The search had been exhausting and disappointing. Months of chasing down every lead. The thieving whore hadn't stayed long anywhere, always a step ahead.

In Memphis, a bass player, an enormous black guy called Boom Boom, had been putting his instrument away at the end of the gig and seen them coming towards him. In a monosyllabic exchange he'd admitted to having a one-night stand with a foxy red-haired chick, then sensed trouble and clammed up. His massive hand lingered inside the guitar case. A blade or a gun? Nobody wanted to find out that badly and Mura settled for an answer to his final question. 'Did she say where she was headed?'

Boom Boom thought about it. 'Might have mentioned something.'

'Something about where?'

'Can't rightly recall.'

So they'd gone home until the next sighting had taken them to Raleigh and an albino hooker who recognised the description, bit into her cheroot, and told them to fuck off – they'd missed her by a day. Maybe it was the truth. Maybe it wasn't. Forty hours later, the prostitute's mutilated body had been discovered in a dumpster. Killing her had been unnecessary but it had broken the monotony of the fucking ego-trip his bosses were on – Bruno had two of them and never forgot it. When the crone died he intended to be tight with her grandson.

Though Beppe's woman had definitely been in Jersey: a former boyfriend, a croupier in one of the casinos, had been surprised to see her and let her sleep in his bed while he'd worked the late shift. When he'd come home in the early hours of the morning, she'd gone. Before Bruno cut his throat and left him to bleed out on the floor, he'd told them about the house she'd lived in with her mother.

Seven and a half hours later they were almost there.

The four men from the second vehicle scanned the barren landscape. They were city boys. To them this felt like a hostile planet on the other side of the galaxy. Yet, they didn't question it – they knew better.

Tony said, 'How much further?'

'Half a mile.'

Bruno's answer seemed to satisfy him. He nodded and dropped the cigarette in the snow.

'Back in the cars. Let's get closer. Then, we'll walk.'

'You think she'll be expecting us?'

'Out here? We're the last thing she's expecting. But we're not taking any chances.'

Night fell in a white cloak as the sky made good on its threat. Snow came down thick and fast, reducing visibility to yards, and it was impossible to be sure they hadn't strayed from the track. Tony Giordano led the way, head bent into the blizzard, driven by demons he hadn't shared and likely never would. Behind him, Bruno Mura kept the others together and followed, conscious of how far they'd travelled from anything resembling civilisation. Without their boss they would have given up and turned back to the cars. The air stung their faces, each step sapping the strength from their thighs; under their coats, they were sweating. One man lost his footing, stumbled and slipped and went down heavily. In the emptiness, the sound of bone cracking was like a cannon.

Bruno knelt on the snow beside him, assessing the extent of the injury, whispering in Cajun to reassure him it would be all right. Anywhere else it wouldn't be a problem; they'd deal with it. Mura guessed his boss's reaction and knew it was a death sentence.

Tony waited for him to bring the news he didn't want to hear. 'How bad is it?'

'Bad. Valoir's broken his leg. He can't walk.'

As Bruno expected, Giordano's decision was instant, without loyalty for a man who'd blindly followed him.

'Leave him.'

'He'll freeze, Tony. We—'

'Don't argue with me.'

Mura said, 'I'll tell him we'll come back for him.'

'Tell him whatever you like, Bruno. Just get on with it.'

The snow was still falling but in a clearing surrounded on three sides by dense woodland that rose to a star-studded sky they could make out a ten-year-old Chevy Silverado 1500 and the cabin; the frame tilted at a crazy angle against the brick chimney breast, and at the other end, the white roof sagged close to collapse. Smoke drifted into the air and disappeared on the wind, a dull orange light glowed in one of the windows, and Mura was reminded of a scene from the bedtime horror stories disguised as fairy tales parents read to their kids. Once, a long time ago, people had lived here, farmed the land and died trying to scratch an existence from it. Tonight, it was the final refuge of the thief who'd been foolish enough to rob the Giordanos.

She'd run far. But not far enough. There was no such place. The family were always going to find her.

Foolish woman: it would all have been so different if she hadn't rejected him for his fat fuck of a father.

Tony signalled his men to fan out and stay low, leaned his back on the trunk of a tall fir and checked his weapon. The well-oiled action was smooth; Mura knew it wouldn't be needed. Giordano intended to obey his grandmother's order: the thief would leave this world slowly and in agony while he watched, but not before his spurned boss had his fun with her; the thought of rearranging Charlene's beautiful face made him stiffen.

An owl – the bird they'd seen earlier or its mate – glided across the clearing and landed in the trees.

Bruno envied the grandstand view it would have of the retribution he was about to exact.

The men surrounded the building, hunched figures darting across the clearing, closing in. Giordano waved them forward. On the wooden porch, a rocking chair that wouldn't be used until spring was glazed with ice. He imagined her curled in it, skirt gathered round her long legs, a woollen blanket draped over her shoulders as a red sun dipped over the horizon.

Was she afraid? Or did she believe she'd lost them and was safe?

Mura listened, hearing only the wind rustling the leaves. He took a step back and put his boot on the door; the wood splintered and swung open. Apart from a cot in the corner and a collection of empty bottles it was almost bare. A woman wearing a grey army coat many sizes too big for her sat hunched in a chair staring into the fading embers of the fire. She didn't turn to look at them – may not even have realised they were there. Her face was so heavily lined it was impossible to guess her age. On the floor at her feet, an uncorked stone jar added to the miserable scene. She didn't blink; at first they thought she was dead. Then, the cracked lips parted and she spoke, the words half formed. 'Who the fuck are you?'

Giordano stood in front of her, keeping his distance. 'Where is she?'

'Who? Where's who?'

'Charlene.'

A laugh gurgled in the crone's throat. 'Charlene? Don't know anybody called Charlene.'

* * *

Mura lifted his coffee cup and let the waitress drag a damp cloth over the table. Up close, with her white teeth and blue eyes, she really was a pretty little thing. Her mouth turned down at the corners: time wouldn't be kind and he saw her as she'd look after she'd sparred a few rounds with life, when what she'd dreamed of becoming would embarrass her so much she wouldn't talk about it any more, and work, kids, and age took their toll.

Mura tried to connect. He said, 'What's your name?'

'Why?'

'Just asking.'

'Thought it was the other girl you were interested in?'

'What gave you that idea? I don't even know her.'

She finished wiping the table and stuck the damp cloth in her pocket. 'You don't know me either, and that's exactly how it's going to stay. You have a good day now, y'hear?'

Mura grinned. Feisty! All right! He appreciated a female with spirit – it made the inevitable conquest so much more satisfying. The old woman had had plenty. Yeah, and courage, too. Not that it had done her any good.

* * *

Tony grabbed her by her scrawny neck. 'So where does the booze come from? Who brings it? No more lies!'

When he pressed the gun to her temple she didn't so much as blink. Even putting one in her kneecap guaranteeing she'd never walk again made no difference. She dropped to the floor, howling like a banshee, more alive than at any time since they'd burst through the door and roused her from her stupor. A second bullet brought a partial result – an admission she had a daughter called Charlene.

Blood from her shattered legs seeped into the wooden floor, staining it red. The pain had to be unbearable but she'd forced herself up on one arm, an incredible feat given her condition, and Mura realised that, yet again, their search had come up short.

The woman screamed, 'Fuck off, whoever you are! Charlene isn't here! And you aren't smart enough to find her.'

Tony put his hand under her chin, forcing the ruined face to look at him. 'Finish her, Bruno. She doesn't want to live. Make some noise. Sound travels. If Charlene's out there let the bitch know we won't give up.'

They watched the fire eat the damp timber, sending clouds of black smoke into the air. Beside him, Tony was a shadow of the man he'd been in New Orleans, weighed down by his failure. Bruno reached for a positive, knowing it wouldn't be welcome. 'She can't run forever.'

Tony answered out of the corner of his mouth. 'Told you before, Bruno. I won't say it again. If there's nothing to say, say nothing.'

* * *

Like his father before him, Tony Giordano was an ungrateful bastard. His men had followed him wherever he'd gone with hardly a word of complaint. All forgotten as he drowned in self-pity. His voice was thick, slurred with tiredness after yet one more sleepless night in a long line. 'What do you want, Bruno? And it better be good.'

'It's a lot better than good.'

'I'll be the judge of that.'

Mura let him wait.

'I'm heading over to tell Madeline. Better she believes she's hearing it first.'

'Hearing what first?'

'I said she couldn't run forever, didn't I?'

'What the fuck are you talking about?'

'Her. I've found the thief, Tony. I've found Charlene.'

7

'I owe you an apology.'

Eamon Brannagan's soothing lilt was at odds with his reputation as an out-of-control drunk who started fights and had been forcibly ejected from several airport VIP lounges. The Irishman's PR people worried when the next public relations disaster was coming. Charley remembered reading an amusing story from Montreal: the actor, out of his head, had wandered around the airport in his pyjamas claiming he intended to sleep through the twenty-one-hour flight to Singapore. On a scale of one to ten, the previous night at LBC had been, at best, a two.

'What for?'

'To be honest, I'm not exactly sure.'

'You had too much to drink.'

Brannagan said, 'You're lettin' me off lightly.'

'Am I?'

'For sure. I'm starin' at a photograph on the front page of *The Sun* and it's not a pretty sight. By the looks of it, I made an arse of myself. Again. So I'll apologise anyway, if it's all the same to you.

I've found that if I kick off with that, seven times out of ten I'm right.'

'Only seven.'

'Okay, more than seven. And before you say anythin' I have to tell you I'm sufferin' for my sins. My poor head feels like it's been leased to a frackin' company.'

Charley smiled into her phone. 'It's only what you deserve.'

'I can't deny it. Any road, I'm sorry.'

'You're welcome.'

'You aren't barrin' me, are you?'

'Not this time. Keep it up and I might change my mind.'

'You've got a heart of gold, so you have.'

There was plenty to like about the Irishman: he was charming, funny, and very handsome. But Charley was hearing the script he used to get him off whatever hook he'd got himself on. It would work with some people. With her it jarred because it was old and she knew where it was going. On cue, he said, 'Have dinner with me.'

'No, thanks.'

'Well, that was quick enough. Why not? I've said I'm sorry. At least pretend you're thinkin' about it. A man has his pride.'

'But I'm not. Come back when you get over yourself, Mr Brannagan. And ditch the blarney. Nobody's buying it.'

* * *

Nina was in bad shape: her nose ran, her head felt like a lead weight and her thinking was fuzzy.

She'd phoned Stevie D from the taxi on the way home from the club. The bastard had let her call go to voicemail and she had a problem. If she contacted one of Luke's guys – Felix Corrigan, maybe – it could be solved. Felix had had his eye on her for years; it wouldn't take much to persuade him to score for her. Except, he'd see how low she'd fallen – recreational drug users didn't run around London in the middle of the night looking for the next fix: addicts did that – and he'd tell. Absolutely, for sure, he'd tell. His fierce loyalty to her brother and George Ritchie would make it impossible for him not to. Luke knew she got high. How high and how often were her secrets and she intended to keep them. If he found out the truth he'd be furious. So what? She was a big girl and big girls did what they wanted.

Traffic was heavy on Borough Road. Nina pinched her eyes and tried to concentrate. A blue Fiat she hadn't realised was there roared past on the inside, freaking her out. Worse was to come. At a red light in Southwark Street, she didn't see a group of pedestrians at the crossing and only just managed to brake in time. A youth in a black hoodie jacket and Dr. Martens banged on the bonnet; a woman probably hurrying to work shook an angry fist and shouted something she couldn't make out.

She'd almost run them over.

The incident brought a suffocating surge of anxiety and an overwhelming need to stop in the middle of the road and get out. Somehow, she made it to the car park beneath the office block, to her designated space, and rested her forehead on the wheel, waiting for the panic attack to end.

Her fingers trembled. She shivered and sweated at the same time.

Drugs were fine until you ran out. Then, it was hell.

* * *

On the eighth floor, Roseanne, Nina's secretary, glanced at the clock on the wall, then at the door; her boss had never been this late. In the beginning it had been fun working at Glass Houses.

Staff meetings sustained with pots of decaf coffee and trays of low-fat doughnuts. Nina would arrive, cheeks glowing from her early-morning gym session, and take her place at the sleek table in the boardroom, every inch the thrusting young executive. Behind her through the window London sprawled to the horizon. The business regularly recorded month-on-month increases and it was easy for everyone on the team to believe they were taking over the world. Nina was an inspiration, performing at the top of her game, holding numbers in her head, rarely opening the folder in front of her, asking for progress updates on high-value sales in two dozen locations across the city. Totally on it. Luke had made his sister an equal partner. The recognition had galvanised her and, impossibly, she'd found yet another gear, determined to justify his faith in her. And she had. Glass Houses had become an elite agency in the capital, specialising in top-of-the-range properties. The hand-picked team had earned substantial commissions. Everybody had been happy. Good times.

Vertically integrating Glass Houses with Glass Construction had made sense. In two months staff numbers doubled and the ninth floor of the building became home to the new team. The sky was the limit, or that was how it had seemed. Until Nina's stellar performance had faltered and the people who were inspired by her example wondered if the pressure and responsibility were too much. Nina had changed. None of them knew why. The decaf and the doughnuts were still there, the money was still coming in, but the vibe from the top was different: working at Glass Houses wasn't fun any more.

* * *

Nina showed up at ten minutes to one and went straight to her office. She pressed her back against its hard surface, her heart beating as though she'd been running; she felt drained and jittery. Nina was crashing.

Last night she'd given Luke sisterly advice about his life – how ironic. If he could see her now...

Roseanne read the signs – the boss was hungover and didn't want to be disturbed. At two o'clock she knocked and went in. The blind was drawn; the room was dark. She peered into the gloom. Nina was sitting behind the desk, head lowered, chin resting on her chest; the secretary thought she was asleep, until she spoke, startling her. 'What the hell do you want?'

'Sorry, I didn't mean to—'

The voice was low and hoarse, intimidating. 'What do you want, Roseanne?'

'The staff meeting was supposed to be this morning.'

'And?'

'I've rescheduled it for three.'

Nina didn't respond.

'Is that okay?'

'Do I look like I'm up for giving a rah-rah speech? Cancel it. And while you're at it, cancel everything else for the rest of the day.'

'Including the architect on the Southbank project? He's coming at four.'

'No, he isn't. He's a tosser. Bin him.'

'If you're sure.'

'I'm sure. Now, close the door on your way out.'

'What shall I tell the girls?'

'What girls?'

'About the staff meeting. They were looking forward to it.'

'Tell them to get on with what I pay them to do. This isn't a fucking holiday camp.'

* * *

Stevie D scanned the underground car park for the blue Renault Alpine A110 and spotted it in a designated space. Nina had sounded near to tears. The dealer pretended he hadn't noticed, telling her he couldn't meet until later. That was when she'd broken down and begged him. *Begged him.* Not many could say they'd heard one of the Glass family do that.

Stevie got by on four hours' sleep a night. When she'd called in the early hours of the morning he'd been lying on his back in his bedroom watching smoke drift from his cigarette to the ceiling. He could've driven to her place and sold her what she wanted. He hadn't; it was too soon. The hurting had only started. Tomorrow, every bone in her body would ache, craving the drug that would make her feel all right. So, he'd blanked her call – part of the plan that had come fully formed the second he'd discovered the identity of the woman behind the wheel of the flashy Renault.

Nina Glass was his ticket into Calum Bishop's operation.

Something for Bishop to hold over her brother, and, for Stevie, the sky was the limit.

Steven Dean had started early in the drug game, initially as a customer spending the wages he earned from a garage off Cricklewood Lane on marijuana and speed. The realisation he could make more money as a dealer had been a cathartic moment for the young mechanic. His new direction had gone well until he'd forgotten the cardinal rule, got high on his own supply and fallen into addiction. Thanks to Father Joseph Conroy, a Catholic priest in Neasden and himself a former junkie, he'd kicked the habit and stayed clean. Father Conroy had spoken to him about a twelve-step programme and a Higher Power. Stevie wasn't interested and parted company with the priest who'd saved him. Since then, to his credit, he hadn't had so much as an occasional toot. The experience could have turned him into someone carrying a persuasive message dedicated to helping victims escape a life of bondage. It hadn't. The opposite, in fact – he despised them for giving in to a weakness he'd overcome and fed the monkey on their backs.

When Kenny Bishop's grip on his north London empire slipped after he ran afoul of Luke Glass, he'd correctly read it as a sign his best days were behind him, brought in his nephew, and retired to concentrate on his golf game. Calum Bishop was a man with a bad reputation who had already served time for assault. Joining his uncle had always been an option. He'd shunned it, choosing to wait in the wings for the offer that would inevitably come. When it had, he'd grabbed hold of his sudden elevation with both hands and overnight become the new king of the hill from Clerkenwell and Finsbury on the edge of the City to the boundary with Hertfordshire.

His first task had been to put his own stamp on his uncle's gift. Lay down a marker. Those who hadn't accepted him paid the price in blood and broken bones and word had gone out that young Calum – he was twenty-seven – was harder than his uncle had ever been.

Stevie D could testify to that.

He'd been on a street corner in Dollis Hill, minding his own business on a rainy afternoon, when a black Range Rover pulled in, the passenger window silently rolled down, and a man with pock-marked cheeks called him over. The conversation had been brief, the long and the short of it – Stevie's little enterprise was under new management and he was out on his arse.

The pockmarked guy had explained in language they both understood how things were and the consequences of not going along. While he spoke, Stevie's gaze had drifted over his shoulder to the figure in the back, and he'd got his first glimpse of Calum Bishop: the new gang boss had been dressed in a tan jerkin, dark-blue T-shirt, and jeans, staring out of the window as though what was being said had nothing to do with him. In the confines of the car, the smell of new leather was strong. Bishop had drawn on a cigarette, tilted his head, and blown smoke into the air. His hair had receded alarmingly for someone his age; he'd be bald before he was thirty.

Without uttering a word, Calum radiated menace, happy to let his minion in the front do his talking for him.

The proposition hadn't left much to think about: walk away or learn to walk on crutches. Pockmark had summed it up in one succinct sentence. 'Take it or leave it, Stevie.'

Not a difficult call to make considering the result was already in.

Stevie D had decided to take it.

'Let me know if you need me for anything. Anything at all.'

Pockmark had enjoyed seeing him beg. 'If Mr Bishop needs a lackey, I'll be in touch.'

The electric window hummed shut and the Range Rover drove away towards Gladstone Park.

Stevie had taken his diminished status well. It was what it was. Nobody said he had to like it.

Bishop would always have a use for men like him and having the sister of Luke Glass on the hook was the ace that would open the door. All he had to do was bide his time and reel her in.

Nina came out from behind the pillar, footsteps echoing in the concrete cavern. Meeting her dealer in the car park underneath Glass Houses wasn't clever for any number of reasons. As she came towards him he saw the hunger in her eyes and turned the screw a little more.

'You look like shit.'

'Don't start, I'm not in the mood.'

'Why didn't you call sooner?'

'I did. You didn't answer.'

Stevie leaned on the roof of a car. 'I'm a popular guy. A lot of people phone me. How much do you need?'

'How much can you spare?'

'Depends.'

Nina's fear took over. 'Money isn't an issue. I can pay.'

The dealer flashed a mirthless grin. 'That's a given. Otherwise, I wouldn't be here, believe me. Meeting freaked-out chicks in underground car parks isn't my idea of living the dream. Powder or crack?'

'Crack. Always.'

Stevie D whistled through his cigarette-stained teeth. 'Then, unfortunately for you, not much.'

'What do you mean?'

He didn't hurry to answer and let his attention wander to a line of Jaguars and Mercs on the far side: fancy cars belonging to the fancy people who worked in the offices upstairs. A fair few would use on the weekend, imagining they were living life on the edge. Wankers! Some would stay in control. Others would lose it. Sooner or later they'd cross his path, sweating and agitated, the same craving in them that was in this woman.

Stevie dropped the news casually, as though he was only vaguely concerned. 'Supply line's been breached. Very little stuff around at the moment and there won't be until the next shipment gets through.'

Nina was holding on by her fingernails; her nerves were shot. This wasn't what she wanted to hear. 'What do you mean?'

'The navy boarded a boat ninety miles off Cornwall and seized two tonnes. A hundred and sixty million pounds' worth. My mobile's red hot. No wonder you couldn't get me.'

'I... didn't know.'

'Considering your level of interest, shall we say, you're surprisingly uninformed.'

Nina brought out a bundle of notes. 'I'll take it all – whatever you've got.' She thrust the money at him. 'If it isn't enough I can get more.'

'You're not the only fish in the sea. This is a favour because I feel sorry for you.' He passed four clear-plastic bags to her and took the cash. 'Best I can do.'

'Aren't you going to count it?'

The dealer grinned. 'No need, I trust you. Besides, I'm guessing we'll be doing business again. Assuming I can get product. If you're short I'll get the difference next time. And, oh yeah, the price has gone up.' He shrugged. 'Market forces, you understand how that goes.'

Nina ripped the bag open with her painted nails, tipped the contents onto the bonnet of a dark-green Audi estate and separated them into white lines with a credit card. Stevie's mouth curled in disgust. He was immune to the pain he caused; he saw the victims of his trade every day of the week. Desperation was par for the course. They were pathetic excuses for human beings lacking the will to straighten themselves out – some of them wouldn't be alive by Christmas. One less addict in the world. Nobody would miss them. The day he got choked up about what they were doing to themselves it would be time to look for a new job. However he made his money, it wouldn't be spent on junk. That lesson had been learned.

He rolled up a twenty-pound note and handed it to her, his voice heavy with sarcasm.

'Remember how precious it is. Don't lose any.'

Snorting wasn't the fastest way to absorb cocaine, though the effects lasted longer. It took a minute for the drug to enter the bloodstream and flow to her brain. When it did, it hit like a thunderbolt; Nina's legs buckled and she stumbled. Stevie caught her, laughing. There was powder at her nostrils, then her features relaxed as the C took effect and the fears that had driven her to the edge of sanity faded. Her eyes fluttered, like a medium waking from a trance.

Stevie D smiled. 'Feels great, doesn't it?'

Nina didn't reply.

'That'll hold you for a while. You've got a couple of days' worth if you go easy on it. Don't leave it so late to contact me next time. Your body's had a hammering – it won't appreciate another one. Give me your number. I'll check in on you tomorrow.'

Some of Nina's old fire returned. 'You don't give a damn about me. As far as you're concerned I'm just another junkie. Why would you "check in" on me?'

The dealer was used to telling lies; this one was easy. 'Because it isn't nice to see a pretty lady like you fall so far.' He held his hands up. 'But if you aren't cool with it, I'll back off. I'm just trying to help here.'

'No, it's fine. I appreciate it.'

She watched him add her number to his directory. 'Expect to hear from me. Meantime, if I were you I'd go home and try to get some sleep. Eating something wouldn't be a bad idea, either. Get some food into you. And drive safely. There are a lot of crazy people out there.'

8

Jocelyn Church hadn't disappointed; for most of the meeting he'd been smooth and unflappable, certain of his ground: everything I'd expected and more. Given my family history, trying to involve me in his shady business dealings wasn't a surprise. Resorting to threats when I turned him down – that was something else. The confidence oozing from every pore wasn't the product of his public school background or even some inbred sense of entitlement. It came from knowing he wasn't alone, that in the shadows behind him the faceless people who wielded the real power in the country had his back. Church wasn't one of them; he was their puppet. His request that I murder someone on his say-so was laughable.

There were any number of villains in this town who'd do what he wanted, no questions asked. So, why me?

Long ago, the office above the King of Mesopotamia pub had been mine. Now, it was George Ritchie's domain and when I arrived the barman was leaning on the counter reading a paper. He saw me, grabbed a cloth and started polishing a pint measure to convince me he was worth whatever we were paying him. At the top of the stairs, the door was open; Ritchie was on the phone. I sat in the chair across the desk and waited for him to finish. Like the rest of us, he wasn't getting any younger: his eyes were hooded and he hadn't shaved; white stubble covered his jaw. In a rough kind of way he was probably handsome, not something I'd given much thought to. Now I had it wasn't difficult to imagine women being drawn to his quiet strength. But I'd never seen him with a girl-friend or even heard him mention one – another part of his life he kept to himself. We were friendly without coming close to being friends, although if I had to choose one guy to be in the boat with, it would be him.

I'd offered him a move up west with more responsibility. That London didn't interest him. He was happier running the streets south of the river and keeping an eye on the horizon in case a rival suddenly decided to go for it.

He ended the call and turned to face me. 'Hello, stranger. A while since you've been here. I'm guessing it isn't just a friendly visit, am I right?'

'Nearly, George, nearly. What's shaking?'

'Nothing worth reporting. When there is...'

When there was it would be too late, he'd have dealt with it and we both knew it.

He said, 'Heard you were rubbing shoulders with some very dodgy people at the weekend.'

'Indeed, I was. And indeed, they were.'

'And that's why you're here?'

'Got it in one, George. What do you know about a character called Jocelyn Church?'

Ritchie studied his fingers and leaned back in his chair. 'About as much as everybody else. What my old mam would've called "a slippery customer worth the watching".'

'I regret I didn't get to meet your mother. I would've liked her.'

'She was the best judge of folk I've ever come across. Have you sussed in two minutes flat. It was a gift and she used it relentlessly.'

'Well, you're her son.'

'I don't have what she had. What's Church done to get your attention?'

'Only asked me to kill somebody.'

'Is that all?' Ritchie smiled. 'Two questions. Who? And why you?'

'Your guess is as good as mine. He didn't give the target's name and was disappointed when I didn't jump at the chance.'

He shook his head. 'Clown. So, what do you want from me?'

'See what you can dig up on a proposal for a Skytrain.'

'Come again?'

'Yeah, that was my reaction, too. Apparently, the idea's been around for sixty years. I'd like to know who's behind it. If we understand that we'll understand who Jocelyn's working for.'

'Okay. Where have you left it with him?'

'As you'd expect, I told him to fuck off, didn't I?'

'Not something a man in his position hears every day. How did that go?'

'Not well. He threatened me.'

'You're joking. Is the guy insane?'

'No, I don't think so. Told me I was making a mistake.'

Ritchie was having a hard time taking it seriously. 'I'll poke around and see what turns up, sure, but is there any way this geezer could be a fantasist? I mean, the whole thing's over the top. And threatening Luke Glass of all people...'

'I'll leave it with you. Come back to me when you have something.'

'Should we be worried?'

'That's what you're going to find out, George.'

* * *

Charley saw him the moment he stepped into the club and felt a flutter of excitement in the pit of her stomach. Eamon Brannagan was wearing a dark suit and a white shirt open at the neck, and even from a distance she saw the difference in him: he was sober. A hostess approached to take him to a seat. He declined and waited for Charley to come over. She picked her way between waiters balancing trays of drinks in the palms of their hands, suddenly nervous at meeting him again. When he'd called she'd been rude. Women threw themselves at this guy. At the world premiere of one of his movies at the Venice Film Festival a fan jumped into the lagoon because she couldn't get close enough to kiss him and had to be rescued by a police boat.

He said, 'Since I'm not barred – at least, not yet – I decided to apologise in person.'

'No need, I told you, it's fine.'

Brannagan smiled. 'You did. You did. But when a lady says somethin' is "fine", I know it's as far from fine as it's possible to be. Am I wrong?'

Charley laughed. 'In this case, yes. I'm pleased you're here.'

He held out his hand. 'So we're friends.'

She took it. 'We're friends.'

'Friends?' He made a face. 'Christ, it gets worse and worse. I'll have to misbehave again to get your attention.' Brannagan hadn't listened to her advice on the blarney. He said, 'I'm jokin'. Stick me behind a potted plant and forget about me. Don't worry, I'll be okay. I won't cause any trouble and you won't have to carry me home on your back. Promise.'

'Can I get you something to drink?'

'Absolutely. I'll start as I mean to go on with a glass of your finest soda water and lime.'

'Anything else?'

'Some ice, and when you get a spare minute make sure I'm okay. Usually, I'm heavily anaesthetised in these situations. I get lonely.'

It was over the top and corny but it made Charley laugh. She said, 'You won't be alone very long. At least half a dozen women have their eye on you.'

Brannagan dropped the act. 'Then, whoever they are, they're wastin' their time. If they come near me I'll be tellin' them the same. Sorry, again, about the other night. I can be a bit of a wanker when I put my mind to it.'

Charley didn't disagree and the actor glanced round. 'I didn't realise how cool this was before. I like it. I like it a lot.'

'LBC belongs to my brother.'

'LBC?'

'The Lucky Bastards Club.'

'Really? Well, congratulate him on his sense of irony. The name's bang on for these eejits. Why're you here?'

'Are you asking what a nice girl like me is doing in a place like this?'

'No, no, that wasn't what I meant at all. Shame on you for puttin' the thought in my head.'

'I manage it.'

'Smart as well as beautiful. And who's this brother when he's at home?'

'Luke Glass.'

'Should I know him? I don't bother with newspapers.'

'You're in them often enough.'

'Which is how I can assure you they're a right load of bollocks. If you don't read them, you're uninformed. If you do, you're misinformed.'

The latest in a string of classic Tamla Motown songs drifted up from downstairs. Charley led him to a table near the bar and missed his eyes wandering to her fingers, checking for a ring. Brannagan took hold of her hand. 'Don't go too far. I wasn't jokin' about being lonely. Or about the anaesthetic. And keep the soda water coming. If you see me drinkin' anythin' stronger, throw me out on my arse.'

Charley's interaction with Eamon Brannagan had run to two brief conversations – one of them when he'd been drunk – and a phone call that hadn't gone well. Not an ideal beginning. Tonight, he was sober, respectful and contrite, working a little-boy-lost charm offensive that was difficult to resist and probably wasn't real. Charley didn't judge; in different ways she'd done her share of using. Wasting energy on insecure ego freaks who measured their own worth by the woman in their bed was in the past. She needed more. The early signs were that Brannagan probably wouldn't have more. But the chemistry between them was undeniable. He was an actor; pretending was what he did. Letting him in close could be a mistake she'd regret, and the fact she was even having that conversation in her head told something about where she already was with the handsome Irishman.

In the meantime, she had a job to do. The waiting list for membership of LBC was as long as Margaret Street – the club was busy every night during the week and rammed at the weekend. Luke had his office in the basement and rarely put in an appearance. There was no need; Charley had it covered. The staff she hired had first-rate interpersonal skills, were well trained and well paid; the chef was an up-and-coming culinary star she'd persuaded to quit a restaurant with an honourable mention in the *Michelin Guide*, and the hookers made more money in two months than most people made in a year.

Charley loved what she did and worked harder and longer than any of them. She glided round the club, seeing everything, missing nothing, aware the bottles of Laurent-Perrier champagne ordered by the party of trust-fund managers celebrating a great day in the stock market were taking too long to arrive, and that an older man with a blonde young enough to be his daughter was getting restless. In a minute, he'd ask for his bill.

Brannagan's eyes followed her wherever she went; she felt herself flush like a schoolgirl and turned to the two men in the booth. Each had his arm around a girl – Zia, a tall ebony beauty from the Gambia, and Aisha, a Malaysian student who'd traded a career in medicine and the Royal London Hospital to make money. They were laughing at something one of the men had said when Charley interrupted them. Her question was asked before she realised who she was talking to. 'Good evening. Are we taking care of you?'

Antoine Giordano looked up at her, older than she remembered but still handsome. Beside him, Bruno Mura untangled himself from Zia's long arms and smiled an empty smile.

Giordano said, 'Long time no see, Charlene. We've got a lot to talk about, you and me.'

* * *

The driver of a grey Lexus drummed the dashboard and waited for the call. When it came, he accelerated to the neon-lit entrance of LBC; two men and two women appeared, opened the door, and piled into the back. The guy behind the wheel didn't turn his head. He'd been around enough to understand curiosity killed a lot more than the cat. Calum Bishop's order had been clear – pick them up and take them where they want to go. The driver caught a glimpse of his passengers in the rear-view – the women were stunning, sensual and perfect, and for a moment he envied the men squiring them. They were strangers, from their accents, American; their identities weren't his concern.

Over his shoulder, Tony Giordano fingered the amber pendant round his neck. 'Did you see her face? Did you see the bitch's face, Bruno? She couldn't believe it.'

Bruno Mura didn't reply. His opinion wouldn't be welcome. Madeline was right: her grandson was a clown. Mura was tired of covering for him. He'd tried and failed to persuade Tony to be patient and stick to the plan, reminding him that showing up at the club wasn't a good idea. He hadn't listened, preferring to witness the thief's reaction for himself when she realised he'd caught up with her. Delivering the sister to her brother piece by piece would have been a fitting end for a beautiful whore like Charlene. Picturing it made Mura hard; he regretted he wouldn't get the opportunity. His dark-skinned companion sensed the change in him and got on her knees. She unzipped his trousers and gasped. Above her head, Bruno's lips parted in a silent snarl, wanting to snap her slender neck and throw her into the gutter for mistaking him for a gullible *idiota* like the rest of the horny imbeciles she serviced for a living.

Instead, he ran his fingers through her hair. 'And it's all yours, my lovely. All yours.'

9

Charley pressed her back to the door and slid helplessly to the floor, breathing in frantic bursts as the panic attack took hold and the awful reality of what had just happened arrived.

They'd found her.

'Charlene'.

Hearing it from Tony Giordano's lips had been like the lash of a whip biting into her flesh.

'Charlene'.

A name she'd almost forgotten had ever been hers. Almost, but not quite. Because the dreams – the hellish dreams – had stayed, reminding her who she really was and what she'd done. And, night after night, in the darkness, Charley had cried out, and wakened bathed in sweat, terrified and trembling. Nobody needed to tell her stealing from the Giordanos had been a massive error. Believing they'd let her go or that she could outrun them, beyond foolish. They were never going to give up. The photographs, the address book, with their damning truths, would've been replaced. New marks identified, the screw turned, the power base fortified and renewed. From Algiers to Lakeshore and all points in between, it would be business as usual.

She felt her face flush with shame at her stupidity, knowing she was responsible. Tony had wanted her, more than once making artless attempts to get her into his bed. Rejecting him for his father had brought her to this. The irony was bitter: she'd crossed the biggest crime family in New Orleans and put her own in danger. And for what? Information she could never use because, even if it wasn't gone, like a trail of breadcrumbs it would have led them to her.

They'd found her without it, hadn't they? Christ!

Showing up at the club wasn't about getting anything back. No, they were here because if a whore could take what belonged to them and live, their reputation would be irreparably damaged and one of umpteen outfits in the city might see a chance to challenge them.

It was revenge, pure and simple. And nine miles from the Canadian border she'd witnessed first-hand how pitilessly they administered it, immune to an old woman's screams.

Luke and Nina would have to be told, that prospect itself enough to bring the shaking back. Charley hugged herself to make it stop. Sweat dried on her forehead; her breathing returned to normal. Upstairs had been them delivering their calling card. Letting her know this might be her family's city but it was their game.

It was too late for regrets; she had to get away or drag them all down.

She forced herself to think it through: Tony and Bruno wouldn't have come alone, there would be others, perhaps many others, tooled up and ready to launch a gang war if necessary. This time there would be no desperate race to escape under cover of a storm.

Like a cat playing with a mouse, the final result would never be in doubt. Better for her to surrender and take what was coming. Except, it wouldn't be quick. In the Big Easy, she'd seen Bruno Mura gut a man with the razor-sharp blade of his knife over a disagreement about cards. She'd heard the anguished screams from the cabin and guessed he was using it on her mother. The same weapon would be turned against her. And when the end came, she'd welcome it.

After their appearance tonight, they'd guess she'd make a break for it rather than wait for them to come. Getting out of London would be a problem. They wouldn't take the chance of losing her again. Wherever she went eyes would be on her until they tired of toying with her and ended it.

Charley sat with her back against the wall; she'd never felt so lonely or so alone.

One man could help, as ruthless in his own way as the Giordanos. He might very well refuse because there was no love lost between them. From their first meeting in the office above the King of Mesopotamia he hadn't hidden his suspicion of her or her claim to be Luke and Nina's long-lost sister. He was wrong, she was a Glass and had proved it. But the relationship hadn't improved and they kept their distance from each other, only meeting when it couldn't be avoided, both accepting they would never be friends. Nevertheless, he was a shrewd operator who knew everybody there was to know in the city and had the contacts to make her disappear, although she was the last person on earth he'd expect to hear from.

Charley took a deep breath, pulled out her mobile, and called George Ritchie.

* * *

Tony Giordano had gone along with Madeline's strategy though he strongly opposed it. His ego demanded the death of the thief and a war that would be talked about four and a half thousand miles away in the parishes, in the bayous, and on the streets of New Orleans, allowing him, at last, to step out of his grandmother's shadow. A not unreasonable ambition, except the battle hadn't begun and already he'd blundered. In any conflict, the element of surprise could be decisive – that edge had been sacrificed to satisfy the whim of a spoiled child whose only interest was proving to himself he was a big man.

Mura cursed under his breath and spoke quietly to the driver. 'Take us where there aren't cameras.'

The wheelman inhaled noisily between his teeth. 'Not easy, mate. This city has five hundred thousand of the buggers. Dozens of them filming us right now.'

'But you know a place, am I right?'

'Tower Hamlets has three hundred and sixty-two.'

'So?'

'Fifty-six of them don't work. Limehouse has only one.'

Mura nodded, satisfied. 'Then, Limehouse it is.'

'It's a bit of a shlep.'

He leered at the girls. 'No problem. We'll amuse ourselves till we get there.'

They'd told the women they were staying at The Dorchester and watched them exchange smiles at the mention of the fashionable address; Mura guessed they'd seen the ceilings of more five-star hotel bedrooms than they could remember.

Heading east along the Victoria Embankment with the lights of the city reflected in the river, Aisha broke from Giordano's pawing hands. 'This isn't the way.'

Mura answered with the speed of a practised deceiver. 'You're right, it isn't. London is one of the greatest cities on the planet. I want a picture of me having fun with two of the most beautiful women in town.'

Zia and Aisha giggled on cue like tipsy teenagers and accepted the explanation. Mura smiled to himself: it was just too easy. He was aroused, for sure, though not by what they had to offer. Zia said, 'You called her Charlene.'

'What?'

'Charley. In the club you called her Charlene.'

Bruno fought the urge to close his hands round her throat and squeeze.

'Because that's her name, honey.'

Tony looked out at the silhouette of St Katharine Docks Marina etched against the night sky. He knew how this ended. He hadn't forgotten what Bruno had done to the albino prostitute in Raleigh or the croupier in Jersey: there had been no need to kill them, but he had. In the cabin, the old woman had died in agony, mutilated beyond recognition. And although it had been on his order, Mura had enjoyed cutting her, relished her screams, knowing her daughter was hiding in the woods listening to every pitiful cry.

The driver shouted, 'We're almost there,' and took a left into the appropriately named Butcher Row. Mura's lust for death wouldn't wait. In Narrow Street, he lost it completely, opened the door of the moving car, jumped out and pulled the still giggling Zia behind him. One of her high heels snapped; she stumbled and fell, ripping her tights, skinning her knees. Bruno bent down and brushed his lips against the bruise, gently lifted her to her feet and led her into the lane behind a pizza place.

Reluctantly, Tony removed his hand from between Aisha's smooth thighs and followed them. There could be no witnesses to what was about to happen. His finger traced a line across her firm breast and led her to certain death. If she was lucky, it would be quick.

What a waste!

Mura stood like the feral creature he was, sniffing the unfamiliar air of an urban landscape. Slowly, his eyes settled back on his companion, almost as though he'd forgotten she was there. She saw his face and whimpered, eyes wide, suddenly afraid.

Zia's voice trembled. 'I don't like this. Take us back to the club.'

She looked pleadingly at Giordano. He ignored her; there was nothing he could do. Mura bared his teeth, grabbed her long hair and slapped her hard across the jaw. Her eyes fluttered and closed; blood trickled from her lip. He screamed at her. 'You don't like it? Who gives a fuck what a whore likes?'

His cool palm closed over Zia's luscious mouth. She bit him and he hit her again, a punch this time, rocking her head on her shoulders like a broken doll, her nose and her beauty destroyed.

Aisha was crying hysterically. 'Stop him! Please stop him, for God's sake!'

Mura refocused his attention from the semi-conscious Zia to her sobbing friend.

'Shut the fuck up, your time's coming.'

Aisha begged a silent Giordano to save her life. Tony roughly pushed her away. Mura wiped his bloodied fingers on a white handkerchief and stepped towards her. At his side, the carbon-steel blade, his trademark weapon, glinted in the lights illuminating the alley from the high-rise buildings of Canary Wharf on the Isle of Dogs. Aisha ran to the car in a futile attempt to escape. Bruno hauled her, moaning, back into the darkness and finished what he'd started up against a wall. The driver couldn't watch – it was too much, even for him. Bishop would go off his nut when he heard.

PART II

10

The pub in Islington had officially closed two hours ago; the people left were locked in and weren't complaining about it. 'Afters' was a perk usually only extended to the diehards – the drinkers who spent most of their lives and all their money here. Early on a Sunday morning, they'd knock on the back door with a shaky hand and when it opened, hurry in, anxious to begin the new week the way they'd ended the old one. Fucking losers to a man.

Spending time with them wasn't Stevie D's idea of fun. Tonight was different. He ruffled the bundle of notes a desperate Nina Glass had pressed into his hand and considered his good fortune: his situation had changed – and not just because he had a pocketful of money. Stevie waved his empty pint measure to get the barman's attention.

'Same again, squire. And a large malt.'

'Any particular brand?'

'The best you've got.'

'Oh, won the lottery, have we?'

'Not quite.'

'What's the occasion? Mother-in-law's parole come through?'

Stevie laughed. 'Wouldn't be pushing the boat out for that, mate. No danger.'

The barman measured twice from a bottle of Ardbeg 10 and set it down. 'This stuff's hard to beat. Been voted Best Single Malt in the World more than once. You'll like it.'

'At these prices, I'd better bloody love it.'

'Shall I join you? Don't mind a decent Scotch now and again.'

Stevie rolled the whisky round his mouth, savouring its smoothness, eyeing him over the rim of his glass. 'You're a chancer, do you know that, John? Under-ringing the till. Short-changing the punters too pissed to notice. Now, you're on the blag with me. Should be ashamed of yourself.'

'What're you on about? I'm being sociable.'

'Is that what they're calling it these days? Yeah, well, forget it. You get more than enough of my money as it is.'

'Is that a no?'

'It's a fuck off out of it, is what it is. Give me another.'

The barman hesitated. 'You sure?'

'Put another one in there and be quick about it before I change my mind.'

'That's top gear. Not how it's supposed to be drunk.'

Stevie felt the skin at the corner of his eyes tighten. 'Your inter-personal skills could use a refresher course, my old son. Not to mention your arithmetic. Save the lecture for somebody who appreciates it. Do your job, pour the fucking whisky.'

Stevie D had been coming to this boozer for as long as he could remember. For years he'd been happy to earn enough to keep body and soul together with the occasional luxury of a hooker who wasn't wasted on the drugs him or somebody else had sold her or some skank giving him a freebie in lieu. Most of the ladies around Camden Town didn't meet the criteria – junkies with well-estab-lished habits – which meant he had to go further afield for what he was after. The prostitutes who plied their trade in the West End were too expensive unless he'd had a windfall. He hadn't. At least, not yet. Snagging Nina Glass gave him reason to hope one was on the way. The dealer had twice found his way to the Chelsea Cloisters building known as 'ten floors of whores' owned by a millionaire Tory donor. Not exactly top-of-the-range pussy. Nevertheless, the girls were so busy servicing clients they went to lunch in groups wearing pyjamas.

Stevie could do better and he would. Mayfair and Kensington were where the high-class prossies hung out – the ones in it for the cash who intended to be out before it got nasty; prepared to kick back and share a spliff with a mark – before, during or after the action – but too smart to get drawn into anything harder.

Further down the line, their gormless husbands wouldn't suspect the scores of times their prim suburban wives had been naked and on their knees while strangers slapped it into them from behind and would think themselves lucky to have married a woman who understood how to satisfy a man.

The dilemma he hadn't resolved was how to turn the circumstances to his advantage. Nina was still at the stage where she was just about able to hold it together. If he kept the supply rolling her dependency would increase without her life going completely off the rails. The trick was to keep her on a tight leash, be gentle, sympathetic, pretend to be falling in love with her if that was what it took. Get to the point where the poor cow thought he was her saviour, maybe even her friend.

The notion made him laugh.

Stevie Dean wasn't a complex man; his plan was simple. Luke Glass was a player in London. Arguably, *the* player – the one every wide boy starting out in the city wanted to be. He'd become a legitimate businessman – no mean feat considering the family's reputation – the last thing he needed was an addict in the nest. As soon as

Nina started putting white powder up her nose she became unreliable: a liability. Family loyalty went out of the window. All an enemy had to do was supply the sister. Her dirty little secret could stay between them so long as she did what she was told. Stevie hadn't a clue what that might be, though a guy like Calum Bishop would have a few ideas. Colin and Kenny Bishop had mugged Glass off. Not the wisest thing they could've done and they got well slapped up for their trouble. Colin – another snowhead – died a slow death. Kenny had seen the writing on the wall, passed what was left of their empire on to young Calum and retired for the good of his health, last heard of sunning it up on one of the Costas. It would be fucking ironic if he teamed up with Luke's missing brother. From what Stevie had heard, Danny could've given masterclasses in being a solid-gold nutter.

Stevie put his empty whisky glass on the counter and called the barman over. 'A nice taste of Scotland that. Appreciated.' His hand closed round the barman's shirt sleeve, digging into the flesh beneath, leaned across and spoke quietly. 'Try it on like that with me again and some friends of mine will come round when you're in bed and torch the place. Got it?'

'I was only being sociable.'

'Yeah, you said. A word in your ear: don't. It isn't what's wanted, John. Not wanted at all.' He released his grip. 'Show some respect, eh? Remember, the customer's always right. Or is that concept too fucking deep for you, mate?'

The barman would remember the exchange. Stevie D forgot about it the minute he stepped towards the machine glinting in the dim glow from a flickering lamplight overhead. For him, nothing could touch the thrill of bombing down a country lane, leaning into the curves, bent against the wind rushing in his ears. That was the best. He ran his hand lovingly over the matt-black chassis of his pride and joy, the Energica EGO, claimed by the manufacturer to be the world's first street-legal electric Italian sport motorcycle. It had cost him £23,000, which he'd paid in cash from the proceeds of selling cocaine. If the police busted him the bike would be considered a criminal asset and confiscated – one reason he was determined not to get caught.

Drugs were a means to an end. His dream was to own a repair shop focused exclusively on motorbikes – a one-man operation until he could afford to bring a couple of like-minded bike-mad geezers on board. He even had a name: SD Bikes. He didn't kid himself it would be easy – most bikers weren't flush with cash – but if the job was good and the price was right word would get round. Dealing would've served its purpose. No more putting up with users, losers and skanks. He'd have a girlfriend he wasn't ashamed to be seen with, go on holidays, a life that didn't have you jumping out of your skin when the door knocked in the middle of the night. Nice one.

Until then, he had this place. Not great but it would do.

The lock-up was as close as he'd managed to get to his goal and he spent more and more time underneath the railway bridge working on his current obsession, a 1982 metallic-silver Yamaha SR250 he was restoring. It sat in the middle of the concrete floor balanced on a lift between two heavy blocks of wood. Japanese motorbikes were simple builds – the only things controlled electronically were the lights, the timing, and the battery charging system. When he'd done the work it needed he'd flog it, stash the profit, and buy another one – something a bit more challenging – and begin again.

The pungent-varnish smell of pure gasoline and oil hung in the air and from a 2019 titty calendar, Miss July gazed seductively at the camera. Stevie remembered flicking through the last six months and deciding he liked her best.

A line of rusted iron hooks embedded in the brick wall gave a clue to the lock-up's vivid past: during the Second World War it had been an air-raid shelter, a century earlier, home to the Great Eastern Railway Company's horse infirmary. Evidence of the stalls, the tethering rings and the farriers' workshops could still be seen; the hooks dated from its first incarnation as a wholesale butcher's before the invention of refrigeration.

Stevie D didn't give a flying fuck about any of that. As soon as he had the money he'd be out of here.

That was where Nina Glass and Calum Bishop came in – they were the fast track to where he wanted to go.

11

On Bayswater Road, George Ritchie pointed the car towards Marble Arch and the city centre. A taxi with its FOR HIRE sign lit was travelling in the other direction, no doubt taking some exhausted party people home. For them, the night was over. For him, it was only just beginning. He rarely slept more than three or four hours and when his mobile rang he was in the cramped basement flat in Moscow Road reading Vincent Cronin's biography *Napoleon*.

He put down the book, checked caller ID, and spoke. 'Charley?'

Her voice was a frantic whisper on the other end of the line. 'I'm in trouble; you need to help me.'

Ritchie was immediately alert. 'What kind of trouble?'

'I can't explain over the phone.'

'Where are you?'

'At the club. In the office. Please, George. Please. You have to get me out of here.'

'Stay put. I'm coming.'

* * *

LBC in Margaret Street was less than three miles. Ritchie drove fast, though not fast enough to get pulled over by a cruising police unit – that wouldn't help anybody – and tried to make sense of the tense exchange. Luke's sisters were strong-willed, impetuous females who did what they wanted and fuck the consequences. Clashing with them was inevitable. Nina was the original wild child who'd never grown up. If her elder brother Danny – one of the most feared gangsters in London – couldn't control her what chance did anybody else have? When the family was under attack, the job of dragging her, screaming and kicking, from the club or the party or the bed of the new loser she'd be better off without had fallen to Ritchie: a thankless task repeated so often it had soured any hope of a cordial relationship. He was under no illusions about exactly where he stood: Nina wasn't a fan; in fact, she detested him and made no secret of it. In her shoes he might feel the same, but she was a deep one, a mystery he wouldn't solve if he squandered the rest of his life trying. Women held grudges forever; they didn't know how to let go. He hadn't seen Sister No 1, as Luke called her, in a while and George wasn't crying about that.

He turned left into a deserted Great Cumberland Place, passed the Hard Rock Hotel, and hung a right into Seymour Street, thinking about the phone call from Sister No 2. Charley had sounded very different from the red-haired enigma oozing sensuality and confidence who'd burst into his office above the King of Mesopotamia, tossed the birth certificate on the desk that said she was a Glass and dared Luke to deny her a seat at the table. She'd been at the top of her game that Saturday morning and hadn't known the meaning of fear. The Charley he'd spoken to tonight wasn't the same person – not even close.

At the club, the men on the door dressed in Hugo Boss suits and black Armani T-shirts recognised Ritchie and stepped aside. He barely acknowledged them. LBC had been Luke's idea and turned out to be a licence to print money: a private club in the centre of the city that had quickly become the hottest place in town. On any given evening, movie stars, rock stars, lesser royals – and Christ knew there seemed to be more of them every time he opened a newspaper – rubbed shoulders with politicians, hedge-fund managers, and other villains paying over the odds for everything from peanuts to prostitutes. Apparently, not everybody was looking for a bargain. Luke had offered him the job of running it alongside the other legitimate businesses. Ritchie had declined, preferring the streets south of the river and dealing with wide boys who weren't concerned with their image or the latest prices on the FTSE 100 – bread-and-butter criminals with their feet on the ground. People he understood.

A guy with designer stubble stood in front of him, barring his way. Ritchie put a hand on his shoulder, leaned forward, and whispered in his ear. 'Do yourself a favour, son. Before you say anything, think about how important the next words out of your mouth have just become.'

The tone was soft but the anger beneath was impossible to miss and the man took half a pace back; he was making the right decision. He said, 'Sorry... just doing my job.'

Ritchie flashed a line of uneven teeth. 'Apology accepted. But do it somewhere else before I break your fucking arm, there's a good lad.'

The throb of an electronic bass line followed him downstairs. George Ritchie wasn't cool and that was okay with him. In his opinion, music – real music – died in 1982 when Benny, Björn, Agnetha and Anni-Frid went their separate ways. Since Abba, if he happened to switch the car radio on all he heard was noise.

He hid his apprehension and tapped on the door. 'Charley, it's me. Open up.'

'Thank God! Oh, thank God!' For a moment he thought she

was going to fall into his arms weeping. Luke's right-hand man wasn't used to women sobbing on his shoulder. He kept his emotions on a tight leash and wished everybody else would do the same. In the north east where he'd grown up, big boys and girls didn't cry. He held her at arm's length. 'What's going on?'

Charley put her head in her hands. 'I've fucked up, George. I've fucked up big time.'

London had softened her accent but the New York drawl she'd arrived with hadn't been lost. She ran a weary hand through her hair and leaned on the desk 'There are men in the club.'

'What men? How many?'

Her answer had little to do with the questions. 'It's a long story.'

Ritchie relocked the door and stood with his back to it. 'I'll bet. Who are they?'

'The Giordanos.'

'Never heard of them.'

'They're from New Orleans.'

'From... what're they doing here?'

'They've come to kill me.'

Ritchie instinctively reached for the gun inside his jacket, reassured by the smooth black Nitron finish under his fingertips. The SIG Sauer P365 was new and hadn't been fired – that might be about to change.

'How many did you see?'

'Two. They won't be alone.'

He drew his weapon, opened the door, and stepped into the corridor, signalling her to follow him to the security office at the end. A bald man in rolled-up shirt sleeves, his jacket draped over the chair, sat in front of a bank of black-and-white screens mounted on the wall.

Hearing them come in startled him. Ritchie wasted no time with introductions and barked orders. 'Contact the entrance.

Nobody leaves. Tell them anything, I couldn't care less, but do it now or start looking for a new gig.'

He turned to Charley. 'Where're they sitting?'

'In one of the booths.'

'Find them.'

She ran her eyes over the screens and shook her head. 'I think they've left.'

Ritchie spoke to the operator. 'Go back thirty minutes. Inside the club and out. Let's see what these jokers look like.'

He did as he was told and Charley shouted, 'That's them!'

Ritchie saw two guys out on the town, champagne glass in one hand, a hooker in the other. Dressed in their sharp suits they might've been twenty-first-century City traders, swaggering barrow boys who'd made it to the big time and were convinced they were the smartest people in the room; carelessly spending the commission from their latest legal scam secure in the knowledge there was more where that had come from. George Ritchie recognised the type; the exclusive clubs and Michelin-star restaurants in London were full of wankers just like them.

He said, 'Who are they?'

'That's Tony Giordano with the slicked hair.'

'And his friend?'

'Bruno Mura. He does Tony's dirty work.'

On cue, Giordano ran a finger provocatively along the soft flesh at the throat of the woman he was with, defiantly staring at the camera, in his eyes an unspoken challenge to whoever would observe him. Charley came into the picture. Giordano said something. As she walked away he made an obscene gesture behind her back that brought a grin from the thug with him. Tony untangled himself from his leggy companion, got up and left with her. Mura threw notes on the table, grabbed his woman by the wrist and went after him.

What Ritchie was witnessing wasn't good: these people were arrogantly announcing their presence. A sliver of anxiety ran through him and he spoke out loud to himself. 'Unbelievable.'

'What?'

'This bastard has balls. He's putting on a performance for our benefit, telling us he's here and he's not afraid. All by itself that says a helluva lot. Fast forward. Let's see what happened outside.'

The screen flickered. In Margaret Street, Mura stepped to the kerb and raised his arm; a car that had obviously been waiting pulled up. The four of them got in the back and the car disappeared towards Cavendish Square.

Ritchie heard Charley gasp and slump beside him. He said, 'Now we know what we're up against. Get the reg and run a check on it.'

Nina's phone was switched off; he called Felix Corrigan. Felix ran the East End, a pro who followed orders without expecting an explanation. Just as well because George didn't offer one. 'Go to Denmark Hill. Something's going down. Until we know exactly what it is we have to be sure Nina's safe.'

Felix whistled through his teeth. 'She won't like it.'

'She never does – but don't take no for an answer, Felix. Get her out of there. And get men over to Luke's.'

'I'm on my way. Have you talked to Luke?'

'He's next on my list.'

Charley grabbed his arm. 'The girls! He'll hurt them! It's me they're after. I'll—'

Ritchie stopped her. 'Forget it. We can't do anything about them. It's too late. You're a Glass. Anybody tries to hurt you they answer for it.'

'But—'

'But nothing. You're family.'

'I haven't told Luke about New Orleans.'

If she was hoping for reassurance, she was speaking to the wrong guy. Ritchie was Luke's man – first, last, always; he wasn't sympathetic. 'Then, that's something to look forward to, isn't it?'

He walked to the other end of the office and phoned his boss. Ritchie said, 'We've got a potential situation developing at the club. Charley spotted a couple of faces she recognised. Looks like something might be about to go down. Felix's heading for Nina's place. She isn't answering her phone.'

'Are we being attacked?'

'Too early to know. Our guys should be with you soon.'

'Who is it, George?'

Ritchie stared across at Charley. 'I'll let your sister explain.'

'What's their move?'

'They haven't made it yet. She's convinced they intend to and I'm inclined to believe her.'

Luke's reaction was predictable. He said, 'Hold it together, George, I'm coming to you.'

* * *

Felix Corrigan had been to the white Georgian house in trendy south London many times without ever seeing the inside. Once upon a time, collecting Luke's sister from some downbeat party and taking her home out of her pretty head had been a regular thing. Then, Mark Douglas had come on the scene and the wild nights on the tiles stopped. It had gone quiet; she'd suddenly started behaving. George Ritchie's orders had been specific and vague at the same time. Not like him. It meant he didn't have anything beyond a gut feeling to shield Nina from a threat that might not even exist. Ritchie was a pragmatist but ignoring his instinct was a risk he wasn't prepared to take.

Felix wasn't alone; six men – experienced street fighters, tooled up and ready – were with him. Her car was parked with its wheels on the pavement. Felix felt the bonnet – cool; it hadn't been driven in a couple of hours. A downstairs light was on in the house, a sign the lady might be home and that he could look forward to being sworn at for 'fucking spying' on her.

Corrigan waved his guys to spread out round the building while he edged under the window and peered through a crack in the curtains. His view was limited though he saw enough: a coffee table had been upended and Nina was sprawled on the floor. Her face was ashen, there was blood at her temple, and Felix couldn't tell if she was alive or dead. Thoughts of stealth were abandoned. He hurled himself against the door, snapping the lock at the third attempt. The hall was dark and silent. Felix felt the reassuring weight of the gun in his hand, gently pressed his finger against the trigger, and listened. He heard his men in the space behind him. Nina's assailants – for reasons he couldn't explain he assumed there would be more than one – might be gone. Anyone left inside would have to shoot their way out. Felix didn't fancy their chances.

He moved clear of the line of fire and pushed the door open.

The silence dared him to enter.

Corrigan stayed low and crept into the lounge, both hands on his weapon, nerves at breaking point. If a shooting war started, he was primed. Nina still wasn't moving; blood from her head had stained the carpet beside her limp body. He searched for a pulse, found it and shouted instructions to his men.

'Check the rooms and round the back of the building! And for Christ's sake, stay sharp!'

Glass from the coffee table that had shattered into a thousand pieces and scattered across the room crunched underneath his shoe. In a corner, an upturned bottle of Absolut vodka that had rolled against the wall caught his attention, a survivor of the fall. His immediate reaction was to order his men back to the cars: the less they saw, the better. An anxious Ritchie chose that moment to call for an update. On the other end of the phone his voice sounded far away.

'Is Nina all right?'

Caught off guard, Felix hesitated a second longer than he should have.

'For fuck's sake, Felix! Is she all right?'

George was an old dog who knew most of the tricks, including the new ones. Something wasn't right; Felix was being evasive. Ritchie trawled his brain for an answer to the question gnawing at him: had they got the wrong sister?

In Denmark Hill Felix forced out a laugh. 'Nina's had a few too many and taken a tumble. Simple as that. She'll be okay.'

'You're sure?'

Nina groaned and he said, 'One hundred per cent. She's got a bump on the head and won't feel too clever in the morning. Apart from that, she's fine. I'll take her to A & E if she needs to go.'

Corrigan chanced his luck. Ritchie didn't take kindly to suggestions – even from him.

'Don't tell Luke. Nothing bad has happened. Nina's bound to be pretty embarrassed. Let's cut her a break. She's had a rough trip.'

'She's his sister. He should know.'

'Know what? That we found her pissed?'

The silence told him Ritchie was thinking it through. Finally, he said, 'You stay with her.'

'I will. For as long as I have to. But keep Luke out of it.'

12

This was my city. All I knew. All I wanted to know. Driving across it in the wee hours it felt like an alien planet. I couldn't focus; my mind was a blur. Since the crazy scenes in Yorkshire it was as though I'd fallen down a rabbit hole into Alice in Wonderland territory. Nothing was as it should be and I was making a poor show of processing it. 'A potential situation developing' was Georgespeak for big trouble on the horizon. We'd climbed to the top of the tree and crossed over into legitimate business. We even paid tax, for Christ's sake! And though there were plenty of gangs – by some estimates as many as two hundred – most of them were happy to fight each other for pieces of tuppenny turf not worth the hassle. The serious competition had been rinsed. Most of it. What was left wouldn't have the bottle to take the Glass family on.

So what the fuck was waiting for me in Margaret Street?

My mind scanned for its next problem. I'd asked Ritchie to find out who the players were in the latest tilt at a London Skytrain, in particular the person standing in the way of Jocelyn Church and his 'people' hoping to make a fortune out of it. The concept was bold; I'd no objection to anybody with drive and vision coming out on the right side of it. Good luck to them. Only, that wasn't what was happening. Church had been chosen to be the public face for two reasons: he was well known, and bent to his upper-class core. Offering me money to eliminate the opposition was beyond stupid. It assumed I was easy to play.

Wrong, Jocelyn.

For all his outward sophistication and expensive education, Jocelyn Church wasn't very bright. He'd put two and two together and come up with five. The mysterious 'people' behind him weren't too sharp either, otherwise they'd have sussed a smooth character like Church's chances of persuading me to do what they wanted were zero.

Career criminals are misunderstood; so much bollocks written about them: romanticised horseshit about a 'code' that only worked in the movies to bring a sliver of humanity to the heartless killers on the screen. Violence, often gratuitous violence, was a fact of life in the underworld. Women, even children who got in the way, were collateral damage. Sad, but true. Anybody who said different was talking out of a hole in their head. If there was a code it had to be Do Unto Others Before They Do Unto You.

None of the Glass family expected Saint Peter to welcome them with open arms at the pearly gates. Danny had been a monster – no other word for it – the rest of us, whether we liked it or not, had been birthed from the same gene pool.

A Volvo pulled in behind me and flashed its lights: Ritchie, as good as his word: the men in the car were ours. By the time I turned left onto Old Kent Road, another had joined it. Seeing them ought to have reassured me. No chance. It meant my fears about what 'a potential situation developing' meant were on the money.

I called Ritchie again, cursing when his mobile was engaged. On Southampton Row, I ran a red light, forcing the two vehicles with me to do the same. My hands were steady but my mouth felt like the inside of a chauffeur's glove and acid burned my stomach. Then, I remembered George's cryptic response when I'd asked who we were up against.

'I'll let your sister explain,' he'd said and left it there. I parked it beside his 'potential situation...' claptrap and raced down Great Portland Street.

The scene at the club was nothing like I'd expected. There was no panic. No gunshots. No bloodied bodies on the pavement. And as I made my way downstairs with the Bunny Sigler version of 'Let the Good Times Roll' in my ears, I couldn't shake the feeling the gods were having a laugh. Maybe the key word had been 'potential'.

The office door was locked. I tapped and it opened. Ritchie rarely smiled and didn't now. Behind her desk, Charley stared at the floor and didn't raise her eyes when I came in.

I said, 'Okay, I'm here. Does somebody want to tell me what the fuck's going on?'

The silence only added to my fears. Ritchie broke it with an amended version of his earlier enigmatic statement. 'Charley will fill you in.'

Sister No 2 was a strong woman; tonight, she wasn't here, and the dread I'd felt on the drive across the city was a lead weight on my shoulder. There were tears in her eyes, genuine regret in her voice, as she falteringly tried to explain. 'Luke... I'm sorry. This mess... what's happening... is all my fault.'

'What's all your fault, Charley? You're not making sense.'

'It's me they're after. I'm the one they want. They—'

I took her hand and went into my big-brother routine while my nerve-ends jangled and demanded the truth. 'Don't worry, sis. Whatever it is, we'll sort it.'

Kindness pushed her over the edge; she couldn't handle it and cracked completely. 'Not this! Not these people! You don't know them. They burned...'

She rocked backwards and forwards, hugging herself. George Ritchie still had the gun in his hand and I guessed the next few minutes weren't going to be easy for any of us.

Charley sobbed and I let her. 'Listen to me. You're my sister. Whatever it is, I'm on your side. Pull yourself together and start at the beginning.'

She looked up, beautiful and broken, her face destroyed by the secret she was about to reveal. 'The beginning? I've no idea where that is, Luke. No idea at all.'

The tracks of her tears were like lines of candle wax. I waited for her to get a grip on herself and began as gently as I could. 'You're going to have to tell me sooner or later, Charley.'

'I don't want to.'

'Why not?'

'I'm afraid.'

'Of me?'

'Yes.'

'You're my sister. Nothing can change that.'

She nodded and took a baby step nearer to opening up. 'Promise you won't hate me.'

She shuddered one final time and spoke so quietly I had to strain to make out the words.

'When Frances Glass was drunk she'd rave like a madwoman about the family she'd left behind, running from our father with me in her belly. Sad stories, driven by anger and resentment, tumbling out of her. Vile, some of them. Graphic stuff no child should ever hear from a parent. Especially, from her mother. The next morning, she'd have no recollection of what she'd said. But I hadn't been drunk. I remembered. I was aware of Danny and Luke and Nina long before you knew I existed. Night after night, while she partied in the room next door with her "new" boyfriend, I lay in bed imagining what the three of you looked like.'

Revisiting the past was hard and for a moment I thought she wouldn't be able to go on. Charley got her emotions under control. 'You've no idea how much I wanted to be part of that family. This family. Growing up, it was all I thought about.'

'For your sins you got your wish.'

Her lip trembled, her voice heavy with remorse. 'It's my sins that have caused this, Luke.'

She closed her eyes and returned to her tale. 'You know most of this. We were living in upstate New York. Frances's marriage had failed. Her and her second husband had separated. She'd got what she wanted from it – a fresh start in a new place. From the beginning, the drinking had been a problem. But when he died suddenly and left her his navy pension and some money, it really took off. She bought an old cabin near the Canadian border – Christ knows what the plan was. I don't think she knew herself. We lasted a month. All I can tell you is she hauled me all over the country through one bad scene after another. I got out as soon as I could.'

We'd been through all this when she'd first got here but I sensed that if I rushed her she'd lose the courage she'd found to tell me what I needed to know.

'You must've been young. How did you survive?'

Charley stared defiantly and allowed me to piece it together without her help. 'Let's just say I managed until I ended up in Louisiana with Beppe.' She saw confusion on my face at the mention of the name. 'Beppe Giordano. Boss of the family who run New Orleans and one of the biggest bastards on the face of the earth. I was with him when he keeled over from a heart attack. It had always been coming. Nobody was surprised. But right away I knew I was headed back to being just another whore on Bourbon Street.'

'So you got out.'

'And fast.' Charley paused. 'The Big Easy is full of gangs. The Giordanos are the kings with a finger in all the usual pies. Their speciality is blackmail. Beppe had a safe in his bedroom where he kept the evidence. He'd just opened the door to it when he collapsed.'

I saw where this was going. It had to be about a lot more than money.

'What did you take? The truth, Charley.'

She shrugged. 'Everything that was in there. A hundred and thirty grand, photographs, invoices; an address book and a memory stick. All of it.'

'And that's why they're here?'

'Yes...'

'Where is it?'

'The money's gone.'

'Not the money, the other stuff?'

Charley stared, her face expressionless. I pushed her to answer. 'Did you get rid of it?'

'Not intentionally, they got too close and it got...' she faltered '... left behind. Luke, I'm sorry, I never meant to bring this mess down on you.'

I believed her. It didn't change anything – the men in the club hadn't crossed an ocean to say hello to an old friend. They'd come to reclaim what was theirs.

Ritchie said, 'We've got them on CCTV. Inside and outside the club.'

'What does it tell us?'

'All we need to know at this stage. Like Charley said, there were two of them. When they left a car picked them up.'

'Are we tracing the reg?'

Ritchie didn't reply and I asked again. 'Are we tracing the reg, George?'

He hesitated. 'They've taken two of the girls.'

'Fuck!'

I paced the floor struggling to get a handle on it. 'If they've got the nerve to show up here, what's their next move liable to be?'

He reassured me. 'Don't worry about Nina, she's safe. Felix is with her.'

'One less sister to be concerned about. Well done, George.'

Charley had her head in her hands, more upset than I'd ever known her. She was scared – I got that – but crying wouldn't help. I said, 'Okay, let's have a look at them.'

We went next door, ran the CCTV footage, and George gave me the first sight of my new enemy: arrogant bastards, even in grainy black and white, drinking champagne and fooling around with the smiling hookers draped over them. The cameras were at the wrong angle to capture Charley's reaction. Picturing the colour bleach from her face as surprise turned to horror didn't take much imagination. They laughed, drained their glasses, and left. Their job was done, or it would be when the girls' bodies were discovered, as they inevitably would be.

George pointed at a screen. 'The car picking them up at the door was a mistake. Either they aren't great at what they do or they're super-confident, which means this is just the advance party.'

'LBC is a private club, so how did they get in?'

The security guard replayed the video and the question was answered: the same car dropped them off; they drew a steward aside; money changed hands and they were in.

I felt anger hot on my cheeks. 'Whoever that greedy fucker is, George, make him regret it.'

'Depend on it, Luke.'

We went back to the office to talk. Ritchie's opinion was always worth hearing. I said, 'So what does it look like to you?'

He took a few seconds before he answered. 'Hard to say without knowing the whole story. These guys have appeared from nowhere. Charley's been here eighteen months? Taken their time, haven't they? And they're punks. Where do they think playing games will get them?'

'We know more than we think.' I counted off on my fingers. 'One: in New Orleans, they're the big dogs – how important does it have to be to bring them over here? Two: they gave up the element of surprise. That says they're pretty sure of themselves.'

Ritchie interrupted. 'Everything says these people are mob-handed.'

It made sense. 'Three: too much water's gone under the bridge since Charley robbed them. They've survived. Now, they're settling an old score. It's about revenge. They've come for her.'

13

From the sixth-floor window of The Dorchester Hotel, the park, lit by an early morning sun, was a verdant oasis in the heart of the city. Below, traffic moved sluggishly from Marble Arch down to Hyde Park Corner at the beginning of another day in the capital. Madeline Giordano gazed north to three young oak trees planted on the island at the junction of Edgware and Bayswater Roads marking the site of the infamous Tyburn gallows. The door opened and Antoine and his attack dog came into the room. Madeline was old-school: her grandson was everything his waster of a father had been and more, yet, in the final reckoning, he was blood. Bruno Mura certainly had his uses, but he was an outsider and always would be. Though the Sardinian didn't know it, his days of working for the family were numbered. All in good time – there were more pressing matters to attend to.

She addressed Tony as though he were a ten-year-old caught playing truant. 'Where did you go last night?'

He dropped into an armchair and brushed cigarette ash from his clothes. Madeline faced him, her eyes hidden behind the unnecessary sunglasses. 'Where did you go?'

The grandson resented the inquisition; he wasn't a little boy who had to be scolded into eating his vegetables. He tossed an arrogant reply across the room. 'Out.'

'Out where?'

Mura saw anger curl the corner of her mouth and realised she already had the answer to her question.

Tony said, 'We went to the club. I wanted the whore to know we'd come for her. You should've seen the bitch's face.' He laughed and dragged a reluctant Mura into the conversation. 'What was it like, Bruno?'

Bruno stared at the floor, his response barely audible. Tony irritably snapped his fingers. 'Remind me what I said.'

Mura cleared his throat that had suddenly gone dry. '"Long time no see, Charlene. We've got a lot to talk about, you and me."'

Tony slapped the chair. 'Yeah, yeah, that was it! Man, was that a good moment.'

His grandmother waited until his laughter subsided. 'Then what?'

'We left.'

'Who with?'

'The girls.'

'What girls?'

'From the club.'

'And where did you go?'

The interrogation angered him. 'I don't have to explain myself to you.'

Her mouth tightened into a hard line 'Answer me.'

Under the challenge, Tony's confidence faded. He shrugged nervously, for the first time suspecting that surprising the thief hadn't been the clever move he'd imagined.

'They were prostitutes. Relax for fuck's sake. Bruno took care of them.'

Madeline spoke quietly, every word a damning loveless critique. 'You're a fool, Antoine, do you know that? A fucking *moun sót!*' She pointed the cane at him. 'If it wasn't for the sweat of your grandfather you'd be just another syphilitic pimp pandering to the tourists in the French Quarter. By yourself, you're nothing.'

Tony couldn't recall, in his whole life, getting so much as a kind word from the matriarch, even on the day he'd lost his mother, yet the unmistakable fury behind the slight caught him off guard and at that moment he knew she hated him and always had.

He defended himself. 'If Glass is half as sharp as he's supposed to be it wouldn't take him long to figure it out. All I did was save him the trouble.'

Madeline pulled her shoulders back and raised her chin. 'No, Antoine, you should've followed the plan like we discussed, and, at the right moment, lifted the thief and settled the score. Her family didn't need to know anything about us. But what you actually did was blow the whole thing.' She hissed her contempt for him through her teeth. 'All because you wanted to show the world you're a tough guy. It's who you are and it's cost us our advantage. Killing those girls was a bad mistake.' She threw a contemptuous look at Mura. 'Your wild dog has drawn first blood. Now, war on the streets is unavoidable and our enemy will be ready.' She smiled, sadly. 'Once again, you've betrayed how unfit you are to lead when I'm gone. You're a child, Antoine, and like a child you prefer games. A warrior has no use for them.'

Tony gripped the arms of the chair, poised to launch himself at his grandmother, the only person on the face of the earth who'd dare speak to him like that.

He snarled his reply. 'If Bruno hadn't found her the whole of Louisiana would be laughing in our faces instead of behind our backs. You forget it was *your* son who caused this. The weakness comes from you! A pity you didn't die in Haiti.'

Madeline's mouth twisted at the memory. 'How little you know. How little you know of anything.'

Mura made the mistake of getting between the grandmother and her grandson. 'This isn't the time for anger. Remember why we're here.'

His conciliatory words fell on deaf ears; Madeline slapped him down. 'And you remember your place, boy. You assume, because this idiot listens to you, you have a voice. You haven't. When this is ove—'

'I'm trying—'

She screamed at him. 'Don't interrupt me!'

Anyone who dared insult Bruno Mura was guaranteed to suffer the consequences; he'd bury the serrated blate of his knife in their heart. Madeline was the exception. Except, the time was coming when that wouldn't be true and, like Beppe's whore, the old bastard would die a slow death. He'd make sure of it.

A knock interrupted the confrontation. Calum Bishop didn't waste time on words, he grabbed Tony by the throat and threw him against the wall. 'I could kill you with my bare hands. Do you have any fucking idea what you've done? Any idea at all, you fuckwit?'

One hand closed round Giordano's throat, hard fingers digging into his windpipe. He pointed an accusing finger at Madeline with the other. 'This isn't what we agreed, Madeline. Nothing like it. Thanks to your idiot grandson and his crazy mate, your advantage has been squandered, two hookers are dead, and Luke Glass will realise I'm involved.'

Tony dragged himself free. 'No, he doesn't! How can he?'

Bishop turned on him. 'Unlike you, he isn't a moron. You don't get where he's got to by being a clown. All he has to do is check the CCTV cameras outside the club and see you getting into a car. Pretty quickly he'll know who owns it and – boom! – my arse is on the line.'

Tony said, 'So what? Between us we can deal with him. Right?'

Bishop balled his fist; he wanted to hurt this guy. 'Between us? There is no *us*. This is Luke Glass we're talking about, not some two-bob hustler. If you want to go up against him, that's your decision, but you'll be making a mistake. I'm not asking my soldiers to bleed for the fucking Giordanos. No chance. When you've fucked off back to where you came from, I'll still be here picking up the pieces because this is where I live.' Calum was done with Giordano and spoke to his grandmother. 'You're in trouble, Madeline. More trouble than your grandson appreciates.'

The matriarch nodded slowly. 'And how do we resolve it, Mr Bishop?'

Calum said, 'There's one thing in your favour: these days, Glass is respectable. He won't fancy reading about himself on the front pages of the tabloids. War is bad for business; he'll try to keep any action contained. Set up a meeting. Talk to him. I wouldn't expect it to change anything, though maybe you can stall him long enough to let us find where they're hiding the sister. Because, make no mistake, she'll definitely be underground by now.' He paused. 'Unfortunately, he has a guy with him who'll be harder to convince. George Ritchie will rip the head off your body and not think twice. You don't want him in your life. I mean, *really* you don't.'

'What will happen when the police discover the bodies?'

'They won't. It's sorted.' Bishop studied the three faces in turn. If they were grateful, they were keeping it to themselves. He said, 'When I signed on to this circus to supply information and back-up you had a plan that stood a chance of succeeding. Two men and an old woman going up against Luke Glass is a suicide mission. I guarantee none of you will come out the other side.'

Madeline said, 'Don't make the mistake of thinking we were foolish enough to come here alone.' She glared at Tony. 'But I agree, the original plan was simple.'

Bishop walked across the room and poured himself a drink. 'And it would've worked. Now, you better think of another one.'

Madeline didn't argue; he was right. 'Okay. We can set up a meeting. Then what? We can have more people here in twelve hours if we need them.'

'*If* you need them?' Bishop laughed and shook his head. 'How many is more? My men aren't doing your work for you. So, yeah, you'll need them. Glass will have his sister guarded like fucking Fort Knox. Without knowing where he's hiding her you could be blasting away on the streets – taking hits all over the place – and not come close to getting to her. Thanks to this clown you also need an exit strategy, unless you're okay with spending the last years of your life in a British prison. The circumstances call for a new financial arrangement.'

He studied the old woman's face. Any dissent and he'd be out of here; he'd leave and they could do what they fucking liked.

'Glass knows I'm involved. I'll handle that. Do like I say – set up the meet and use the time to get your people here.'

Madeline said, 'Obviously, this shouldn't have been so complicated. Our guys can't be carrying when they get on the plane. We're going to need guns.'

'Leave that to me.'

Tony didn't like it and glanced at Mura for reassurance. 'We don't need him or his soldiers. We can take her by ourselves.'

His grandmother had had enough. 'Shut up, Tony. You're the reason we're in this mess. Just for once, do as you're fucking told, boy!' She turned to Bishop. 'It's a deal. I'll make the calls myself.'

'Good.'

'And this new arrangement, how much is it going to cost?'

Calum said, 'I'm guessing you had a figure in your head a minute after I came through the door. You're a realist. You know this is one you have to win, so it's an impressive number, am I right?'

'Yes.'

'Yeah, well, triple it and you won't be far out.'

* * *

When they left, Madeline went back to stand by the window. Outside, the sky was clear, the sun shone on Hyde Park, and although the room was warm she felt cold: old age didn't come alone. The girl from Haiti had had a long life and been a Giordano for almost sixty years, most of them good years. Now, she was in a strange city thousands of miles from home depending on a north London gangster she barely knew who had his own agenda.

Madeline saw the futility of it and laughed: she'd be dead soon – but the family name would be buried with her. Antoine wouldn't live to drag it through the mud like his father before him; she'd fought too long and too hard to let that happen.

* * *

She was young, still two months from her eighteenth birthday, when they left from Jérémie, a coastal city near Haiti's southern peninsula, in darkness and desperation. There was so little space on the boat they slept in turns on the slatted seats in the cramped cabin they'd been given. In the morning, with the ocean stretching endlessly to the horizon and the comforting putt-putt-putt of the diesel engine, it was easy to believe Haiti and the nightmare were behind them.

To afford the trip they'd hawked everything they owned. Everything except the long, lustrous locks, her pride and joy, fixed in place by a five-inch brass hairpin with a pearl top that had belonged to her grand-mother. The hair would've brought good money – money they needed –

but her mother had forbidden her to sell it to the wig-makers in Port-au-Prince. And in so doing, saved her life.

Running wasn't a choice: the Tonton Macoute – Papa Doc Duvalier's death squad – were rounding up anyone deemed a threat to his regime, from peasants who'd supported another political party to market traders refusing to comply with extortion. Every night opponents disappeared; others were stoned or burned alive; their brutalised bodies hung from trees as an example to the rest. Madeline's father was a trade union activist and a fierce critic of the government.

It was only a matter of time.

Placing their lives in the hands of the unwashed strangers who owned the boat had been a risk. They claimed to have made the crossing, promising it would take four days to reach the Florida Keys – the first of many lies. In fact, at around five knots per hour, it took more than eight. They rarely spoke, these men, even to each other. Madeline caught them looking at her when they thought she didn't see. Sly glances at first, then openly staring at her bare legs, making lewd remarks, and laughing.

By the fourth day, there was no disguise; their intentions were in their eyes.

That night they came for her: she was on deck, resting her head against a tar barrel, following shooting stars as they raced across the dark sky. Her parents were asleep in the cabin below, frightened for their children and unable to hide it from them. Madeline shared their fear but she was excited, too; she'd heard stories of America, the home of glamorous movie stars and millionaires, a land of opportunity, especially for a beautiful young woman.

The fishermen's whispers carried on the warm air. She heard them planning their attack, knowing they'd move together and it would be quick. When they were done with her, they'd slit her throat and drop her quietly over the side into the sea. Crabs and small fish would feed on the softer parts of her face; tiger or bull sharks would consume the rest.

They edged closer, bent low, creeping like jackals along the deck, their *presence betrayed by their foul body odour. Madeline pretended to be asleep, until she smelled fetid breath on her neck. Her timing was perfect. Her fingers freed the pin securing the hair her mother had protected; she spun round and buried it in the would-be rapist's eye all the way to the pearl at the hilt. He cried out and staggered backwards, falling against his partner, knocking them both overboard in a crazy tangle of arms and legs. The one she'd stabbed was dead before he hit the water, the other thrashed and desperately tried to get back to the safety of the boat. He screamed. 'Help me! Help me! I can't swim!'*

Madeline watched terror mark his cruel face and was unmoved: this vermin would have raped her and fed her to the fish. Saving him never crossed her mind. He disappeared into the darkness behind the boat and was gone.

Five days later they landed on Little Torch Key in the Florida Keys, washed up on the beach in the middle of the night: strangers in a strange land. Exhausted and parched and lucky to be alive.

Her father couldn't forgive himself for leaving Haiti like a coward: fifteen months after the Touissant family arrived in New Orleans, he was dead. Her brother, anxious to prove he was a man, joined a street gang and was fatally shot in the Behrman neighbourhood of Algiers over a card game with some Creole street performers high on the LSD they'd scored in the Quarter.

Her heartbroken mother lost the will to live and soon followed her husband, leaving Madeline – not yet twenty – penniless and alone.

* * *

A tragic history that could so easily have been the end. In fact, it was just the beginning. At a po'boy stand in the French Market a handsome young man had started talking to her. He'd told her his name was Silvestro Giordano. They'd sat on a bench on the waterfront and eaten their sandwiches together; Louisiana sausage and fried crawfish had never tasted so good.

A year later, she was his wife.

* * *

Nina lay still under the bedclothes. Opening her eyes would be an admission she was alive when what she wanted, more than anything, was to be dead. Hangovers were old news; she'd had scores of them and survived. All they needed were a couple of paracetamol, a hair of the dog, a gallon of strong black coffee and she'd be ready to carry on. This was more. She put it off for as long as she could before throwing off the duvet. Felix Corrigan came in and got both barrels full-on.

'What the fuck are you doing in my house?'

Felix recognised the aggression for what it was – a coping mechanism to cover her confusion – and kept it light. 'So you're back with us. Good. For a while we thought we'd lost you.'

'We? Who's we?'

He sat on the bed. 'I thought I'd lost you.'

Nina struggled to make sense of it. 'Luke sent you, didn't he?'

'As a matter of fact, no. George Ritchie sent me.'

Ingratitude was Nina's stock in trade. 'That bastard, I might have known.' She ran a hand over her naked body. 'How did I get here? I can't remember.'

'It was either that or leave you bleeding on the floor in the lounge on a blanket of broken glass.'

Nina could be the Queen of Mean. She said, 'So you stripped me and put me to bed. Enjoy yourself, did you?'

Felix's expression emptied as if he'd been slapped. 'Not much. I prefer my women sober. You didn't come close to qualifying.'

The rebuke hit home. Nina said, 'What happened? I remember pouring a drink. After that...'

'I'm not sure. There was trouble at the club. Ritchie ordered me to check you weren't part of it. I found you unconscious on the floor – you'd taken a flyer across the coffee table. You got lucky, all you hurt was your head.'

'Did any of the guys see me?'

The modesty was out of character. Yet, it seemed the bold couldn't-give-a-fuck-rebel-without-a-cause Nina had her pride. Felix put her out of her misery. 'They know you were drunk but that's all. They didn't see you. I managed to keep them out of the room.'

'And George? Has he run wagging his tail behind him to tell Luke his alkie sister's back in town?'

Felix stood; the criticism of Ritchie wasn't right. More than once he'd saved Nina Glass, mostly from herself. 'I wasn't expecting you to thank me, that would be too much to hope for. But George has been as good a friend to you as you're ever likely to have. He deserves better. So does your brother, who incidentally doesn't know about your latest fuck-up. And so do I. Over the years a lot of people have put their lives on the line to dig you out of the latest crazy-arsed scene you've got yourself into. Next time, I won't be one of them.'

He stopped at the bedroom door and turned. 'I'll be downstairs for a while. If you need anything, just shout. One more thing. For the record, you're not my type.'

Nina pushed herself upright, letting the covers fall away to reveal the pink nipples of her breasts. She smiled a mocking smile. 'And what kind of women are your type, Felix? Tell me. I'd love to know.'

His reply was barbed, intended to cut. 'Grown-up ones. So you're in no danger from me, Nina.'

14

Bruno Mura ran his finger over the tiny black-and-gold cup, eyed their men lounging around the room, and waited for Tony to get to what was bugging him. They'd left Madeline upstairs in the suite and were drinking espresso at a table in The Promenade, The Dorchester's long elegant entrance, where they could talk without being overheard. Giordano was on a short fuse, tearing anxiously at the napkin in his lap, finding imaginary fault with one of the most iconic hotels in the world. Like his father, the son's mood swings were violent and extreme. All it needed to tip him over the edge was the wrong word. Calum Bishop had said plenty of those. And he was right. The club was a schoolboy stunt that had given away their advantage. Bad enough, but calling it out in front of Madeline made it ten times worse.

Combining resources would put the north London home boys in a position of strength if the shooting started. Tony had pulled his little stunt expecting Bishop to be gagging for war. He hadn't been. But he wanted what Giordano wanted in New Orleans – to be the undisputed king of the city.

Clearly, Madeline had been impressed, listening while he'd

destroyed her grandson with a series of scathing verbal attacks aimed at marginalising and humiliating him. By the end, as Bishop and his grandmother discussed the future, Tony's contribution to the conversation had been zero; he might as well have been invisible.

In the extravagantly decorated lobby an expensively dressed couple ordered tea and ignored each other; the man opened *The Times*, she checked messages on her phone. Tony finished his coffee and leaned towards his lieutenant. Mura sensed a change in him beyond the fury that had drained the colour from his cheeks. 'What did you think of him, Bruno? What did you think of Bishop? Is he somebody you'd want with you?'

The question sounded straightforward but it was fraught with danger. Giordano was wounded and volatile. Mura couched his reply carefully. 'He talks a good game.'

'Not the same as playing one.'

Mura took his cue. 'Maybe. Glass is his main rival, which means Bishop has his own agenda. And it isn't the same as ours. We'd all do well to remember that, especially your grandmother, who's obviously impressed by him.'

Tony liked what he was hearing. Any criticism of Madeline was okay with him.

'She bought right into his bullshit, didn't she? Bought right into it.'

Mura fanned the flames of Giordano's resentment. 'Madeline's from an era that's gone and isn't coming back any time soon. Old ladies like her believe an expert's a guy from out of town. She doesn't appreciate what's under her nose.'

The compliment confirmed Tony's high opinion of himself. He said, 'Bishop's looking for a free ride – we soften up Glass, then he moves in and picks up the pieces. Well, he can forget it. Unless he's prepared to accept collateral damage, he's out, we don't use him. Don't tell me there aren't more contenders in a town this size.'

'Good luck explaining that to your grandmother.'

Tony sat back in his chair. 'That won't be a problem, Bruno.'

'I'm not so sure; she's a tough old bastard.'

Giordano laughed. 'She absolutely is, Bruno, no denying it, but not for much longer. Madeline won't be leaving London. For her, this is the end of the line.'

Mura couldn't keep the shock out of his voice. 'You're going to kill her?'

Tony rejected the question. 'Me? Of course not, she's my grand-mother, my own flesh and blood.' He looked meaningfully at his lieutenant. 'But it will happen.'

'And what about Bishop?'

Tony finished his drink and peered over the top of his cup. 'Him and I got off to a bad start. Speak to him, Bruno. Put him in the picture. Point out the dynamics. Tell him he's got his money on the wrong horse and it would be unwise to leave it there.'

* * *

Nina peered from behind the bedroom curtain, immediately spotting the two men in a car parked further down the street: they wouldn't be alone; there would be more. Felix hadn't shown up in the middle of the night with half a dozen men just because she wasn't answering her mobile. Something was going on. Luke wanted to wrap her in cotton wool. Some sisters might find his concern touching. Nina saw it for what it was: an attempt to control her she was determined to resist.

Felix Corrigan had left without saying goodbye, slamming the door angrily on his way out. He hadn't deserved how she'd treated him. More than once she'd had the phone in her hand, silently rehearsing the apology he was due, only to change her mind. As the day rolled on her attitude had hardened, the embarrassing details of the previous night had receded, until the episode didn't seem important: she'd had too much to drink and passed out. So fucking what?

Nobody asked Corrigan to undress her and put her to bed; that had been his idea – a peep show he'd enjoy telling his friends about.

If Luke tried his guardian-angel act she'd tell him where to shove it.

When she'd wakened there had been shadows on the wall. Her wrist was bandaged – she hadn't noticed earlier. Felix again. The hangover wasn't the worst ever but it was bad enough to have her searching the bathroom cabinet for aspirin and drinking water straight from the tap. London's water had a bitter aftertaste that made her want to throw up. Nina considered going back to bed and abandoned the idea. It had suddenly become unbearably hot; her hands felt clammy, her mind raced; fear washed through her and with it shards of memory she'd have preferred to forget, forcing her downstairs. She pushed the door open. The lounge was fine. The only thing missing was the coffee table; everything else was as it should be.

Felix had been busy.

Nina poured a large brandy, gulped most of it down; her hands were shaking. She dropped into an armchair, rocking slowly backwards and forwards, hugging herself, moaning softly as the reality of her situation dawned. There were men outside. To keep her in or to keep someone else out? Either way, she was a prisoner – a prisoner in her own home.

The thought brought fresh anxiety: if she couldn't get out, how was she going to score? She dragged the cushions off the sofa onto the floor, frantically searching for her handbag. In the kitchen, she found it next to her mobile and emptied the contents onto the granite work surface, sifting them with quivering fingers, hoping against hope to discover something she could use – the packet of blow she'd been saving; a couple of amphetamines that had slipped through a hole in the lining; a knob of Afghan Black tightly wrapped in silver paper to keep it from drying out.

There was nothing; she'd taken it all. Nina lurched back to the lounge and called Felix. He'd shielded her so far. Maybe he'd be prepared to go the extra mile. The number rang out: he wasn't answering – he was blanking her and who could blame him?

Nina drained the brandy and poured another: a new nightmare was about to begin.

* * *

The man lying on the couch in his underpants checked his watch and yawned. Working at LBC was a decent number, all things considered. Being polite to rich punters and their foxy ladies wasn't the worst gig he'd ever had. Now and again, a female with too much champagne down her neck would give him the come-on, usually just before the guy she was with poured her into a car. After a while, he'd stopped being disappointed: classy chicks didn't go for guys like him. Women were a touchy subject. His last girl-friend, a lap-dancer from Sunderland, had dumped him in a What-sApp message; he wasn't in a hurry to repeat the experience. In the bedroom, the Hugo Boss suit and the Armani T-shirt – supplied by the club – were on a hanger ready to put on. When he'd showered, shaved and washed his hair, the transformation from sofa slob would be remarkable. His hand slipped into the jacket pocket and fingered the six crisp Bank of England fifties the geezer with the American accent had given him while his partner with the slicked hair stood beside the alabaster statue of Fortuna. The goddess of luck had certainly smiled on him last night: three hundred pounds for doing less than nothing on top of his wages was a nice little earner in anybody's book. Twenty minutes later the two guys had come out, grinning as they though they'd heard the funniest joke in the world, got into a car, and driven away.

Sneaking a couple of non-members into the club wasn't a big deal.

No harm done. Nobody had died.

He heard a knock on the door and assumed it was the window cleaner collecting his money – the lazy bastard could whistle for it; half the time he didn't do a proper job. The letterbox rattled; he pulled on trousers and shouted down the hall. 'Okay! All right! I'm coming!'

Through the opaque panel, shadows from the landing played on the glass and a worm of disquiet wriggled in his belly. The window cleaner was a thin guy who did his round by himself. Whoever this was, it wasn't him.

He could count his friends on one hand. This was the sixth floor of a multistorey block of flats in Tower Hamlets, arguably the most dangerous area in London: graffiti was plastered on the roughcast walls, misspelt and obscene; every third window was boarded up – none of them would come here unless they had a reason.

A black umbrella with LBC printed on it in gold letters stood where he'd left it against the wall. What the hell good did he think that was going to do?

'Who is it?'

'Delivery for two down. They're not home.'

'Leave it there.'

The response came easily, casual and convincing. 'No can do, mate, it'll go for a walk. Need a signature. Otherwise, I'll have to take it back to the depot. Your call.'

He unlocked the door, still wary, and peered round the edge. Someone booted it and caught him full on the face, breaking his nose in two places. Four men rushed in and dragged him by the ankles into the flat. The beating was administered professionally, without anger.

Nothing personal – they were only carrying out George Ritchie's orders.

The blows found their mark: his ribs cracked, the pain was unbearable, and he screamed. When they were done, they lifted him by his arms and legs to the balcony and threw him over.

He was dead the second he hit the ground.

The message had been delivered.

15

Stevie D was a patient guy; if he'd learned anything from selling dope it was that junkies were predictable fuckers who didn't deviate from type: sooner rather than later they all came back because they had nowhere else to go. Addiction councillors talked about 'the bottom' as if it was a destination. Every drunk, every crackhead, had their own version. For some doomed unfortunates it was beyond death. He'd been expecting Nina Glass to contact him. Druggies – and he'd come across plenty in his time – were disassociated, lonely losers, drawn to the slightest kindness. A performing addict would do literally anything short of quitting. Nina was a fine woman – there were a few things he wouldn't mind her doing for him. She would, too.

Cocaine was the drug that kept on giving.

Santa Claus settings, people!

He let her first call go unanswered, stone-cold certain she'd phone again. In a city of close to nine million souls, he was the one Nina Glass trusted: the only one.

Not her brother. Him.

He heard her nervous laugh on the other end of the line when she recognised his voice and imagined her relief as the anxiety ebbed away and hope returned. This was what it was like to be God. He forced cheerful into his words. 'Nina? How's it all going?'

'Stevie. Stevie.'

'What's happening?'

'I'm trapped. Luke's men are outside. I can't leave the house.'

He guessed what was coming. 'And you want me to bring the shit to you? That's not how I operate, sweetheart. Not what I do, you know that. This is your mess, you have to sort it.'

'But I'm hurting.' She blurted out her disappointment, near to tears. 'You said you'd help me! You promised! In a few hours I'll be climbing the walls. I can't go through that again. I can't! Forget everybody else. If you need money, I'll give you money. As much as you like. Please. I'm in Denmark Hill.'

Stevie teased it out. 'Tonight's tricky. People are in pain out there. Some of them old friends. I can't get to all of you.'

'If you don't I won't make it.'

The dealer said, 'I hear you. But how do I get in?'

Her faith matched her selfishness. 'You'll think of something.'

* * *

If Luke hadn't asked George Ritchie to work for him, George would've retired to a cottage in Devon and waited for the end. With no family, no hobbies and no interests outside his job it wouldn't have been long. Ritchie never forgot he owed Luke Glass. Protecting the family was his responsibility. Luke was the top dog in the city, which meant there was always some ambitious upstart who fancied his chances and needed a good slap. George made sure they got one.

He'd spent the day in the office above the King of Mesopotamia and he was concerned: the crew from New Orleans didn't fit that description. From what Charley had said they were serious operators, not street punks out to make a name for themselves. The guy who'd let them into LBC had broken the rules of the game and paid the price. Ritchie had no regrets.

His mobile vibrated on the desk. He reached for it. 'What's happening?'

'Nina's hungry, she's ordered pizza. We've got eyes on the delivery guy. Want us to lift him?'

'How does he look?'

'Like a guy delivering pizza.'

'Don't be smart; it isn't appreciated. Tell me what he looks like.'

'I am. He's on a bike. There's a box on the back and he's wearing a crash helmet. Want me to lift him?'

'No, if you're sure he's okay it's better she doesn't realise we're watching her. We'll take her to the safe house in the morning.'

* * *

Stevie D hadn't bought the Honda PCX 125 because he liked it. His other bikes, a Royal Enfield Meteor 350 – a beautiful piece of engineering – and a Kawasaki Ninja 650, were like a wild animal roaring between his thighs when he raced through Headley Heath's open woodland or bombed down the M25. Compared with them, it was a child's toy. Except the Honda had something they didn't. Apart from being better for getting round the city, it made him anonymous. Nobody, but nobody, paid attention to a guy on a scooter. Exactly how he wanted it to stay.

He'd pulled up outside the house, dismounted, and removed his helmet. Further down the street he'd seen the silhouettes of the men in the car Nina had told him about and remembered this was

Luke Glass' sister he was messing with. Stevie wasn't worried – he'd run this scam hundreds of times. It was fool proof: if they stopped him they'd find half a dozen pizzas in the delivery box and a piece of paper in his pocket with the Denmark Hill address scribbled illegibly. Calling the Italian deli would make no difference; they were in on it, primed to say the right things should anybody ask.

As he walked towards the front door it opened and Nina stood in the hall, wide-eyed, lips drawn in a thin smile, rubbing the palms of her hands together.

Stevie went into his act. 'Spicy jalapeno?'

'Yes.'

He pretended to count the money she gave him and spoke out of the side of his mouth.

'Go easy on this. There are a couple of disappointed blowheads in London tonight. Heartbreak settings, darling. Think yourself lucky.'

'I do. Thanks.'

'And the price has gone up. Nothing to do with me. Told you already – market forces. Supply and demand.'

'You aren't saying not to contact you again, are you?'

Stevie glanced over his shoulder. 'Of course not. I want to help but it isn't easy. Call me.'

* * *

I'd watched my sister work the room scores of times, drifting through the club like the hostess at a private party – waving to the people with more money than sense who'd just ordered a second bottle of Dom Pérignon P2, throwing her head back at a joke from a businessman on the tiles with his Middle Eastern partners. That she'd heard it before didn't matter; out of the corner of her eye she'd be checking the guests over his shoulder were being taken care of. In any walk of life the great ones made it look easy. I'd realised Charley was good – I'd had no idea how good. Putting myself in her place was a mismatch made in hell: I could schmooze well enough and tell all the right lies, but in the mine-host stakes she was a natural. I wasn't in the same division.

Beside me, George Ritchie had the expression of a celibate teetotaller who'd stumbled into a Bacchanalian orgy and couldn't find his way out. The drink in front of him, compliments of the house, hadn't been touched; I doubted it would be. Twenty-odd years in London couldn't change the working-class lad from the north east. George was a guy who didn't owe anybody anything and paid for his own booze. Parting with a month's wages for a bottle of bubbles wasn't something that was ever going to sit well with him. Given a free choice, the club was the last place he'd come. Tonight, he was sticking close to me and we both knew why.

Around the room, Charley's girls 'entertained' middle-aged men who were probably doting grandfathers in daylight. For the hookers, LBC was the best gig in town – the money was great; it would have to be. They didn't know about the two dead girls – when they did it would rock their world. We'd need Charley back to stop them from quitting.

A High Court judge was deep in whispered conversation with a barrister famous for his involvement in cases splashed across the front pages of the tabloids. Their heads were close together, and, whatever they were cooking up, I was glad the silk wasn't representing me.

In the booth next to them, a face flushed and bloated by alcohol proved it was possible to have too much of a good thing. Rupert Neville – aka. Lord Holland – stared balefully at nothing through eyes dulled by an excess of Veuve Clicquot. He was drunk. Very drunk, even by his standards. I'd last seen him in the library of his north-country house when he'd introduced me to Jocelyn Church as 'the one who can help with our problem'.

Neville was so out of it he seemed unaware of the Filipina beauty nibbling his ear. In the not too distant future, his online credit-card statement would jog his memory.

At the bar, four men waited to be called to their table, leaning in to hear the story one of them was telling, laughing in unison at the punchline. Three were strangers to me. The fourth was Assistant Commissioner Robert 'Beano' Kirby – one of a select band of four or five ACs holding the third-highest rank in the Met behind the deputy commissioner and the commissioner. The 200k he was pulling down from that scam wasn't enough; he was as bent a bastard as anybody on the force.

The policeman caught me watching him and waved me over, smiling. 'How's it all going, Luke? Still fooling some of the people all of the time?'

'Like yourself, Beano?'

He shook his head, amused at the use of his nickname, and swirled the liquid in his glass. From the colour I guessed he was on Remy Martin. And it wasn't his first of the evening.

'We can only hope nobody's recording this, eh? They'll assume we're friends and that would never do.'

'No, they'll realise one of us is doing their job, being nice to the customers. What they'll make of a senior officer in the Metropolitan Police hobnobbing with a known criminal is anybody's guess.'

'Fuck 'em. They can think what the hell they like. I'm beyond caring. This is the best over-priced bordello in the city, although, I have to say, it's not ticking the boxes tonight.'

'Really?'

'Yeah. Service has gone downhill.' He checked his watch. 'Been waiting since half-past eleven to get seated. Not impressed.

Couldn't sort it out, could you? Never have this hassle when Charley's around. Where is she, by the way?'

'Night off.'

'Fair enough, except the place shouldn't come to a fucking standstill.'

'I'll see what I can do.'

Beano patted my shoulder like a faithful dog. His mates were listening; he was playing to the gallery. Fortunately, the policeman realised he'd crossed the line in time to save himself from a broken arm. 'She's something, that sister of yours.' He gave an exaggerated wink. 'Prefer watching her walking away from me than you. The view's better.'

I started to leave. He called me back. 'How's business? Maybe you and me should powwow.'

Not if he was the last man on earth.

'Enjoy your night, Assistant Commissioner.'

'I always do, Mr Glass.'

I repeated the conversation to Ritchie; he wasn't amused. 'Don't poke the bear unless you're ready to lose a hand. Kirby's bad news. He should've been nabbed a long time since. It hasn't happened. It won't because he's a slippery bastard. And he's lucky.'

'A lucky bastard? Then he's come to the right place.'

Ritchie didn't smile. 'Stay out of his way. We don't want to go down that road again. And while we're on the subject of who to avoid.' He nodded in the direction of His Lordship teetering towards the exit supported by the sultry beauty he'd have no use for tonight. 'Your friend there is pimping for some serious people on the Skytrain proposal. I'm hearing one of them has influence. Unfortunately, he's greedy – aren't they all? – threatening to pull the plug on the votes he can bring to the table and bury it in one committee after another so it sinks without trace the way the idea's done before.'

'How much does he want?'

'Too fucking much.'

'Will he get it?'

Ritchie wouldn't be drawn. He said, 'You're not the only one who shouldn't poke the bear. The people in the shadows I mentioned won't take prisoners.'

16

It was twenty minutes to three in the morning and we'd adjourned to the office. Well past George Ritchie's bedtime. Mine, too, come to that. Upstairs, it was all over bar the shouting. I'd done all right in my new role but my respect for Charley and what she did every night in the club had grown. We needed her back.

On his way out of the door, Beano Kirby had turned and waved goodnight, grinning like a drunken orangutan. While characters like him were heading up the Met there wasn't too much to worry about.

My mobile vibrating on the desk startled me. Ritchie pulled his chair closer and stated the obvious. 'We're about to find out what they want.'

The owner of the voice coming down the line chose his words carefully. Thanks to Charley and our CCTV, I knew who Bruno Mura was and what he looked like. He spoke slowly, as though speaking to a child, and I imagined him smiling. Turning up at the club had been intended to frighten my sister. It worked; she was terrified. They hadn't rushed to move to the next stage, an indication of how secure they felt. Now, they had. This was it.

Mura was making contact on behalf of his boss. All part of the plan.

'You have something that belongs to Mr Giordano. He'd like it back.'

'You've lost me. I've no idea what you're talking about.'

He ignored me and carried on. 'This isn't your fight. Mr Giordano has no quarrel with you. Taking another man's property is a crime, an affront to the family that has gone unanswered for too long. Unless—'

He'd been speaking for less than thirty seconds and already I was tired of listening to him. I said, 'I'll decide what is and isn't my fight and if Tony has anything to say to me, tell him to say it himself. I don't deal with lackeys.'

I hung up. On the other side of the desk George Ritchie's face was expressionless. He didn't comment and kept whatever he was thinking to himself.

'I know what I'm doing, George.'

'I believe you. How these people will react is something else.'

'We'll find out soon enough. If they ring back they don't want a shooting war, if they don't...'

Ritchie was ahead of me. 'We can't hang around while they make up their minds. We have to act. Everybody who works for us knows the score and there are men on standby in Liverpool and Newcastle who can be here in three hours.'

George was a veteran of gang wars, usually on the winning side. I'd met all kinds, from the foolish to the wise and every stop in between. Brave men were hard to find. Ritchie was one. Maybe the only one I'd come across. He read my mind. 'We've seen two of them. For certain more will be ready to crawl into the light as soon as Giordano says the word. I'm guessing that isn't what you want and not just because we might lose.'

'You're right, George. Giordano hasn't come to London to take in a show and see the sights. The "something" he wants is Charley. Any advice?'

'Yeah. Buy him off. Life's too short.'

'What if that isn't enough?'

'Then, tell him to go fuck himself and we'll see him in the streets.'

* * *

Ritchie didn't add to his earlier statement and we sat in silence for the best part of an hour. When my mobile went off again it was like Big Ben ringing in the new year. I was more rattled than I cared to admit, which wasn't good. An animal clawed inside my skull. Its name was doubt and I realised the root of my unease: my sister had been selective; I suspected I hadn't been told the whole story. It was the parts she'd missed that disturbed me.

Tony Giordano was an angry man lacking his lieutenant's wolfish charm. The first words out of his mouth set the tone for the rest of the conversation. 'I'm very disappointed in you, Glass.'

'Sorry to hear that.'

He went on as though I hadn't spoken. 'Before I came to England I asked just exactly who is Luke Glass. I wanted to understand who I might be going up against.'

Tony liked the sound of his own voice. He was the only one.

'The reports were... shall we say... mixed. Praise for how you've held your family together after your brother left. I hear you're a respectable man. Well done.' He paused. 'Unfortunately, as I'm starting to discover, that isn't the whole story.'

He was pissing me off. I said, 'Listen, Giordano, I haven't got time for this. What do you want? Spit it out.'

'We need to meet.'

'Why? Why would I meet you?'

He sighed – I was disappointing him again. 'Because, if you don't, we'll leave this town smoking.'

'I'm shaking in my shoes, Tony.'

He lost his temper and shouted down the line. 'Your sister made a big mistake in New Orleans! She stole from our family! That can't stand! We're here to square the account! Tomorrow. Eleven o'clock at the club. Alone.'

'I won't be alone.'

He laughed, as though I'd just said the funniest thing he'd ever heard. When the laughter petered out he said, 'Neither will I. Be warned, Glass. If you don't show, the shooting starts.'

I hung up and faced Ritchie. 'Might be an idea to get the men from up north you mentioned onto trains, George. We need eyes on these guys round the clock.'

* * *

In almost one hundred years little had changed in the restaurant. They knew him here, called him Sir Harry, and treated him like a friend. As usual, dinner had been excellent. London at its finest: oysters, a dozen of them – rock rather than the superior native because of the time of year – followed by a splash of gastronomique theatre, Dover sole served on the bone at his table and a sumptuous pistachio soufflé with Madagascar vanilla ice cream to finish. Even in his days in the officers' mess he'd rarely drunk alcohol and didn't now. When he finished eating the maître d' organised a taxi to take him to Green Park. On Piccadilly, he asked the driver to stop and got out, straightened the blue-and-burgundy-striped tie, a symbol of his regiment, and walked the rest of the way to Half Moon Street.

People hurried by without noticing the discreet gold sign on the wall that said everything and nothing in two words: JADE HEAVEN.

He pressed the buzzer and waited to be allowed to enter. Inside, an oriental lady wearing a flowing red and black silk robe with cloud motifs – the Chinese symbol of never-ending fortune – appeared from behind a bamboo curtain. Her features were delicate, almost childlike, yet he knew she was in her sixties. Madam Chang had been uncommonly beautiful thirty-five years earlier, when Rupert Neville had told him about the place and recommended her. Rupert had been bumming around London, biding his time for his father to kick the bucket so he could inherit. He was reckless back then – up to all sorts: women, cocaine; he even was a member of the Communist Party for a while – but it had to be admitted he'd been fun. Now, he was an overweight buffoon in riding breeches with gout and a drink problem, knocking around that draughty bloody mausoleum of his in the frozen north with his horror of a wife and his nympho sister, taking orders from Jocelyn Church – another jumped-up fucking ninny who could do with spending a few hours here.

Church was the problem. If it had just been him and Rupert they would've reached an accommodation over Skytrain and moved on. Jocelyn wasn't a man you could do business with, a superior, inflexible bastard who acted as if it was his money they were talking about. The last two meetings had gone badly – angry voices and raised fists. But they knew the form: the proposal would be controversial – the left would vigorously oppose it because it wasn't their idea, the traditionalists on both sides of the chamber would be against anything so radical. Even the fucking Greens would come up with some reason to object. Getting it over the line in umpteen parliamentary committees would be a brown-envelope bonanza. And all it would take for it to hit the skids would be a word dropped in the right journalistic ear about the real origin of the funds to have everybody running for the hills. The scandal might even bring down the government itself.

They'd been warned; now it was up to them.

The madam bowed and welcomed him even more warmly than the head waiter but then, their relationship had gone beyond grilled calf's liver and chocolate fondant.

'Wonderful to see you again, Harry. How are you?'

Her English was flawless, spoken without an accent, and when she smiled her cheeks dimpled in a way men found irresistible. He said, 'All the better for seeing you, my dear.'

'And what would you like – your usual?'

Harry's 'usual' involved two females – the younger, the better. He waved a playful finger.

'You know me so well.'

She accepted the compliment with a tight smile and gave him a key. 'No need to tell you what to do. Shower first. Someone will show you to the room. Tonight, we have a surprise for you.'

Harry grinned. 'Really? I love surprises.'

In the changing room he opened the locker, took off his clothes and went to the shower, already aroused. Normal man/woman sex had never been enough and still wasn't. His needs changed from session to session. Jade Heaven satisfied them without judging him. They also employed some of the best-looking girls in the city.

Everything an unfettered mind could imagine was for sale. At a price.

The hot water cascaded over his head and shoulders and down his thighs, immediately relaxing him. He turned his face towards it. From behind, fingers that had never given a massage grabbed his throat, a hand holding a damp cloth cupped his mouth and there was a sweet smell. He felt dizzy; his arms flapped, his eyes closed and he collapsed.

17

Since her arrival as a young woman, Madeline Giordano had never been out of the United States. Until now. The memory of the journey as a teenager in the tiny boat from Haiti to the Florida Keys with her family still haunted her; against the odds they'd survived, but, one way or another, it had killed them and Madeline couldn't shake the fear that if she ever left the city on the banks of the Mississippi, she'd return to a wasteland where her life had been. The world beyond New Orleans might as well not have existed.

London held no interest for her; the landmark hotel on Park Lane failed to impress. She wouldn't be here if her idiot son had been more careful who he'd used for sex. Since Beppe's death not a day passed when she didn't curse him for dragging the family's reputation through the mud. It wasn't possible to mourn a flawed, weak, incompetent fool unfit to lead, whose only strength had been a bottomless capacity for cruelty and self-indulgence. Yet, his mother didn't deceive herself. The mistake had happened long before. And it had been her mistake: when Silvestro died she should have grieved for him, then taken control, leaving their son to wallow in the dissolute pleasures so available on the streets of New Orleans. This was the result.

She lay on the bed, staring at the powder-blue ceiling, regretting she'd waited until it had come to this before acting. The years weighed heavy with the added burden of knowing she was to blame. It would end – one way or another – as all things did. It had taken time but they'd found the thief. Her fate was sealed, though the meeting with Antoine and Calum Bishop was in her mind. Any last hope she'd held for her grandson to become the force the Giordano family needed had died in the room.

Madeline laughed, grimly amused at her self-deception. Who was she kidding? It had ended the minute he'd brought the Sardinian thug who never left his side on board, a poor choice of confidant. His kind didn't understand the meaning of honour. In any dispute their only concern was how they might profit. The signs were clear, impossible to ignore, even if his grandmother had wanted to: while a reptile like Bruno Mura was in the picture her grandson was destined to be a failure like his father before him. She was aware her grandson saw her as a danger to him, and he was right; thinking he could crush her like a mosquito on the bayou was an error he'd realise too late.

Madeline closed her eyes, a silent promise on her lips that the Giordanos would once again be respected in New Orleans. In seconds, she was back in the boat with her parents and her brothers heading for the Keys and her destiny.

* * *

The property in Kentish Town didn't feature on the website and wasn't listed on the Glass Houses portfolio: it wasn't for sale. Nina had bought it anonymously on Luke's instructions from the old couple who'd lived in it all their married life. The strange house and the unfamiliar bed were ready excuses for why Charley hadn't slept; she didn't kid herself – they weren't the reasons. In the club, Luke had accepted her explanation without probing for the details that would expose its discrepancies. He'd asked where the blackmail material was and hadn't questioned her when she'd said it had been left behind when they'd come close to catching her. Luke was smart. He'd revisit her story and discover the awful truth, then the lie of omission, rehearsed for that moment and delivered in a strong voice, would be laid bare.

The four kids Frances Glass had brought into the world shared in the wealth the family had created. It had all been going so well. Until Tony Giordano walked out of the past and royally fucked it. Because of her they were all in more danger than even George could handle.

* * *

George Ritchie hadn't reacted when Felix offered to drive Nina to the safe house on the other side of the river. On his way out of the door he'd called after him. 'If she throws a strop, say it's just George overreacting like an old lady, as usual. She'll believe that. Blaming me works for her. She's bound to ask what it's about. Don't give too much away. Luke will tell her what he wants her to know.'

Felix had nodded his agreement. Inside, he didn't feel good. Ritchie was the father Felix Corrigan had never had. Keeping the truth from him didn't sit well. Unfortunately, it was too late: as ridiculous and impossible as it seemed, he was falling in love with Nina Glass. Maybe he'd always been in love with her. Corrigan didn't fool himself it was reciprocated: it wasn't. Most of the time she didn't even realise he existed.

Denmark Hill was 'nice' London: trendy bars, cool restaurants and open space. The view of the city was spectacular: on a clear day it was reckoned you could read the time on the clockface of Big Ben. The area was named after Queen Anne's husband, Prince George of Denmark, who'd hunted there.

Like anybody gave a flying fuck!

Nothing had changed since the previous day – the street was quiet and further down another two men kept watch from a parked car. Felix had done his share of stakeouts and remembered the bitter taste of cold coffee, the suffocating cloud of cigarette smoke permanently hanging in the air, and the arse-numbing boredom. The original crew would've been relieved. Even so, it was a bastard of a gig that took days to get over.

In daylight, the white Georgian house was impressive and must have cost a small fortune. The girl had style as well as money. He knocked on the door and waited for her to open it. When she did, Felix couldn't hide his disappointment. She was dressed in a satin robe trimmed with fur. Her pupils were dilated, her hair hadn't been combed, and she moved languidly like a diva in a twenties movie.

Nina was drunk.

She smiled a knowing smile. 'Well, well. Back for another look, are we? Glad I made such a lasting impression.'

Felix squeezed past into the hall and lost it. 'For Christ's sake, woman! How the hell did you manage to get this bad? I'd hoped you'd learned your lesson the other night. No chance, you're worse.'

She brushed against him and went into the lounge. 'Fuck off! I don't answer to you.'

He followed her. 'That's the problem, you don't answer to anybody. We're busting our humps trying to keep you in one piece while you do your best to make it as difficult as you can.'

She sat on the end of the sofa, crossed her legs and put her fingers in her ears like a little girl on her way to a well-deserved spanking. Felix hunkered down beside her; close up the smell of alcohol was strong. It hurt him to see her destroying herself, almost as though she didn't want to live and was determined to go out in a blaze of glory. Except, there was nothing glorious about it.

He said, 'This can't go on. At some stage you'll have to deal with it. I'd make it sooner, if I were you. Play the game, Nina.'

She turned, chin jutting defiantly under a snarling mouth. 'Speaking of games, what's yours?'

'I don't know what you're talking about.'

She moved to within inches of him. 'Of course you do. The private peep show you treated yourself to when I was out of it. And now little Felix Corrigan is upset because... because of what, exactly?' She got up and stood in the middle of the floor, hands on her hips. 'In case you've forgotten, you work for my brother. One word from me and you'll be at the bottom of a freshly dug lime pit in the New Forest.' She laughed. 'From what I remember you're lucky to be in the land of the living as it is. Danny wanted to put a bullet in your head in the King of Mesopotamia when you didn't do your job. Luke persuaded him it wasn't his best idea.'

The snarl softened to a sneer. 'Or have I snorted too much snow and got it wrong? Not the pervy bit. That's why you're here, isn't it? Want another swatch at my arse, Felix?'

She drew the robe up to her waist, turned and bent over. 'You only had to ask.'

Felix grabbed her wrists and threw her on the couch. 'Stop it! Fucking stop it, Nina! People care about you. I care about you. You really don't deserve any of us. What you do is your business except when it puts the family at risk. Right now, me and a handful of Ritchie's guys might be all that's standing between you and the end of your life. My orders are to take you to a safe house. Charley's already there.'

The words reached her. 'Safe house? Safe from what?'

'Believe me, Nina, you're better off not knowing.'

She staggered to her feet. 'Safe from fucking what? Tell me!'

'I can't. George says—'

'George! Fuck George! This is me we're talking about!'

'Luke's got a problem. He's on it but he has to be sure you aren't in danger. He'll explain later. I wouldn't want to be you when he sees the state you're in. He's got enough on his plate. He doesn't need... this.'

'He can't.'

'He will. And he'll go up like a rocket.'

She clung to his lapels; pleading. 'He can't see me like this. He can't.'

He took her hands away. 'I've tried, Nina. We've all tried. You make it impossible.'

'Please, Felix, please.'

'You're asking too much.'

She fell to her knees, abject and broken. 'Help me, Felix, help me!'

* * *

The white leather couch was elegant to look at and fine for sitting in. Trying to sleep on it would be another story. On a normal day, Nina was a stylish lady who drew admiring glances wherever she went. The house she lived in was just one more desirable residence in a street full of them. Her position at Glass Houses hadn't been unhelpful; owning something like it was beyond most people. The surprise was the interior, exquisitely furnished, especially the lounge, an unexpected extension of her taste. The original mantelpiece was the focal point of the room, the walls lined with charcoal etchings and black-and-white photographs of Victorian London; a five-panel Rio Silver banana-leaf mural dominated the space, complementing the polished hardwood floor. The home of someone who had it all going on.

Only, that wasn't the truth. Nina was a screwed-up mess slowly falling apart in front of him. She was asleep upstairs leaving Felix to toss and turn and ponder the latest lies told on her behalf. Asking George Ritchie to believe she still wasn't well enough to go anywhere was pushing it. Ritchie had played along, pretending to accept what he was being told. Before the call ended, he'd added a warning betraying he hadn't been conned.

'On the level, Felix. Is she really ill?'

'Yes.'

'Okay. I hope you know what you're doing.'

'So do I, George.'

'For Christ's sake don't get it wrong, eh? If you do, I can't save you. Nobody can. She's Luke's sister, the past will count for nothing. Nothing, Felix. Do you understand what I'm saying?'

Felix Corrigan did understand, the reason he was awake at ten to four in the morning. He lay with his eyes closed, torn between the woman upstairs and his duty to her brother. The first time they'd met Luke had stopped Danny putting a bullet in him in the bar of the King of Mesopotamia; without his intervention, he'd be dead. He heard a noise and listened hard. When he heard it again he tiptoed across to his jacket and took out his gun. Ritchie had men guarding the front of the house and the back. Experience had taught Felix that guaranteed little. If an enemy was mob-handed and determined, it wouldn't be enough.

Feeling the cold grip in his hand reassured him and George Ritchie's warning flashed through his mind.

...don't get it wrong, eh? If you do, I can't save you. Nobody can

He crouched behind the arm of the sofa and held his breath. Slowly, the door opened. Felix's index finger curled round the trigger, ready to halt the intruder in his tracks. The figure edged silently into the room and leaned provocatively against the frame, long bare legs tapering to slender ankles in high heels. Light from the street found the smooth skin at her neck and the firm breasts beneath: Nina was naked.

She took a step towards him, repeating his name in a throaty whisper, and fell to her knees, desperately scrabbling to release the zip of his trousers. Giving in would've been easy; her need was a match for his own. Felix Corrigan almost did until a sad realisation made him push her away, disgusted by his desire. Alcohol was bad enough. Where the drugs had come from, he'd no idea – they must've been hidden in the bedroom. She threw her arms round his neck, pressing her body against him with an urgency that took him by surprise. Felix shoved her off and she fell to the floor, weeping.

He dragged her upstairs. 'Give me your stash. All of it, or I swear I'm calling Luke.'

She clung to him, pleading. 'No. Please, no. I can't. I need it.'

He manhandled her across the bedroom and pulled the contents of every drawer onto the carpet, his anger melding in harsh, unforgiving words. 'You stupid bitch, can't you see you've made a fool of both of us? I want you but not like this. Never like this. You've wasted my time. Everybody's time. But no more! You're not worth it, Nina. Get some rest. In six hours you're going to Kentish Town – no excuses – even if I have to carry you on my back.'

18

During the day, without people, LBC was a gauche, soulless testament to bad taste and I had to remind myself that opening the club had been one of my better ideas. Certainly one of the most profitable. I'd questioned Charley's judgement when she'd insisted we double the membership fee. She'd been right. The more we asked, the more the well-heeled hedonists and poseurs fell over themselves to pay. Inflation, the government's latest job figures, and all the rest of the guff that filled the evening news sending fear through the rest of the population who worked for a living, didn't affect them. They were above it, miles above it, breathing the rarefied air that came with real wealth. The truth was that London – the London they inhabited – was drowning in a sea of money, some of it – admittedly, not very much – honestly come by. Difficult to believe if you were unfortunate enough to be hunkered on the steps of the National Gallery in Trafalgar Square at one in the morning, waiting for food to be distributed with another night on a busted mattress under a railway bridge in front of you.

Relieving the privileged wankers of their cash was almost as much fun as spending it.

Almost.

George Ritchie arrived at twenty to eleven and took a seat beside me in a booth near the bar. The cleaners were done, the smell of last night's sweat and stale perfume had faded and we had the place to ourselves. He glanced at the half-finished coffee in front of me, shaking his head. Coffee wasn't Ritchie's thing. He said, 'Any chance of a tea?'

'Only if you make it yourself, George.'

He nodded. 'In that case, I won't bother.' He let a minute go by. 'Nina's still in Denmark Hill.'

Not what I wanted to hear. 'Don't tell me that. The people coming here are the real deal. I need her tucked up in Kentish Town.'

'She's under the weather.'

'Sick or just hungover? If she's sick get her a doctor. If she's hungover, toss her into a car and take her where she's supposed to be.'

'Felix says she's got a bug or something. Feeling pretty ropey. Our men are outside. He'll stay with her. As soon as she's better he'll drive her himself. And before these jokers arrive there's something else. That Skytrain guy I told you about – the greedy fucker, remember?'

'Oh, yeah. What about him?'

'They fished him out of the Thames this morning.'

The surprise was how quickly they'd moved after Jocelyn Church reported his lack of success with me. The 'people' he represented had hired somebody else to do their dirty work, which meant I wouldn't be hearing from the slippery bastard again. Good.

At such an early stage, details were few. Ritchie supplied them. 'The police were called to Lower Thames Street just after 5 a.m. They found the body of a man washed up at low tide on a stretch of sand near the Old Billingsgate Market.'

'What's the thinking?'

He sighed as though replying required energy he didn't have. 'Looks like he was beaten to death and thrown in the river.'

* * *

Giordano didn't show at eleven or even quarter past. At twenty-five minutes to twelve, he strolled in with his pet poodle trailing behind him and slid in the other end of the booth. He bowed his head in mock apology. 'We're late, sorry. Got caught up watching your toy soldiers and their changing of the guard thing. Nice uniforms, by the way.' Giordano waved an arm at the deserted club. 'Looks different, doesn't it, Bruno?'

Mura put his mobile on the table and made a disapproving face. 'Reminds me of the morning after in a Vegas brothel.'

'What do you want, Antoine?'

He smiled a slow smile, as though I'd said something clever he was only just getting.

'Antoine? My real name. Impressive. Only my grandmother calls me that. You've done your homework. Good to know my opponent is thorough. As to your question, you already have the answer. We want what the thief stole from my family. There can be no doubt about what happens to whores who cross the Giordanos.'

'Don't disrespect my sister.'

He bowed again. 'She is what she is. I want what's mine.'

'Then, you've come a long way for nothing... Antoine.'

'What're you saying?'

'She doesn't have your stuff. I'll pay back the money and add a sizeable chunk to cover her mistake.'

He dismissed my offer without even thinking about it. 'I don't believe you. Do you believe him, Bruno?'

His henchman grinned his wolfman grin. 'He's joking, Tony, got to be. She's got them.'

Ritchie weighed in for our team. 'Mr Glass never jokes, especially where his sisters are concerned.'

Mura tapped a button on his phone and three men came through the door, guns drawn, aimed in our direction. Giordano's grin was as oily as his hair; he flashed it again and shook his head at our naïvety. 'I warned you I wouldn't be alone.'

Nobody moved. Tension hummed like tinnitus in the air. Giordano was still smiling when Ritchie said, 'You did. Got to give it to you, you did.'

His eyes fixed on the American as he raised an arm and snapped his fingers. Figures rose from behind the bar with the synchronicity of a flash mob, more appeared from under tables across the room where they'd been hiding; a couple edged out of the kitchen. In total, I counted ten, all of them armed and ready to shoot.

Ritchie spoke with the calmness I'd come to expect from him. 'And as you see, we believed you.'

The American's expression froze; he'd been out-manoeuvred and didn't like it.

George said, 'Now, why don't we put the weapons away and start again? Does that sound like a plan?'

Giordano was always going to agree. There was nothing to think about; he had no choice. That didn't stop him taking his own sweet time about it. He bit back his anger, bowed his head, pretending to be gracious in defeat, and managed to bury himself even deeper.

'Everything I've heard about you is true, Mr Ritchie. If you want to feel the sun on your old bones, come and work for me. You'll love New Orleans.'

George folded his arms – he'd won this round and was enjoying it. 'No, thanks, the English weather suits me, I'm happy with the job I have, and, apart from that, I don't like you. Next time you try to be clever we'll put you down.'

Giordano took the threat and the rejection in his stride. 'Pity. I can always use a good man.'

I repeated what I'd said. 'Charley hasn't used what she took and never will because she doesn't have it. We don't have it. All you can walk away with is the money and your lives. Your decision.'

Mura gave a disbelieving laugh and spat on the floor. So far, he'd said little, content to let the scene play out. He carried himself well, appearing relaxed when, in reality, he was poised to strike if the opportunity came. Mura wasn't handsome though he wouldn't be short of female company; plenty would find his lean face and spare frame attractive. But it was the eyes that revealed who he was. From across the booth they ignored Ritchie and focused on me, piercing and unafraid, and I knew I was looking at a man who intended to kill me if he could. His kind made their move in dark streets and back alleys. His weapon of choice wouldn't be a gun; he'd strangle his victims with his bare hands, or gut them with the knife I guessed he was carrying now, cruelly twisting it as he savoured every agonising second until it was over. Loyalty to his master wasn't his motivation; the dispute between Giordano's family and mine would resolve, one way or the other. Mura would be there when it did.

'He's lying, Tony. She spread her legs and waited for her chance. When it arrived, she went for it. Expecting us to believe after all that she somehow lost what she'd risked her life to steal tells me our host thinks we're idiots.'

Giordano said, 'Is he right? Is Bruno right, Mr Glass? *Is* that what you think?'

'Sorry to disappoint. I don't have time to waste on you. That's what I pay George for.' I nudged Ritchie. 'They're asking if you think they're idiots. Tell them.'

'From what they've shown so far, it isn't looking great.'

'I agree, but we'll know the answer in the next sixty seconds, won't we?' I leaned forward and spoke quietly. 'My sister has nothing – repeat, nothing – that belongs to you or your family. Accept it and go home or suffer the consequences.'

Giordano sighed. 'Your sister is a thief. She doesn't deserve your protection. Give her to us and this can end before it even begins. We'll leave London. I promise you won't hear from us again.'

'You're not getting it. Whatever Charley did or didn't do is unimportant. She's family.'

'Is that a no?'

'An absolute no.'

His thick lips drew back in a sneer. 'I wish I could convince you you're making a mistake. You don't understand just how big a mistake.'

'Pack up your tent and disappear while you still can.'

Mura said, 'You're expecting us to leave with a few bucks? Go to NOLA with marginally more than fuck all? You really can't be serious. Your sister's a whore and thief. Who she fucks is her business – I don't have a problem with it. But she should've been more careful. Robbing the Giordanos has brought those consequences you mentioned down on her pretty head. If we can't have what she stole, we'll settle for her.'

Ritchie answered for me. 'Don't bet your house on it. I'm fine with the cleaners earning a bit of overtime.'

Giordano stood; for the moment, there was no more to be gained. He said, 'It's a difficult decision, I understand that. I'll give you three days to hand her over. Otherwise, your blood will be on the streets. Three days, Mr Glass.'

I nodded. 'Three days or three years, Giordano. I can't give you what we don't have. But I'll make a deal with you. Forget the money; that offer closed. Crawl back to the rock you were under and I'll forget what you did to the girls from the club. It's either that or join them.'

* * *

Felix Corrigan saw Ritchie's men in the rear-view two cars back following them up Camden High Street. In Kentish Town Road, a green Mondeo slipped into the traffic and he tensed until it turned off near the Regent's Canal Towpath. Across in the passenger seat, Nina scowled through the window at an unfamiliar London. She hadn't said a word since he'd lost it with her after the demeaning performance in the middle of the night: silence was her revenge. And nobody, but nobody, did surly better than Nina Glass.

She was pale and looked tired, her face thinner than it had been, her mouth reduced to a hard line by a seething resentment that wouldn't let go. The encounter in the dark had been painful for both of them – a stain not easily removed or forgotten.

On top of the usual withdrawal symptoms – exhaustion, restlessness, and irritability – Nina had to be feeling stupid and rejected. Felix tried to reach her. 'We're almost there. As far as George is concerned you've had a bug that wiped you out. You're better but still not great. That's the story. Everything else stays between us.'

She stopped biting a ragged nail long enough for the old Nina to surface and snarled a reply. 'When this – whatever the hell it is – is over, stay away from me. I never want us to even be in the same room. Do you understand? Never! I fucking hate you!'

Corrigan had had as much of her ungrateful shit as he could take. 'I told you before and I meant it, you're in no danger from me. Babysitting a spoiled brat isn't fun. Your antics are tolerated because of who your brother is. Don't you get that? Anybody other than Luke Glass and you'd be selling yourself on the street to feed your habit.'

'Don't talk to me.'

He pulled to the centre of the road, indicated and turned right. 'Somebody bloody needs to, because you're in trouble, Nina. Bad trouble. Unless you do something about it, it won't end well. Unless—'

'Are you deaf? I said don't talk to me.'

Felix lifted his mobile and pressed Ritchie's number. 'We're two minutes out. No problems so far. Nina's been up all night vomiting. She needs to get some sleep, George.'

He dropped the phone into his jacket pocket and stared ahead. 'That's the last lie I'm telling for you. From here, you're on your own, Nina.'

19

Madeline Giordano stood at the window above Park Lane as she'd done in St Charles Avenue on the morning of Beppe's death and drew the shawl round her shoulders. She hadn't cried for her son and wouldn't – a mother's love for her child was unconditional but, even as a baby, she'd struggled to care for him. The heart attack, predictable though it had been, had triggered memories buried by time. More and more she found herself reliving the past, returning in her mind to the early years when her husband was tightening his stranglehold on the parishes from Terrebonne to Caddo, Beauregard to Madison. The French Quarter in Orleans – where the real money was – had been the last to fall. With her by his side, Silvestro had taken the Quarter one street at a time – Royal, Bourbon, Decatur, Toulouse. For three months during winter a bloody battle had raged over Chartres, finally ending when he'd put a bullet in the back of the gang leader running towards Jackson Square and ripped the amber pendant from his neck. From then on, the family had ruled unopposed.

Dark-brown liver spots on the back of her wrinkled hands were reminders that those days and the girl she'd been were gone – her own demise wouldn't be far away. Age was supposed to bring consolations; Madeline had yet to discover them. Antoine was his father's son – differently flawed, but flawed nevertheless. Left to himself there was no knowing what damage he'd do. Silvestro had been fearless, the cleverest man she'd ever known. With Beppe and Antoine, genetics had taken a holiday; the future depended on her. The house of Giordano was crumbling. In time it would fall. But she'd be damned if it happened while there was breath in her body.

She heard them come into the room and spoke without turning. 'I hope you have good news – we could use some.'

Mura forgot his place and blurted out, 'News, yes. Good isn't how I'd describe it.'

Her reply was brutal, worthy of Beppe at his dismissive best. 'I wasn't asking you, *sót bata*. My grandson will tell me. Or are you happy to let someone speak for you, Antoine? What happened? Has Glass agreed to give up the thief?'

The words were delivered in a defeated whisper. 'No, Madeline, he's agreed to nothing.'

She faced them. 'Really? Then, it was a mistake to let you talk to him. Why am I not surprised? You haven't presented his position clearly enough.'

Mura forgot the warning so recently given. He said, 'They were ready for us. They made us look like children. They could have killed us and sent our heads to you in a box.'

Madeline inhaled noisily through her nostrils. 'I won't say it again.'

Tony was still reeling from the shambles in the club. The threat confidently tossed at the London gang boss on their way out had been an act; he'd listened to Calum Bishop's assessment of Glass, believed it, and still managed to under-estimate him.

Madeline tapped the back of the sofa with a wrinkled finger. 'I'm waiting, Antoine.'

Tony slumped into an armchair. 'Like Bruno says, they were ready. We walked into a trap.'

'Did you really expect anything less from a man who has London in the palm of his hand? We were warned. Glass isn't an idiot. He won't be intimidated. Not by us. Not by anyone. How did it end?'

Tony pinched the corners of his eyes and let the criticism roll over him; he'd been listening to some version of it from his grandmother all his life. 'I gave him the three days we agreed to hand his sister over.'

Madeline crossed the room and poured herself an Amontillado from a crystal decanter, letting the dark liquid climb the glass almost to the top. 'I've already made calls. Mr Glass is about to find out the odds have changed.'

Tony ignored the uncertainty growing in him since the meeting and took courage from her words. 'For sure. This might be his town, but he'll be eating dirt when we're finished with him.'

Bruno Mura was used to having his opinions heard and couldn't keep quiet. 'We don't know this city. We need Bishop to crush Glass and settle the score with the sister.'

Madeline sent her drink crashing into the fireplace; it shattered in a hundred shards of diamond light that fell to the floor in a drum-roll cascade. She gripped the chair, barely able to contain her fury. 'I told you to shut the fuck up, Sardinian!'

* * *

Three and a half miles away in Finsbury Park, Calum Bishop was being given a blow-by-blow account of the ambush in the club, laughing, pounding the arm of his chair when he heard about the gunmen rising like spectres out of the mist.

'Magic! Total magic! Tony Giordano hasn't a fucking clue what he's got himself into. Luke Glass will have him on toast. Him and his family are about to get a slap they'll never recover from. And all because his old man couldn't keep it in his trousers.'

The guy telling the tale waited for his boss to get a grip on himself before he went on. Bishop said, 'How did it finish? Was there blood on the carpet?'

'No blood. Giordano talked tough and gave Glass an ultimatum.'

'Brave lad. Rather him than us, eh? What did he say?'

'He has three days to hand over his sister or it's war.'

Bishop had suggested the meeting and it could hardly have turned out better. However it ended, both sides would be weakened, creating an opportunity for him to step in and pick up the pieces. 'Well, well. It seems we're going to be busy. Good. Now, get your arses out there and help find that sister. She's the trump card.'

* * *

Felix led Nina from the car to the house; she ignored him and stared sullenly at the ground. Her hair hadn't been combed, her skin was ashen and the normally elegant woman looked as if she'd slept in her clothes. Ritchie was waiting to quiz Felix. 'Nobody followed you?'

'If they did, I didn't see them.'

'How's Nina doing?'

'She's weak. Hasn't eaten in days.'

Nina resented being discussed like a senile old lady and lashed out. 'I'm right here, George, in case you haven't noticed. If you want to know anything about me all you have to do is ask. I'm big and ugly enough to speak for myself, thank you very much.'

Ritchie smothered his irritation – he'd been here before. It wasn't a popularity contest, and if it was he wouldn't be the winner.

Inside the house, Charley ran to Nina and hugged her. 'I'm sorry for putting you through this.'

Nina didn't understand what she was talking about. 'Why, what've you done?'

'I assumed you'd know.'

'Nobody tells me anything. How long will we have to stay here?'

Ritchie overheard and answered. 'Until Luke's sorted out some stuff.'

'What stuff?'

He didn't elaborate. 'Charley will show you to your room.'

When the door closed behind her sister Nina crawled under the bedclothes without bothering to undress. She said, 'Let's talk later. I'm too tired.'

* * *

20

A warm breeze caressed the dense crowns of the Canary Island date palms lining the approach to Departures at Louis Armstrong International Airport. At thirty feet high, they would take years to reach full height. The woman behind the wheel of the Volkswagen Passat wore jeans and a red off-the-shoulder top showing her slim neck and flawless decolletage. The kiss she gave the man in the passenger seat lacked passion. They'd quarrelled the previous night and hardly spoken on the drive from Chalmette in St Bernard Parish, down river from New Orleans.

The exchange was dry. She said, 'So, I guess I'll see you when I see you.'

He reached into the back for his suitcase and answered as he opened the door. 'That you will, honey.'

Inside the terminal, he joined the queue at the British Airways check-in desk and ignored the three men ahead of him he'd worked with before, then strolled to the end of Concourse B and Emeril's Table, studied the menu, decided he wasn't hungry, and headed to a bar and his last cognac for a while. Alcohol made him sluggish; he needed to be fresh. On the flight he'd have nothing stronger than coffee and not too much of that, either.

Tomorrow morning, he'd be in the capital of England.

* * *

At the same time, two young Creole guys were boarding an Air France jet to Hartsfield-Jackson Atlanta. They stored their carry-on luggage in the overhead locker. One of them lifted an old lady's case and stowed it for her. She thanked him for his kindness.

He flashed a smile – 'Happy to help, mam,' – folded the spine of a battered copy of James Lee Burke's novel *Cadillac Jukebox* and picked the story up from where he'd left off. His travelling companion closed his eyes and listened to Marc Broussard's rasping cover of Otis Redding's 'These Arms of Mine' through earbuds. In ninety minutes, they'd be in Georgia. Eleven hours after that, on the other side of the Atlantic Ocean.

* * *

Ahead, an Iberia Airbus A330-200 to Charlotte Douglas taxiing on one of the three asphalt runways included men on its passenger manifest who weren't strangers to each other. They sat apart and during the two-hour stopover kept their distance before reboarding the seven-hour-fifty-five-minute flight to Heathrow.

* * *

The two guys wandering around Toronto Pearson International had never been to Canada: Pierre Honoré was a loose-limbed twenty-four-year-old graduate of the St. Roch neighbourhood of New Orleans, where three out of four children were raised in poverty; a gig with the Giordano family was a lucky break. Boudreaux, his partner, was a stocky Cajun from the Desire area who sold women and dope to tourists in the French Quarter. A criminal conviction of longer than twelve months would disqualify them from entering another country. Remarkably, given their backgrounds and history of violence, they were clean – the reason they'd been selected, along with the fact they had passports.

* * *

When the Finnair stewardess came round offering champagne and chocolates, Roberta Romano had already slipped out of her shoes and was asleep. In ten years she'd clocked-up more Air Miles than she could spend and learned early that the key to successful travelling was to forget the in-flight food and drink, the movies, the umpteen music channels, or whoever was seated nearest her even if he was as handsome as George Clooney in his prime. None of that helped if she wanted to be fresh and rested when the plane touched down.

At thirty-four, slim and dark, with painted nails and long hair, she looked like a model on her way to a photo shoot, an illusion that shattered when the hair parted to reveal the jagged scar on her right cheek – a souvenir from the one hit that had gone wrong.

Roberta Romano was an assassin who worked freelance, charged a lot of money for her services, and was worth every penny.

Originally from Cane River country where free people of mixed-race descendants had settled before the Civil War, she lived alone in a modest house in the Garden District bought with her first pay check from a job in Atlanta. There was no man in her life – an easy decision, given her skill-set. She restricted herself to two or three contracts a year, all within the continental USA, and rejected everything else. At night, she played the piano, favouring the music of Chopin and Rachmaninov. During the day she worked her way through *The Escoffier Cookbook*. In both cases honing her technique.

Known in the underworld as 'La Réponse' – the answer, a nickname she'd earned seventeen times – she carried no weapons of any kind for her first trip abroad.

That was being taken care of in London.

Roberta had discovered early on she was attracted to the finer things in life: Chopin's 'Nocturne No. I in B flat minor', a Thomas Keller chocolate soufflé prepared by the master himself; the lyrics of Stephen Sondheim, and hotels like the Mandarin Oriental Hyde Park. In her work she was cautious and never took an assignment until she'd scouted the location and figured out the approach – Tony Giordano had persuaded her there were exceptions to every rule, the offer he'd made impossible to turn down.

The job was different from anything she'd taken on. But that didn't mean it couldn't be done.

PART III

PART III

21

THE FIRST DAY

George Ritchie's call from Kentish Town was meant to reassure me. It didn't work. I'd known him a long time, long enough to spot the trace of uncertainty in a voice that was usually rock solid. Ritchie was concerned. Before I could ask what was worrying him he all but admitted it.

'Where are you?'

'At the club.'

'Don't go walk-about. We need to talk.'

'As long as you're satisfied everything's under control.'

'It is – your sisters are okay. I'll see you in thirty minutes.'

* * *

As soon as he opened the door I saw the anxiety on his face. Ritchie's caution was legendary – I hadn't been to his house and didn't know anybody who had. In fact, I couldn't have told you where he lived – if he was worried, I should be, too. He took a seat across the desk and drew a hand through the stubble on his jaw. 'Kentish Town's sorted. Our guys are inside the house and outside.

Nina and Charley are as safe as you can be without being dead. I'm not expecting anything we can't handle.'

So why was he worried?

I said, 'Have you spoken to Nina?'

'Not directly. Felix is handling it.' He paused, considering how to word what he was about to say. 'When this is over let's discuss the way forward with Nina.'

'What does that mean, George?'

'There's a lot of water gone under the bridge, Luke.'

'She's my sister.'

'Maybe she'd react better to somebody else.'

'I'm not getting this. What's she done?'

He stared and I realised I'd had as much as I was getting from him on that subject.

The criticism was unexpected coming from him, though it was the truth. I guessed he'd run out of patience. 'What's brought this on? What's she done, George?'

He shifted the conversation to something less controversial. 'We've identified the reg of the car that picked them up outside the club.'

'Give me a name.'

'Calum Bishop.'

I hadn't come across the nephew who'd taken over in north London. By all accounts he was everything his uncle had been and more.

'What's the word on the streets?'

'There isn't any.'

'Really? I'm surprised.'

'Me, too. There's always somebody who can't keep his mouth shut. Bishop's new at this game. Everything he has is down to his uncle Kenny. Young Calum's keen to make a name for himself in his own right. Fair enough, except going up against the Glass family at this stage in his career would be an error that could finish him before he's even got started. The last time his family fucked with us didn't turn out well for them. He's got a score to settle but he's not ready.'

I let Ritchie speak. I had nothing to say.

'The Americans are a way in. When this is over they'll go back where they came from.'

'And Calum will be in pole position here.'

'I'm guessing that's the thinking.'

'I'm more interested in your thinking, George.'

He took a beat before he answered. 'However you dress it up it isn't great news for us, that's for sure. But it explains Giordano's front. Knowing Bishop's behind him, he has to be feeling pretty good about getting what he came for.'

'Charley.'

'More. If that was his ambition he didn't need to show himself, yet he did.'

'What does your gut tell you?'

He pounded his fist in his palm. 'We've seen him and his Rottweiler at the club. The big unknown is how many more are in the city. Add Bishop's men and we have a problem. If they've roped in that old IRA sympathiser in Kilburn it's hard to see us coming out ahead.'

'Bridie keeps herself to herself.'

The familiarity didn't escape him. 'Bridie? You sound as though you like her.'

'Better than some I could mention.'

For reasons I didn't understand, the atrocities committed by the Irish Republican Army were a red rag to Ritchie. 'Can I respectfully remind you she's a murdering rebel bastard?'

'Ancient history; the best part of fifty years ago. She isn't part of this.'

'I wish I had your faith. We did for his relations. Could be young Calum hasn't let it go. Before he does something he'll regret, perhaps a reminder of how it went last time might be in order.'

George had a point. I said, 'Arrange a meet with him. Today. I'll deal with Bridie myself.'

* * *

Nina's skin crawled; she fidgeted and couldn't sit still. A feeling of dread swamped her as the withdrawal symptoms started, leaving her on edge and ready to take it out on whoever was handy, in this case her sister. When things were going her way she was the sweetest person anyone could meet. When they weren't...

They were in the lounge. Charley closed the door so, at last, they could talk without being disturbed, and sat across from her, more nervous now than when she'd confessed who Tony Giordano was and why he'd shown up in the club. What she had to say wasn't easy. Luke already knew the story; Nina deserved an explanation and Charley was determined to give her one. From her expression, she wasn't in an understanding mood but that couldn't be the excuse to not tell her why she'd been hauled across the city. She owed her sibling that much.

Charley could count on one hand the times she'd been in the same room as her sister in the last few months. And when they were together Nina was unapproachable and monosyllabic, only speaking when spoken to. Easy to understand: Mark Douglas had been the love of her life. Making sense of what had happened, trying to go on, would be beyond difficult. The safe house was an unexpected opportunity for them to connect, except Nina wasn't interested; she was agitated and distracted, in and out of her bag every five minutes, searching for Christ knew what.

'I'm sorry if you've been dragged away from something important. But it gives us a chance to talk.'

The response was disappointing. Nina said, 'Wouldn't you know it? I'm out of bloody cigarettes. Sod's fucking law!'

'Tap a couple off one of the guys.'

'I'd rather go for them myself.'

'That's ridiculous. You aren't serious – you can't be? We're in this place because somebody wants to kill me.'

Nina wasn't getting it. She said, 'How long do you think we'll have to stay?'

It was the wrong question and Charley lost it with her. 'Oh, for God's sake! Is that the best you can do?'

Nina dismissed the rebuke with a shrug. 'What do you want me to say? Whatever it is, Luke will sort it like he sorts everything.' Her eyes welled up, her voice cracked and faltered. 'Like he sorts everything for this family.'

Charley put her arms around her and let her weep. 'I'll send one of the guys for cigarettes.' The slim body seemed to fold in on itself with her next words. 'You aren't going anywhere, d'you hear? Not anywhere, Nina Glass.'

* * *

Bridie O'Shea was everything Ritchie had said and more. At seventeen, driven more by oestrogen than patriotism, she'd followed Wolf Kavanagh, a bomb-maker for the Provisionals two decades older than herself, to London and played a significant part in at least four bombings in the early 1970s. How heinous acts that left bystanders dead and maimed squared with her staunch Catholic beliefs was beyond me. When fervour in the Cause faded, Wolf stayed in the capital, turning his hand to extortion, prostitution and robbery. Bridie – Mrs Wolf by now – was in it with him up to her twinkling Irish eyeballs. The Bridie I knew was a card-playing pub landlady in Kilburn High Road, who sipped port and lemon and bottles of O'Hara's stout in a cubbyhole and followed the happenings in the world without leaving her chair.

We weren't friends, but we weren't enemies, either.

At least, not as far as I was concerned.

No one just showed up expecting to be ushered into her presence; that wasn't how it worked in this part of west London. The man behind the bar recognised me and went to petition on my behalf. An unnecessary rigmarole for my benefit: Bridie O'Shea would've known I was coming to see her while I was parking my car.

I'd expected her to look older; she didn't, she was exactly the same: the cards and the booze were still there; the cigarettes weren't. Maybe she'd decided to change the habit of a lifetime and obey the law of the land on smoking in a confined public space, though I seriously doubted it. More likely, shortness of breath and a tightness in her chest one morning had forced her to accept she wasn't indestructible after all. From there, a diagnosis of incipient emphysema and a stern warning from some doctor who'd refused to be intimidated by her reputation had forced the old rebel to reconsider the damage she was doing to herself and ditch the Capstan Full Strength.

She kept her attention on the cards and asked a question that didn't need an answer. 'Did you hear about the Irishman who meets a leprechaun in the forest?' And she was off. 'The leprechaun likes the look of him and grants him three wishes. Paddy says, "I love women, especially blondes." The little fella snaps his fingers and a luscious platinum blonde appears. "That's marvellous," says Paddy. "And I love Guinness." A bottle appears in his hand and the little fella says, "This is no ordinary bottle. Every time you drink from it, it'll fill up to the top again." Paddy says,

"That's grand. What a thing." The wee man smiles. "Tell me your third wish." Paddy thinks hard for a minute, then he says, "Give us another of them bottles of Guinness.".'

Bridie laughed a throaty laugh, snapped the four of diamonds on the five of spades, and lifted the port and lemon to her lips. The laughter died. 'Understand somethin'. Any Irish jokes in this boozer, I'll be the one makin' them. What brings Luke Glass to this godforsaken neck of the woods? And don't lie to an old woman, because she won't believe you.'

'I wouldn't dream of it, Bridie.'

The laugh came back, louder and longer than before. 'Like hell. You're a man. You're all the fecking same. Can't help yourselves. Spit it out and let me get back to my game.'

'There are people in London who shouldn't be here. I'm guessing you know that.'

Her eyes shifted from the cards, grey lasers boring into me. 'Startin' with the stupid stuff, are we? All right. I haven't seen you since Brigid left Tipperary so I'll humour you and pretend I didn't catch what you just said. If you're askin' if I'm with them you've got a funny way of going about it.'

'Are you?'

The corners of her mouth twitched and reset. Nobody dared challenge Bridie O'Shea, especially in her own boozer; she didn't appreciate it. 'My Wolf used to say, "The best friends are the ones you don't meet too often."' She lifted the port and emptied it in one go. 'For years I didn't understand what the damn he was on about.'

'But now you do.'

'But now I do.'

The barman appeared at her elbow with a refill: quite a trick. I wondered how it was done. Bridie chose her words. 'My dear departed husband had the right of it. Just like he had with so many things.' Her fingers searched for the cigarettes they wouldn't find; at any rate, not today. She tilted her head. 'Have I done anythin', said anythin', to make you believe I'd go against you?'

'No.'

She turned the word over, exploring it. 'No. No. Yet, here you are, standin' in my pub suggestin'... God knows what.'

'I'm not suggesting anything. I'm coming right out with it, Bridie. And before you go off the deep end let me remind you that if I thought you were in with the enemy, I wouldn't be here.'

She topped up the stout and blew on the creamy foam. 'I'll say this and I'll say no more. You and I have a relationship that works. Friends, no, but a long way from enemies. Only a fool would waste something like that. I'm a lot of things, Christ knows, a fool isn't one of them.' She started to smile and stopped. 'Once upon a time, I'll grant you, maybe that wasn't true. The young are allowed to be foolish. Not these days. You have nothin' to worry about from Bridie.'

'And if it turns out I need somebody watching my back?'

She shuffled the cards and didn't look at me. 'It seems you're determined to offend me today. You heard me say we have a relationship that works, didn't you? The reason it works is because we can depend on each other if circumstances go against us.'

Bridie lifted her head. 'Or do I have the wrong of it, Mr Glass?'

With her jokes and her quotes from the long-dead Wolf, the Irishwoman was a plausible old fucker. She'd just proved she could turn it on and off like a tap. I didn't believe she was involved with the Giordanos but if they made her the right offer it might not stay that way.

* * *

I had a theory that there was a secret factory churning out policemen by the dozen, winding them up and sending them into the world to annoy people. Lookalikes with short-back-and-sides heads, and hands that had never done a hard day's work and never would, buried in the pockets of identical trench coats; robots programmed to introduce themselves with, 'Excuse me, sir, can I have a word?' delivered with all the personality of the speaking clock. The two coming towards me were fresh off the production line and before they'd left New Scotland Yard on the Embankment, they'd known more about Luke Glass than I did. These guys were minnows. Even if they got lucky, detective inspector was as high as they'd go. At LBC we regularly had the big fish in – bottom-feeding jolly boys out on the razzle, gleefully pissing the taxpayer's money up against the wall – every one of them as bent as a nine-bob note. Once upon a time I'd believed coppers were the good guys, on the side of law and order. My brother had slapped that nonsense out of me. Danny had been a lunatic but he wasn't always wrong.

They glanced around, mild amusement in their eyes, a couple of planks with nothing better to do than rattle my cage. Except, their smug expressions said they were pretty confident about whatever they were pushing.

The routine they were about to run began with questions and ended with a polite invitation to accompany them to the station. All very civilised. Until it was just me and them in the interrogation room at three o'clock in the morning.

Then, the kid gloves would come off as the evening took an ugly turn.

I knew. I'd been there.

The nearest flashed a warrant card and told me his name. I did an impersonation of the alabaster statue of Fortuna in the foyer and waited for him to say the magic words. He didn't disappoint me. 'Can we have a word, Mr Glass?'

'Should I call my lawyer?'

He faked surprise. 'Your lawyer? Why would you need a lawyer?'

'I expect you're going to tell me.'

His colleague dispensed with the introduction and got into it. 'Where were you two nights ago?'

'No idea. Where were you?'

Irritation made his mouth twitch; he'd practised his spiel and was determined to get it out uninterrupted. 'The body of a man was washed up near the Old Billingsgate Market. He'd been beaten to death and dumped in the river.'

'Sorry to hear that. A friend of yours, was he?'

His mate took up the interrogation. 'I'll come straight to the point, Mr Glass.'

'Do.'

'We've had a tip-off you were involved.'

Well, well, Jocelyn. Not smart. Not smart at all.

'Really?'

He looked away, immediately defensive, coughed into his hand and revealed why detective inspector was probably beyond him. 'Because a call is anonymous doesn't make what was reported untrue.'

'What was reported?'

His lips tightened in a grim smile. 'We're getting ahead of ourselves. Please answer the question.'

I could've told him but that would've been too easy. Instead, I said, 'You know, before this goes any further maybe I should give my lawyer a bell.'

The reply was dismissively casual. 'Of course, you're perfectly entitled if you think it's appropriate.'

I forced concern into my voice and lifted the mobile. 'Just to be on the safe side, eh?'

They came closer, sharks sensing blood in the water, and I

revisited my original thoughts: not a clone factory, a woodcarver called Mr Geppetto had created them in a Tuscan village. The one who hadn't introduced himself dashed his hopes of becoming a real boy with a series of lies so outrageous I almost applauded. 'Don't take this visit personally, Mr Glass. When an anonymous caller mentions a name in connection with a suspicious death we don't have a choice. As police officers we're duty-bound to follow it up. You aren't under arrest or anything like that. We simply need to ask you some questions. Now, again, can you tell us where you were?'

He stopped short of adding 'on the night in question'. It would've been fun to string it out a bit longer and some light relief at this tosser's expense wouldn't be unwelcome. But I was tired. And I remembered the state Rupert Neville had been in on that same night: morose and intoxicated to the point of stupor. Because he'd known what was going down and discovered talking about murder was very different from actually being a part of it. The hooker and the over-priced bubbles hadn't softened the reality.

I said it for him. 'On the night in question I had a conversation with someone who can confirm I was here all the time.'

'Who?'

'Assistant Commissioner Kirby.'

The light went out of their eyes. Blood drained from their gormless faces. Only moments ago they'd been peddling an under-rehearsed version of good cop/bad cop, picturing themselves walking into the Curtis Green Building with Luke Glass. It had all gone wrong and they felt sick. Disbelief fell from the copper's mouth like tainted meat. 'The AC?'

'He is now. Beano and I go way back. First ran into him when he was a sergeant working out of Peckham. I hadn't seen him in ages. Had a laugh about how well we'd both done.'

His mate clutched at a straw. 'You're sure it was the same night?'

'As sure as I can be. Beano's credit-card bill will nail it down.' I threw in a bluff. 'Call him. If you haven't already got it, I can give you his number.'

They couldn't hide their disappointment and I almost felt sorry for them. They were shell-shocked, trying to make sense of the bomb that had blown their plans for promotion out of the water.

I smothered a smile and rubbed salt in an already salty wound. 'The club's CCTV will confirm it. We keep the footage for three weeks. You're welcome to check. I'll set it up for you.'

Having an assistant commissioner of the Metropolitan Police as my alibi was more than they could stomach. 'That won't be necessary. We'll speak to AC Kirby at the Yard.' He tossed a final observation at me. 'Somebody doesn't like you, Mr Glass.'

'They can join the queue. Who was it, by the way? The guy in the river?'

He coughed into his hand again and trotted out the stock reply. 'The chief inspector will be making a statement in due course.'

'Yes, of course he will, but between us.'

'Sir Harold Clifford.'

I put Jocelyn Church's amateur attempt to frame me aside and focused on the main deal. Tony Giordano's ultimatum had been a desperate attempt at saving face. As George Ritchie's men appeared from all over the club, the American realised he'd been out-manoeuvred and resorted to threats. Empty words, maybe, but I didn't dismiss them. London wasn't their patch. My family's hold on it was hardly a secret. Yet, Tony hadn't tried to hide. Far from it – twice he'd gone out of his way to shout his presence. In their shoes I would've lifted Charley off the street and been heading back to the USA in hours. Job done. The road they'd taken put them directly in conflict with us, which meant they were incompetent idiots or, for reasons of their own, they *wanted* a showdown.

This city had more than its share of gangs, street outfits whose territories bordered each other leading to tension and, inevitably, to violence. They lived in a world of their own and it was a small world: Bridie would swallow them whole without missing the black jack on the red queen in her cubbyhole in Kilburn. My interest in them was zero. O'Shea was levels above them – a wily old bird who lived by her own rules; deciding to trust her or not was a judgement call I'd make in due course. So were the Bishops: the baton had been passed from Kenny to his nephew and, according to reports, Calum had adjusted to his new status without dropping a beat.

Arranging a powwow should've been simple. It was early in the afternoon and we were in the office above the King of Mesopotamia. I had my feet on the desk watching tiny particles of dust float in the shafts of sunlight streaming through the window. Ritchie was talking to Bishop's guy – Calum wouldn't come to the phone – and relaying the gist of what was being said to me.

George put his hand over the receiver. 'This boy thinks he's Reggie Kray. Five minutes in the door and already acting like he's royalty. They're insisting we go to them.'

'Where?'

'The North Star on Finchley Road. I'm against it.'

'Why?'

'For the same reasons they're for it.'

'We don't know their reasons.'

'Exactly. We should catch them off guard and insist on somewhere else.'

I overruled him, although I didn't expect him to like it. 'The North Star's fine. When?'

'They're saying tomorrow.'

'No use. Tell them it has to be today.'

Ritchie made the arrangements and closed his phone. He was a pro who'd earned his stripes in a score of conflicts and, understandably, wasn't happy about his advice being so readily disregarded. 'Time I wasn't here. What's the point? You aren't listening.'

'I am.'

'Can't be. Otherwise, you'd get what I'm saying. Kenny Bishop was a snake. Calum's his nephew. He might be minded to make a name for himself by taking out Luke Glass. The reason I get out of bed in the morning is to protect the family and the business. Let me do what you pay me for.'

'I can handle this. It's no big deal.'

He slammed his fist on the desk. 'All right! You don't need me! I'm gone!'

Ritchie was the one man I could rely on, a cool head in the storm, reasoned and unflappable. Losing his temper forced me to reconsider. There might be a day when I could stand to be without him. This certainly wasn't it. I softened my approach. 'Listen, George, ignoring your instincts would be a mistake, perhaps a fatal mistake. We'll both go. As for quitting, forget it, you'd be dead in six months.'

Ritchie's ability to get a grip of himself and calm down was impressive. He immediately turned his focus on the meeting. He said, 'We'll have people in the pub. So will they. Power is still a novelty for Calum. If that fiasco on the phone is anything to go by, he thinks he's God Almighty. Young and bloody bulletproof. Be easy to step over the line and discover he's just little Calum Bishop, same as he always was. But by then, you might be on the floor with a knife in your back.'

'How long will it take to get there?'

'Finchley Road is one of the main arteries out of London. Traffic's always heavy. I'd say an hour plus.'

'And we're meeting them, when?'

'Half-past three.'

I checked my watch. 'We should get going.'

He disagreed. 'Our guys need time to get in position before we show up. The wait will do Bishop good. Remind him he isn't as important as he thinks he is. No bad thing. We asked for the meet. They decided the where. Right at this moment they believe they're calling the shots. Turning up late will change the dynamic.'

'And when Calum sees you he'll run out of the door screaming for his mother?'

Ritchie gave a rare smile. 'If he knows what's good for him.'

'By the way, George, I had a visit from Scotland Yard.'

'Anybody I know?'

'Two detectives – Tweedledum and Tweedledee – asking where I was the night they fished the guy out of the Thames.'

The smile on Ritchie's lips faded to memory. 'How did your name get in the frame?'

'An anonymous phone call.'

'Sneaky. Who do you reckon?'

'Jocelyn Church, for sure. Fortunately, I could prove I was in the club talking to Beano Kirby.'

'That would go down well.'

'Yeah, the original lead balloon.'

'So, what do you want me to do about it?'

'Keep digging. I want as much as you can find on anybody even vaguely associated with the Skytrain project. I told Church I wasn't interested but I'm starting to change my mind.'

* * *

I'd passed The North Star a few times without ever having been inside – a typical boozer from the Victorian era. Growing up, south of the river had been my stomping ground. Central London was a tourist trap best avoided, the West End too expensive. Only the lucky bastards could afford it. As for the rest: why bother when everything a teenage boy wanted could be found on Tooting Broadway? Since then, my eyes had been opened. The lucky bastards were still around, a new generation living their golden lives, only now they spent their money in my club. The irony didn't escape me.

In the car on our way across the city, Ritchie slowly morphed into the man I remembered when he'd worked as Albert Anderson's enforcer and I was scared of him. His jaw set hard, he stared ahead, unblinking, and didn't speak.

Finally, he broke his silence and let it all come out. 'The car reg proves the Giordanos aren't alone. Bishop's in this with them. Long odds to beat. O'Shea helped us once because she'd been caught in the crossfire. Otherwise, she'd have stood on the sidelines, drunk her stout, and happily made peace with the winner.' Ritchie warmed to his subject. 'St Patrick banished the snakes from Ireland. Okay. Where did they go?'

I had a feeling he was going to tell me.

'A fair few landed in Kilburn.'

'Not what the legend says.'

'Fuck the legend. We aren't dealing in legends, we're dealing in facts, and the fact is that that old soak is just one more bastard in this town who can't be trusted.'

He stopped the car on the other side of the street from our destination and checked his gun. 'Please tell me you're tooled up.'

'No worries.'

'Thank Christ for that.'

'Relax, George. All we're going to do is talk.'

He shook his head, frustrated and unconvinced. 'This is hard and it hasn't even started.'

* * *

A plaque outside told the pub's history to anybody who was interested. Apparently, it had been around since 'Brigid left Tipperary', to quote Bridie O'Shea – and had been among the first buildings to grace the new Finchley Road in 1850. Bishop's guys frisked us on the pavement, a pointless exercise to reassure themselves they were in control. One of them made a move to take Ritchie's gun: George forced his arm up his back and pinned his face to the wall, whispering in his ear. 'You're an inch away from a dislocated shoulder. You don't want that, trust me. Be a good boy and tell your boss Luke Glass says to get real or forget it.'

We didn't have long to wait: a minute later he was back, rubbing the top of his arm, the grin replaced by a sullen nod. Inside, I counted ten people, five at the long, polished-wood bar, the rest spaced out in booths. Nobody looked up at the new arrivals: a clue that few, if any, were actual customers.

Calum was wearing a tan leather jerkin and blue jeans. The family resemblance wasn't obvious; Kenny Bishop's nephew was very different from his beanpole uncle. With his heavy frame and thinning hair, I saw no likeness. He watched us come towards him, lifted his pint and put it down again without taking a drink. By itself, a small thing, but an indication he wasn't quite as confident as he appeared.

'My men are a bit over-zealous at times, you know how it is. They prefer it's their finger on the trigger.' He laughed at his joke.

Ritchie let it fade. 'A finger isn't much use unless there's an arm attached to it.'

Bishop took his attention off him and turned it on me. 'You asked for this meet. What do you want? Make it short, I'm a busy man.'

Dancing around it was a waste of time: we both knew why we were here. Calum was keen to present himself as a tough guy and that was okay; maybe he was. The day would come – perhaps sooner than he imagined – when he'd get an opportunity to prove exactly how tough. I wasn't looking for a new enemy. On another day this young Turk could strut his funky stuff from Belsize Park to Brent Cross and all points in between, so long as he stayed well away from me. The moment he stepped over the line I'd come down on his balding head like a proverbial tonne of bricks.

Explaining the past wasn't necessary, but I tried. 'Your uncle got into bed with the wrong people. Don't make the same mistake.'

Calum toyed with a beermat, matched my cliché with one of his own and tossed it at me. 'It's an ill wind.'

He was right; his uncle's defeat hadn't done him any harm. Indirectly, I was responsible for his elevation. I said, 'Your little arrangement with the Giordanos is blown. They're using you; when they've got what they came for, which they won't, by the way, they'll return to their own turf.' I kept my eyes on him so he got the message loud and clear. 'It'll be just you and me. And I know where you live.'

'Sounds as though you're trying to frighten me.'

'Am I succeeding?'

His tough-guy impersonation was getting plenty of practice. Bishop said, 'What do you think, Glass?'

'I think the day you heard of the Giordanos was a bad day for you.'

'Yeah? On this side of the river nobody cares what you think. Why don't you fuck off to your fancy club? LBC? What's that?'

'It's from something my brother used to go on about. The Lucky Bastards Club. In other words, people like you. Fuckers who didn't get where they are through their own efforts. Fortunate dickheads. No wonder it's rammed every night. London's full of them.'

'Thanks for the history lesson. I'm guessing you've got a few more stories even better than that one.'

He was trying my patience. 'I'm prepared to overlook your lack of judgement. This time. Once the shooting starts, there's no going back. I'm giving you a chance to reconsider your position, Calum.'

Bishop dropped the beermat and kicked it across the floor: an outward show of what was going on inside him. The stakes had just got higher. Losing would cost him everything and he knew it. He replied like a surly teenager on the wrong end of a lecture.

'Any more advice or is that it?'

'No, that's it.'

'Then, see yourselves out.'

On the drive into the city, Ritchie was silent, though I had a fair idea what he was thinking. He left it until we were crossing Marylebone Road before finally saying what was on his mind. 'Bishop's learned fuck all from his uncle. He wants to run before he can walk. We were always going to have to deal with him. As for helping the Americans – he's relaxed because he's sure he's picked the winning side.'

'Then, we'll have to disappoint him, won't we?'

* * *

Nina had retreated into herself, withdrawn, chain-smoking the cigarettes Charley had tapped from one of the guys, curled in an armchair with her eyes closed. When they were open they searched for demons that existed only in her fevered brain. Seeing her, it was hard to believe this was Nina Glass – the tough cookie who didn't give a fuck and didn't care who knew. Pale and thin, she'd fallen farther than it was possible to imagine.

How could Luke not have noticed his sister was in trouble and got her the help she so obviously needed? How could he? The answer was one Charley didn't want to admit, that the family she'd longed to be part of – the Team Glass she'd heard Luke talk about – was no more than individuals inhabiting their own disparate worlds, a family in name only. Uniting for as long as they needed to if some outside force threatened them, then drifting away from each other when it passed.

There was no Team Glass; it was a myth.

They'd be in this house until George Ritchie said they could go. Tomorrow, a month down the line, or whenever the Giordanos returned to Louisiana. Charley looked at Nina and swore a solemn vow under her breath: she'd be damned if she was giving up on her. One way or another Nina was going to get well.

She sat on the floor, back against the wall, her head in her hands, bitterly regretting the choices that had brought this down on them. If only she'd stepped over Beppe's body and left New Orleans that night none of this would be happening. Tony would be king of the French Quarter and their mother might still be alive. Guilt was hard to bear. Anyone who disagreed could ask her sister.

Nina spoke for the first time in hours and Charley realised she hadn't been asleep. 'I'm starving, aren't you?'

'Ritchie will have organised something.'

'Forget what he's organised, I want pizza. Fancy joining me?'

'If you like. I'll tell the guys.'

Nina overruled her. 'No, they don't take a leak without his permission. They'll insist on asking if it's all right.'

'Yeah, but still...'

'Why wouldn't it be? It's only pizza, for Christ's sake. We'll tell them when it's on its way.'

'How can anybody deliver when we don't know the address?'

'Don't be stupid. It was me who bought it. Luke got me to do a deal with the old couple who owned this place. One of the first bits of business I was involved in.' She tapped her mobile and the screen lit up. 'So, what kind? I'm having pepperoni and cheese.'

23

They waited for the traffic lights at Great Cumberland Place to turn green, then drove past Marble Arch into Park Lane. In the back seat, Calum Bishop wasn't a happy man. The meeting with Luke Glass hadn't gone as well as expected and he was more nervous than he was keen to admit. His involvement with the Giordanos was always bound to come out but he would've preferred it to stay hidden a while longer. The Americans were a disappointment – not at all what he'd imagined. Calum had thought he'd be hooking up with serious bad guys, not a couple of psychos and some old coffin-dodger, although from the steel in her eyes he guessed she'd been something in her day. And if he'd known they were going to show up at the club, he'd have told the cocky bastards to fuck off out of it and take a taxi. Not smart.

Despite that, Bishop recognised the deal with the Giordanos was the best chance he was likely to get to make the south London mob eat some of the same shit they'd dished out to his family. Until every Glass was history and he was standing at the bar in LBC, drinking Luke's champagne and getting ready to fuck his hookers, Calum wouldn't relax. The crew from New Orleans had their own reasons for being in London. He had no interest in them; they could cut off the sister's tits and leave her to bleed out for all he cared, then with Glass beaten and broken he'd step in and deliver the final blow. And when her celebrated brother was history anybody who objected to the new arrangement was dead. The Giordanos were convinced he was on a mission to settle his uncle's unfinished business. Wrong! To hell with revenge! He wanted what was good for Calum Bishop. As simple as that.

George Ritchie was another name high on Calum's hit list. The Geordie was a legend in his own right: he'd had a good innings, but his time was up. Persuading him to jump ship and join forces would've been the cherry on the cake. Not happening; he was Luke's man. Yet, coming face to face with the old fucker, it was impossible not to have a sneaking pang of regret. In The North Star on Finchley Road, despite being outnumbered, Ritchie hadn't flinched. Glass and George Ritchie were a formidable combination – tough-as-boots bastards. If Calum had just one man half as good, the sky would be the limit.

The car drove around Berkeley Square into Curzon Street and stopped on the corner of Curzon Place. Bruno Mura was waiting on the pavement. Unlike Ritchie, Bishop had no grudging admiration for the man getting into the back seat; he disliked Mura and sat as far as he could away from him. If Mura noticed he didn't let it show. He took a piece of paper from his pocket and handed it to Calum.

'Madeline asked me to recap what you discussed. She assumes you've already got most of it.'

'She assumes right. I'm waiting on a couple of outstanding items. Your kind of guns are illegal in this country. Can't just go down the shops and tool up with whatever you fancy. Handguns have been banned outright since the Dunblane school massacre in 1996. Getting hold of them isn't easy. As for semi-automatic and fireburst – forget it. This isn't Chicago in 1929. Quick and quiet is how it's done. Anything else and I'm out.'

Mura didn't argue. Madeline was living in the past; her shopping list had stupid written all over it. He'd tried to tell her and got the usual dismissive reply. Fuck her!

Bishop pressed his point. 'What you're buying isn't cheap, by the way. Speaking of which...'

'When you've delivered.'

'That wasn't the deal.'

'What can I tell you? Deals change. You'll be paid then and not before. Don't worry; the Giordano's are good for it. You won't get stiffed.'

Calum couldn't believe what this guy was trying to pull. Mura dipped into his pocket and came out with a second piece of paper, smaller than the first one. Bishop held up his hand, silencing him before he could get started. 'Am I hearing right? Do you seriously imagine you can come onto my turf after the cock-up you made and take the fucking high road with me? What the fuck are you people smoking?'

Out of sight, Mura closed his hand round the knife never far from his reach, imagining the shock on the other man's face as the blade slid into his belly, gutting him as easily as a catfish in a Louisiana bayou.

Bishop said, 'If I didn't think you might actually be of some use to me, I'd do you right now.'

The Sardinian let the insult slide. When the business with the thief was over there would be one last score to settle. He continued. '*This*... this is something else. A late addition to our plans, separate and apart from the rest.'

'By "separate and apart" you mean...?'

'The funds to pay for it are coming from another source.'

'You mean the old lady's in the dark?'

'I mean another source. Draw your own conclusions, just keep them to yourself.'

Mura passed the note across. Calum opened it. 'This stuff doesn't just fall out of the sky.'

'Really?'

'Yes, fucking really. How the hell do you people survive in New Orleans? You couldn't organise yourselves out of a wet paper bag.'

Bruno Mura recognised the show for what it was: a move to up the price. He opened the car door. 'If you can't supply, say so now and we'll go elsewhere while there's still time.'

He paused in the frame and Calum felt the balance of power shift. 'And a word to the wise – when you're picking a side, choose as though your life depends on it. Because, trust me, it does. I'll expect your call.'

* * *

Bruno Mura strode through the main door of The Dorchester's Park Lane entrance into the long, outrageously lavish gold leaf and marble lobby. The hotel's star-studded history didn't impress him. As an only child in the city of Cagliari he'd spent his young days running barefoot through the city's streets; until he was nine years old he hadn't owned a pair of shoes. When his widowed father killed a man who was 'connected' to the mafia in a late-night bar brawl, it had been the end of the family. Three nights later, they'd gunned him down as he'd bought flowers from a stall outside the cemetery gate on his way to visit his wife's grave, leaving Bruno to make his way in the world. He'd grown fast and learned faster. He'd had no choice – it had been that or perish.

On the fifth floor, Tony Giordano had changed into a blue polo shirt and dark grey trousers. He looked relaxed but wasn't, immediately bombarding him with anxious questions.

'How did it go with Bishop? Did you give him his instructions?'

'Yes.'

'What did he say?'

Mura slumped into a chair. 'He made a song and dance about it and tried to hike the price. I told him to fuck off.'

Giordano waited before he spoke. Mura had never shaken the attitudes of the sad parochial little island of his birth. Everything was about strength; reason played no part so long as he was allowed to satisfy his baser instincts – like killing the two hookers for the fun of it. He was a mongrel loyal to no one.

Tony said, 'This is the first commission La Réponse has taken outside the States. She's making an exception, breaking her own rules. Normally, she doesn't move without studying the target and deciding exactly how to bring them down. With this there is no plan. The slightest deviation from her demands and she'll walk away.'

'So why take this one?'

Giordano smiled and rubbed his thumb and forefinger together.

Mura said, 'Bishop claims he needs more time. I told him to forget it or we'll go elsewhere.'

'There is no more time. We've got two days. After that...'

'Don't worry, he'll get us what we've asked for. La Réponse won't be disappointed.'

* * *

The dark-haired man at the bar was a long way from home. His name was Stanley, a Hong Kong-born Chinese from Sham Shui Po District, who'd chosen not to settle for being one of the twenty-three million people in the city living in poverty. Instead, when he was still a teenager, he'd decided to get rich and gone into business buying second-hand cameras and reselling them from a stall in Temple Street Night Market in Kowloon next to a lady reading tarot cards. Stanley Tang was in his late thirties, slim and dark, with teeth that cost more than anybody in his old neighbourhood earned in three years. His tech company, ST Development, specialised in renewable energy; Tang was in London to meet a group of venture capitalists he needed to take the business to the next level. Roberta Romano gave no sign she'd noticed him although every detail had been recorded: the beige Armani jacket and guru collar, the black Tom Ford T-shirt, and the two-tone handmade leather ankle boots. He emptied the glass in front of him and signalled the bartender for a refill from a bottle of Johnnie Walker Blue Label on the gantry. Roberta saw the pale outline of the wedding ring he'd removed from the second finger of his right hand and knew he was a player.

She ordered a Double 12, a cocktail made from Beefeater London Dry Gin, maraschino liqueur, lemon, basil and honey, and gave him the opportunity he was looking for.

Tang said, 'Let me get that.'

Roberta reacted as though this was the first time a stranger had offered to buy her a drink. 'Oh, that's so kind, thank you.'

He slid off the stool and made his move. 'Not at all. May I join you?'

'Please do.'

Tang flashed his perfect smile and offered her his hand. 'Stanley.'

'Roberta.'

'From your accent you aren't one of the locals.'

'Right back atcha.'

He laughed. 'What're you doing over here?'

'Working.'

'Doing what? Let me guess, you're a model.'

A corny line in any circumstances.

'I wish. No, I'm in personnel.'

'An international head-hunter?'

Roberta sipped her drink. 'Something like that.'

* * *

Stevie D understood two things better than anything else in the world – bikes and addicts. Motorcycles spoke and it was important to listen; noises, vibrations, grinding, rattling, rubbing, rasping, whistling and flapping told the owner to pull over and take a look. Junkies were the most predictable people on the planet, and, like fuel tank and fork oil leaks, the signs of trouble were there. Before Nina had snorted through her stash she'd be worrying where her next hit was coming from; physically she'd deteriorate and her behaviour would become more reckless. She'd make contact, desperate for more, and he'd have her exactly where he wanted. When he bumped the price and with a straight face asked her for funny money, she wouldn't object even if she noticed. It was a seller's market and always would be. Cocaine was Class A: a no-messing serious drug, the damage it did pure evil. Somebody had said it took a clear head to take it and a clear head to leave it alone – for sure they'd known what they were talking about. Once it had you in its grip it was close to impossible to shake the monkey off your back.

He was in his workshop underneath a railway bridge slugging from a bottle of Beck's, adjusting the chain on the Royal Enfield, checking the brake and transmission fluids on the Kawasaki Ninja with the rusted roller door up and shadows lengthening on the concrete floor, when his mobile vibrated. He recognised the caller ID, wiped his oily hands on an old dishcloth and went into his breezy act, faking it for Nina's benefit.

'At last. Thought you'd got yourself another boyfriend. Kicked me into touch.'

She didn't rise to it, only just holding it together. She said, 'A large pepperoni and cheese and a medium Neapolitan.'

He understood she couldn't speak freely and played the game. 'Is the pepperoni for you?'

'Yes.'

'Extra cheese?'

'Extra everything.'

'Denmark Hill?'

'No, I'll give you the address.'

And suddenly, Stevie D wasn't relaxed: Kentish Town was Calum Bishop country. If he was spotted dealing – there of all places – God alone knew what Bishop would do to him.

'It'll be an hour, is that okay?'

Nina didn't reply; she'd hung up.

* * *

The Honda weaved through traffic on York Way, completely anonymous, barely getting above thirty miles an hour – just a delivery guy on his little scooter doing his thing. At The Rose and Crown in Torriano Avenue, Stevie headed left towards Kentish Town Road. If this had been about earning a few bob and nothing else he'd have opened another Beck's and let it pass. The sale wouldn't have been lost; when the withdrawals started in earnest, whoever was hassling him would be prepared to crawl on their hands and knees to get what he could give them.

But it wasn't. There was more to it. A helluva lot more. Luke Glass' sister was a fucking doper. His fucking doper.

Stevie checked the address against what he'd written down – he'd come to the right place.

What was a south London girl doing this far from her stomping ground? Of course, he could be wrong, it might all be perfectly innocent, but Nina hadn't mentioned a boyfriend – which didn't mean there wasn't one. Yet, the conversation over the phone hadn't felt right: if somebody was in there with her, Nina didn't want them to know pepperoni and cheese was code for heavy-duty drugs. Her caution was justified. 'Possession with intent to supply' could get you life in prison. Even holding a small amount warranted an arrest that could lead to a seven-year sentence.

If that didn't concentrate the mind, nothing would.

Stevie took off his helmet and got the pizzas out of the box on the back. The tall wrought-iron gate creaked on its hinges and swung open. With the curtains drawn and a light in a downstairs window the house seemed no different from others on the street and he wondered again why Nina Glass was in this part of the city. Halfway down the path he got his answer: the front door opened and a huge guy dressed in a denim jacket, white T-shirt and jeans held a hand as big as a shovel in the air. 'Where do you think you're going, sunshine?'

Stevie lifted the carboard boxes up for inspection. The rhodo-dendron bushes lining the garden rustled; he sensed a presence behind him on the path and a maggot of fear crawled in his belly.

'How the fuck did you get in?'

'The gate… was open.' His voice faltered. 'Just doing what they tell me, squire. Delivering a large pepperoni and cheese and a medium Neapolitan. And before you start complaining, don't blame me if they're bloody stone cold. I got here as fast as I could.'

The guy saw a nonentity and dismissed him; he turned and spat his disgust at the men.

'Who the fuck ordered this shit?'

Nobody answered. He rolled his sleeves back to reveal meaty forearms covered in tats, a match for the pot belly drooping over his belt, making everything he was wearing look two sizes too small. Everything except the Beretta 9000 in the waistband of his jeans.

His eyes were hard; anger was his default position and Stevie D realised he'd stumbled into something he wasn't intended to see.

'Which one of you ordered pizza? Who the fuck was it?'

'I did. So what?'

Nina was at the bottom of the hall, arms folded defiantly across her body. She walked to the door and eyed the interrogator like shit on her shoe. This was the Nina Glass Stevie D had yet to see – a lady used to being obeyed, crushing anybody – man or woman – who got in her way, firing questions that didn't require answers to intimidate them into silence. 'Do you expect us to survive on whatever muck you decide to give us? Is that how you think we live? Who we are?' Her laugh was brittle. 'You're confusing us with yourself. It's bad enough we're forced to stay here, it doesn't mean we can't eat what we want.'

'George Ritchie gave orders that—'

Nina's scream echoed in the hall. 'Fuck George Ritchie and his orders! He's not my boss and neither are you! Got it? If that's a problem, take it up with my brother. We fancy pizza so we're having pizza. And wine. Send somebody out for a couple of bottles of red.' She clicked her fingers at the nearest guard without taking her gaze from Stevie. 'Give this man his money and let him get on with his work before the stuff's not worth eating. Make it a twenty. In fact, make it twenty-five. He's come a long way.'

Over Nina's shoulder a door opened and a red-haired woman stood with her back to it, hesitating about coming closer. Nina shook her head and she stayed where she was. Stevie didn't recognise her but even from a distance she was beautiful.

It was time to let Calum Bishop in on his secret.

* * *

She stood backlit in the bathroom doorway, aware of the effect her
nakedness was having on the man she hadn't known existed an
hour ago. On the king-size bed, Tang's pulse quickened; his hungry
eyes savoured the full breasts, the dark areolas and already-erect
nipples. For Stanley Tang a good day had just got better.

He'd impressed the investor group with his insights into the
target market, his grasp on numbers, ability to think on his feet,
field questions, and justify his ambitious projections. They'd made
encouraging noises loud enough to convince him he'd be hearing
from them in the very near future. At the hotel, he'd called his wife
and told her he loved her. A celebration was in order: he was
exhausted and had considered settling for sandwiches and a
chilled bottle of Sauvignon Blanc Reserva from room service.

What an error that would've been.

Roberta drew her nails through the tight black curls on his
chest and straddled his white thighs, pinning him to the bed. Tang
arched his back and took her weight. Out to the corner of his eye,
hidden by her hair, he saw the ragged tissue of a scar running half
the length of her cheek. 'Jesus Christ, what's that?'

Her answer was an open palm that caught him full on the
mouth, rocking his head back on his shoulders. Blood trickled in a
red line from his lip; he panicked and tried to throw her off, but she
held him with more strength than he would've thought possible
from a woman.

Suddenly, Stanley Tang was afraid – this wasn't how it was
supposed to be. He whimpered. 'Who... who the hell are you?'

Roberta didn't reply. She lowered herself onto his cock and bit
his finger where his wedding ring would be this time tomorrow on
the other side of the world. Then, she started to ride him.

24

THE SECOND DAY

The men had failure etched on their faces. They were tired; it had been a long night and they had another long day ahead. Some of them studied their shoes and let the tongue-lashing from their boss wash over them. The rest accepted the harsh words were justified and bowed their heads. They'd been ordered to find the Glass sister and hadn't come close. Calum Bishop wasn't known for his patience; his reaction was predictable. He paced the room throwing insults and accusations into the air. Charley Glass hadn't been seen since the night Tony Giordano decided to show up at the club and take the drama to a new level. If the idiot had done the simple thing and just lifted her off the street, none of this would be happening.

Bishop stopped in the middle of the floor and took a draw from the cigarette in his hand.

'In case I didn't make myself clear the first five times, I'll try again. This isn't rocket science. Even morons like you should be able to understand it. Glass has his sister stashed. Somebody in this godforsaken city is in on it. Get out on the streets, break as many bones as you have to, but don't come back till you've found where she is. No fucking excuses. Giordano's expecting us to turn her up. Now, hop to it!'

His minder, a guy with pockmarked skin, said, 'There's somebody here to see you.'

Bishop stubbed the cigarette out under the heel of his shoe. 'Tell them I'm not available.'

'I did. He says it's important.'

'To him or me? Who is it?'

'Stevie D.'

Calum was in a foul mood. 'No bells.'

'You've met him.'

'Have I?'

'He had a nice little dealing scene going in Islington until we took it away from him.'

'It's a hard old world.'

'Been told to make himself scarce but he's a stubborn bugger. Insists you'll want to hear what he has to say.'

'Then, kick his arse down the road because he's wrong. I've got enough on my plate without listening to a sacked dope pedlar. Tell him again to get on his bike, I'm not—'

Raised voices on the other side of the door interrupted the conversation. It flew open and Stevie stumbled into the room. He glared at Bishop's soldiers and turned to the man himself. On his way across London he'd almost changed his mind. Now, standing in front of Calum Bishop, Stevie was strangely calm.

'Sorry for barging in.'

Pockmark snarled and balled his fists. 'Are you fucking deaf? I told you Mr Bishop wasn't available.'

Calum said, 'Hold it. Let's hear what he has to say for himself.'

Bishop looked the same as he had in Dollis Hill – still wearing the tan leather jerkin, still going bald at a rate of knots. Stevie D took his time, knowing his power was temporary, savouring it while it lasted.

Pockmark angrily hurried him along. 'Come on, come on. Mr Bishop doesn't have all fucking day.'

'Nina Glass is a junkie.'

Bishop came towards him and stopped when they were inches apart. His eyes were bloodshot and he smelled of cigarette smoke. 'Say that again.'

Stevie remembered who he was addressing and suddenly it didn't seem like a good idea. His throat went dry and he faltered. 'Nina Glass... is a junkie.'

Calum Bishop nodded slowly. 'And you know this how?'

'She scores from me.'

'How can she when you're out of that business?'

'She's an old contact. I'd no idea who she was until recently.'

Bishop placed a hand on his shoulder. 'So supplying her was just a favour?'

'That's right, just a favour.'

The knee to the groin was the most pain Stevie had ever known. He cried out and fell, doubled up, to the floor. Bishop dragged him onto his feet and pinned him against the wall.

'Don't try it on with me, sonny boy. You were told you were out of business, yet you carried on. That's the truth, isn't it?'

When Stevie didn't answer he slapped him hard across the mouth, splitting his lip. 'I said, that's the truth, isn't it?'

Stevie nodded. 'I thought it was a one-time thing. But she's hooked on coke. Can't get enough. I've just delivered to her again.'

'Delivered where?'

'A house in Kentish Town.'

'And you're coming to me with this because?'

'You can use it against her brother. She's hiding it from him. He's no idea how much she's shoving up her nose.'

Bishop let go of him. 'Your information is a crock of shit. It's worthless.'

'No, how can it be?'

'Clearly, you don't appreciate what would happen to anybody who harms Glass' sister. The world wouldn't be big enough to hide them.' He laughed out loud. 'As our American friends are about to discover. My question is why Kentish Town?'

'I don't know but something's going on. There are men with guns crawling all over the place. They're dressed like workmen but there isn't any work going on.'

Bishop felt his interest quicken. 'How many guns?'

'Hard to say. I saw two or three inside, more in the garden.'

'Is George Ritchie one of them?'

'Don't know him. If he is, what would that mean?'

Bishop led Stevie to the chair and barked an order at his lieutenant. 'Get this guy some water. Be quick about it.'

He sat on the edge of the desk. 'I won't lie to you... Stevie. This could be important. Tell me everything. Don't miss anything out. Even the smallest detail might be significant.'

When the water arrived, Stevie D sipped it and started to relax. It had been scary for a minute. Now, Calum Bishop was hanging on every word, eating out of his hand. He started with the call from a woman desperate to score and lied about his reluctance to get involved.

'We arranged to meet in a pub on York Way.' Stevie scratched behind his ear, feeling more secure than at any time since he'd decided to seek Calum Bishop out. 'If there's one thing I know about, it's junkies. She was different.'

'Different how?'

Stevie didn't have an answer that made sense. 'Just different. Her attitude, how she carried herself even when her addiction was eating her alive. Nothing I could put my finger on, but it was there.'

He paused. 'I guess you could say she came across as being somebody.'

'I don't know what you mean.'

'Not the usual strung-out druggie. So, I got her car reg.'

'And discovered she was Nina Glass. After that, it was about building a relationship with her. Getting her to trust you.'

'More. Getting her to depend on me. Making her believe I was her friend. The only one who cared. After that was easy. She said her brother had men at her house.'

'Did she tell you why?'

'She's Luke Glass' sister. I assumed it was normal and did what she wanted – ran the pizza delivery number and sold her enough flake to last her a couple of days.'

'And?'

'Last night, she called like I knew she would, except the address wasn't Denmark Hill or a pub. It was a house in Kentish Town.'

'Did you use the pizza thing again?'

'Absolutely. She made a big deal about the pepperoni and cheese being for her so I'd put the gear in the right box. Still waiting to get paid for it, by the way. The guards weren't happy with her phoning out. And I don't mind admitting when the door opened and I saw who was there, I nearly threw the boxes at them and ran.'

'Instead, you came here?'

'Yeah, it seemed like the only thing to do. I'll be honest with you, Mr Bishop, I need a job. I'm kind of hoping you'll give me one.'

Bishop considered his reply. 'I'm sure we can do something with you.' He included Pockmark in the conversation. 'We can do something with Stevie here, can't we?'

'Sure we can.'

Behind his eyes Calum Bishop's sharp mind processed the information. 'You said boxes.'

'That's right, two of them.'

'Who was the other one for?'

Stevie shook his head. 'I was focused on getting out in one piece. There was somebody with her but I only saw her for a minute: a redhead, stunning looking. That mean anything to you?'

25

The strident ring of the mobile on the bedside cabinet woke Charley, depressed and exhausted, from a night broken by dark dreams. The Giordanos – Beppe, Tony, and his witch of a grandmother – were in her head. When she'd arrived from nowhere at the King Pot and announced she was his sister, Luke had been unconvinced and quizzed her about where she'd been. Charley had answered with as much of the truth as he'd needed to know, leaving out New Orleans, the cabin near the border, and their mother's terrible death. But the lies of omission had caught up with her in the club and now, men would die because of them.

She stared at the phone, willing the damned thing to stop. The Irishman was persistent – over the last few days Eamon Brannagan had tried a dozen times to contact her. Charley would've gladly fallen into his arms and confessed the whole sorry saga, knowing he'd listen without judging. But not yet; she'd been responsible for enough trouble. The nightmare she'd brought to Luke and Nina's door would end, one way or another. Until then, for his own safety, it was better to keep the actor at arm's length.

Remembering the sincerity of his apology made her blush:

what she'd done was much worse. The best thing for all concerned would be to give herself up to the Giordanos and suffer the consequences of her actions.

At the bottom of a drawer Charley found a scratchy pen and a sheet of paper. At first, the words wouldn't come; the page stayed as empty as the wilderness all around her on that last day. When they finally arrived it was like a torrent breaking and she was back in the woods with freezing air stinging her cheeks and her enemies just beyond the horizon.

* * *

Her boots thudded dry and dull on the wooden boards, the only sound other than the rustle of her fur-lined parka. Behind the cabin a pile of logs, cut and split during the warm summer months by backpackers in exchange for a bed, would see them through the worst of winter. Come spring, she would fell a few saplings and the process of preparing for the next one would begin. She brushed snow off the top, lifted an armful, and hugged them to her chest. On the ground, a brown mouse, its tiny body slicked with frost and hard as stone, had taken shelter between them and perished in the unforgiving temperatures. Only a few creatures had the capacity to survive up here; this one had failed the test.

She paused on the porch and looked up at the sky that had been a brilliant blue earlier in the day. Now, it hung low and heavy. Above the treeline, a flock of northern shrike took to the air and soared away into the distance. Something had startled them. A cougar or a lynx, maybe, on the hunt for rabbit or hare. Every year there were sightings all over the state.

Charlene listened; she heard nothing, but her instincts whispered the truth.

It had been too good to last. They were coming.

She dropped the logs and hurried inside. The old woman sitting in a chair by the fire had been asleep under a grey army coat. She wore black corduroy trousers, brown shoes and two pairs of socks; bony fingers closed round a cloth stained with patches of red. On the floor at her feet a half-empty bottle of Jim Beam sat like a sentry beside a white mug.

She roused herself when the door opened. 'Didn't you bring wood?'

Charlene ignored the question. 'Get your things. We have to go.'

The woman reached for the bourbon. 'It'll be dark soon, we'll need it. Tonight, it'll drop all the way. No point going outside if you don't come back with wood.'

'Didn't you hear what I said, Frances? We have to go.'

'Go? What the hell are you talking about? Go where?'

'Leave. Get out of here.'

'Why?'

Charlene wondered if she really didn't remember. Lately, she'd been forgetting. 'You know why. I told you why. C'mon.'

Frances topped up the glass with a shaky hand; some of it spilled and she cursed. 'Damn! Damn, damn and damn! This stuff costs too much to be slopping it around.'

'We don't have time for this.'

'Speak for yourself. I've had enough time. More than enough. I'm staying put.'

Charlene's frustration boiled over. 'Have you finally gone fucking Looney Tunes? We knew this could happen. We discussed it. They're coming. We have to go and go now.'

Frances looked into the fire. Golden light played across her hollowed-out cheeks and the glazed eyes sunk deep in her head: a face that had once been beautiful. She spoke to the flames. 'Chill, I won't tell them if that's what you're worried about. Depend on it. I won't tell them a thing.'

'No! No! That isn't it. We have a deal. You promised.'

'And you believed me because you wanted to believe me.' The laugh was like ice cracking. 'Christ's sake, Charlene, this is me we're talking about.'

Charlene cried like a disappointed child. 'But you promised.'

The reply was harsh. 'Oh, grow up. I haven't kept a promise in my life. Why would I start now?'

A coughing spasm wracked Frances's body. She put the cloth to her mouth and wiped blood from her lips. Charlene knelt and clung to the chair, pleading with her. 'Don't you understand? Don't you understand what I'm saying? The people I told you about. They're here. They'll hurt you.'

Frances blinked and regained control of herself. ''Course I heard you. Now, you hear me. I'm not going anywhere, Charlene. I'm done running, do you understand? Even if I wanted to, can't you see I don't have it?'

'They're animals. They'll kill you.'

'Then, I'll die. There are worse things. Nobody knows that better than me.'

Charlene grabbed the coat's lapels. 'Fuck you and your noble sacrifice. You're too late. Years too late. You think it'll make a difference. It won't.'

Frances put a frail hand on her daughter's arm. 'It'll make a difference to me.'

'No, no, please, no.'

'Why don't you and I tell the truth for a change, how about that? Take a good look at me – go on. Now tell me why I shouldn't just stay here and let whatever happens happen.' She extended an arm, so thin the skin seemed like a gossamer veil over the bone. 'I'm not lasting much longer and we both know it. A couple of months, maybe weeks, and I'll be gone. These bastards will be doing me a favour.'

Charlene shouted. 'This is crazy! You're coming even if I have to carry you!'

Her mother slowly shook her head. 'What little money I have is in a pickle jar under the sink. Take it. Use the back door. Get moving.'

'I can't. I can't.'

The emotional exchange had drained the older woman. She said, 'Listen. You deserved a better mother than the one you got landed with. I was never worth a damn in that department. Wasn't much of a wife, either, come to that. This is my chance to make up for it – the first decent thing I've done. Don't deny me. I need it. And not just for you.'

They held each other until Frances pulled away. *'Go. It's for the best. I love you, honey.'*

At the door, Charlene turned and watched her mother for the last time. Frances said, *'These fuckers don't mean to but they're doing a service for an old woman who ran out of road a long time ago. If you ever meet your brothers and your sister, tell them I said hello.'* Her lip trembled. *'It was never about them. I couldn't cope and ran away. Tell them I'm sorry their mother was a fuck-up.'*

The blizzard had stopped. In the fading light, shadows stretched into deformed black fingers on the white ground. Charlene quietly closed the door, scanning the trees for a sign that would confirm she'd waited too long, left it too late. There was no one. Since she'd seen the birds, the temperature had plummeted and was still falling.

'Tonight, it'll drop all the way' was how Frances had described it and she'd been right.

The hill behind the cabin was steep. Charlene climbed, expecting at any moment to slip back to the bottom. A huge grey boulder, its smooth surface weathered by a million years of wind and rain, offered her a place to hide; she crouched behind it. It had only been minutes but already her lungs were raw from the freezing air and an overwhelming silence hummed in her ears. Most of Beppe's money was still there – in a scarf tied round her waist under her clothes. But in her haste she'd forgotten the memory stick and the photographs hidden in the bottom of the wood bin. Too late to do anything about that now. Perhaps they'd find them and let it end there.

She laughed at her naïvety. Then it began: the first scream was short and sharp; the second longer, trailing off at the end. Charlene imagined the scene inside – Giordano and Mura towering over the helpless body on the floor, too weak even to crawl – and hated herself. Coming here had *brought this but guilt wouldn't make it better. Her mother had embraced death trudging towards her through the snow. It represented, not pain and suffering, but release from the cancer and salvation for her choices. What she said or didn't say was unimportant. They'd kill her because that was who they were.*

The sound of the gunshot ricocheted in the trees and echoed in waves around her. Charlene bowed her head and whispered a prayer. Bruno Mura's guttural Sardinian dialect carried to the hillside followed by another scream, longer and more anguished than the one before.

It wasn't over. Dear God, her mother was still alive.

At this time of year night fell like a curtain, plunging the world into darkness. Suddenly, she caught the earthy smell of wood smoke drifting in the air and a crackling like a heavy step on dry twigs. Charlene felt the blood leave her face: they were burning the cabin. All she could hope was that Frances was dead. The alternative was too terrible to contemplate.

The house had stood in the clearing since the Civil War, more than a hundred and sixty years. The farmer who'd hammered the frame together, dressed the walls and carefully laid the roof had been returned to dust, yet his labour had lived on. Until tonight.

As the inferno reached to the sky, Charlene huddled under a majestic American sycamore, terrified and alone. Where could she go now? Beyond the flames on the other side, Giordano and his men would watch their handiwork char and blacken and begin the search. The falling snow had covered her tracks almost as she made them. But they wouldn't give up. Ever.

When she was certain they'd moved on, Charlene warily approached what was left of her mother's house, more afraid than she'd ever been in her life about what she'd find.

She was empty. Too numb to weep. Too sad to mourn.

The smouldering fire spat and cracked like the gunshots of a retreating army. Mercifully, the roof had collapsed on the spot where she'd last seen Frances and Charlene mouthed a silent thank you to a God she didn't believe in, a stranger who had abandoned her long ago.

Her boot uncovered shards of bottle glass and the stone jar, crushed by a rafter, that had sat on the earth floor at her mother's feet. And tears came for what might have been.

She whispered, 'I love you, Mom,' the words torn by the wind from her lips.

As she turned to go, the twisted-metal buckle of Beppe Giordano's blackmail diary almost buried in the ashes caught her eye: it had all been for nothing – the New Orleans gangsters had lost. Again. But sooner or later her luck would run out. Charlene took a deep breath, walked past the smoking shell of the old pickup and headed for the road. By morning, she'd be in Canada. Then, she'd seek out the family she'd never known and hope they had a place for her.

The door to the office above the King of Mesopotamia was like a portal to my past: on this side, I was Luke Glass, club owner and entrepreneur, a businessman and a respectable law-abiding member of society. On the other, the guy who'd cut gang boss Albert Anderson's life short by sending him into space one sunny morning off the forty-third floor of an office block in Bishopsgate and into folklore south of the river. I didn't completely identify with either.

26

The door to the office above the King of Mesopotamia was like a portal to my past: on this side, I was Luke Glass, club owner and entrepreneur, a businessman and a respectable law-abiding member of society. On the other, the guy who'd cut gang boss Albert Anderson's life short by sending him into space one sunny morning off the forty-third floor of an office block in Bishopsgate and into folklore south of the river. I didn't completely identify with either.

George Ritchie sat behind the desk that had been there for as long as I remembered, his clear-blue eyes as inscrutable as the Buddha. We were living through strange times but he seemed calm. Trouble had found us – we hadn't gone looking for it – and we were on the edge of something that had been beyond our control from the beginning. Tony Giordano had given me three days to hand my sister over to him. An impossible demand.

Tomorrow was the third day. After that, anything could happen.

Usually, we marked our meetings above the King Pot by sharing a whisky from the bottle Ritchie kept in the bottom drawer. He didn't offer and I didn't ask. He wasn't surprised to see me; he knew why I was there. Whatever went down twenty-four hours from now, he'd be at the heart of it, reminding anybody too young or too stupid to recall why I'd offered the right-hand man of a defeated rival a job.

I had a dozen questions in my head, none of them worth a damn. When the enemy was positioned to wage guerrilla warfare, the best you could do was second-guess him. Guerrilla – Spanish for 'little war' – depended on surprise, the element Tony Giordano had so recklessly given away. Yet the odds were still with them. Our interests sprawled across the city; they could strike and run and strike again.

Ritchie anticipated what I was about to say. 'The troops from Liverpool and Newcastle arrived late last night. Can't be every-where but men will be at the club, the Glass Houses building and two construction sites. We'll be as ready as we can be.'

'What about the safe house?'

'I'm treating it as the main target. The Giordanos don't know about Kentish Town. They can huff and puff so long as they don't get close.'

'And if they do?'

Rather than answer he brought out a three-quarters-full bottle of Long John and two glasses. I sensed a diversion and repeated the question. 'And if they do, George?'

'It won't be the best day they've ever had, believe me.'

I did believe him though my sense of unease remained. 'I'm getting a bad feeling about this. Maybe we should get Nina and Charley out of there?'

'Okay. Suppose we did. Where can we 100 per cent guarantee they'll be more secure?'

His chilling logic stopped me in my tracks, because he was right. For the Giordanos to know about the safe house someone would have to betray us.

'You don't think...'

'No, I don't. The guys on this have been with us for years, I'd bet our lives on them.'

'Except, it isn't *our* lives we're talking about, is it, George?' I stood. 'I'm heading up to check on Charley and Nina.'

'I'll be doing the same later tonight.'

From somewhere I found a grin. 'Be nice. They could be your new bosses.'

'No offence but that cottage on the coast just got more attractive.'

Ritchie was laughing. I was serious. 'And so you're in the loop, I've spoken to the accountant. If this goes pear-shaped he knows what to do.'

* * *

Calum Bishop lit a fresh cigarette off the one in his hand and inhaled down to his boots: the future looked bright. This morning he'd barely been able to keep his anger in check when his men reported they hadn't found Charley Glass. Now – thanks to an over-ambitious oily rag, a clown with no understanding of the value of his information – he knew where Luke Glass was hiding, not one, but *both* his sisters. According to Stevie D, Nina was a hopeless addict on her way to the bottom helped along by him. Interesting. On another day something he could've used against her brother. That titbit had been relegated to a footnote.

Calum ran his free hand over his almost-hairless head: the next few hours would be crucial, the most significant since his uncle Kenny met him in a Brent Cross car park and announced he was retiring. Maybe it had been the light but he'd seemed thinner. And he'd been edgy, nervously looking out over the deserted space during the brief conversation that ended with him gifting the empire it had taken twenty years to build to his nephew as though he couldn't be rid of it fast enough.

Stevie D's news was Calum's chance to make his own mark on the underworld landscape.

Pockmark misread the moment. 'When do you want the guns and ammo delivered?'

'What?'

'The guns and that... when are we delivering them to Giordano?'

Bishop turned on him. 'If it's questions you're into, answer me this: why the fuck do I keep you around?'

'I'm just—'

'Our American associates will get what was promised when I see some money from them and not before. A prick just handed us a game-changer. Solid-gold information. I'm asking myself how much that's worth.'

Bishop's eyes ran over the mini-arsenal in the corner. Everything he'd been asked to supply was there – enough firepower to blow Luke Glass into next week. On a table to the side, the 'late addition' Bruno Mura had insisted on sat apart from the rest. Bishop lifted a box of ammunition from the stack on the floor and weighed it in his hand. Unless the Giordanos came across, the weapons cache would stay where it was and they could go against Glass with rolled-up newspapers.

Pockmark hadn't learned his lesson. 'Will you tell them...' he hesitated, remembering it might be better to keep his mouth shut '... you know where she is?'

Calum was done talking. 'Of course. That was the deal.'

27

I was crossing Waterloo Bridge with sunlight cascading on the river in golden shards when my mobile rang on the seat beside me. There were no prizes for guessing who it was and I considered letting it go. Instead, I answered it and got an earful of Assistant Commissioner Robert Kirby's familiar growl. In LBC, after a few decent cognacs had gone down his neck he'd been amused and amusing in a sleazy-bastard kind of way. Beano was a natural-born performer, at his best when he had an audience. I was all there was but it didn't stop him inflicting the usual jokey unpleasantries on me that made his boozing buddies think he was the life-and-soul.

'Beautiful morning, isn't it?'

'Yes.'

'I'm in my office on the fourth floor of the Yard. A lot of coppers weren't keen on shifting from Victoria. Not me. The view's spectacular. On a day like this I can see right into your cell on the Isle of Wight.'

'What do you want, Kirby?'

'Someone's just been in here asking about you.'

'Really?'

'Yes, fucking really! And in case you haven't twigged, I don't appreciate being quizzed by a detective sergeant about my association with one of the biggest villains in London. Not quite the look my superiors are aiming for from their senior men.'

'Then, don't go to his club. You won't be missed, I assure you. They're queuing out the door and down the street to get in. My advice would be save yourself the fees – bloody extortionate anyway – and donate the money to your favourite charity. Assuming you have one, Beano.'

The last time I'd dropped his nickname he'd smiled – the alcohol doing its work. Kirby spluttered down the line and I imagined his stubby mitt gripping the receiver as his overfed jowls darkened to an unflattering puce and he ground his teeth together. George Ritchie's warning about poking the bear had come too late. And he was wrong: if this bastard decided he was having you, there wasn't a lot you could do about it. Kirby was a snake who'd slithered up the greasy pole and understood the importance of covering his arse. Providing me with an alibi – however inadvertently – wasn't something he fancied having on his CV when they were interviewing for the assistant commissioner's job.

He poured contempt into his voice that was meant to cow me into remembering who I was talking to. 'Don't give me your fucking backchat, Glass, I'm not in the mood. I'll go where I feel like going. I'm telling you this once. I won't say it again. Leave me out of whatever shenanigans you're involved in or, believe me, you'll be seeing a lot more of old Beano than either of us would like. Got it?'

Kirby had no idea what 'shenanigans' I was involved in.

The problem was, neither did I.

* * *

I drove for ninety minutes on a crazy tour of north London rather than go directly to the house, checking every few seconds for unwelcome strangers in the rear-view; Neasden, Golders Green, South Hampstead, Belsize Park and Chalk Farm passed in a blur before I turned the car towards Kentish Town. When I arrived, I counted seven men downstairs, more would be in the building and the garden. Apart from them and my sisters the house was empty. It didn't reassure me. George Ritchie had promised that if the Giordanos discovered the safe house, we'd be ready for them. In other circumstances, especially coming from him, that would be more than good enough. Except he'd hesitated, avoided looking at me, and I understood why.

He didn't know what was marshalled against us and was too much of a pro to guess.

Tony Giordano could have manufactured a macho stand-off in the club and given me twenty-four hours to surrender my sister. Instead, the bastard had played his own game. Three days wasn't some random figure pulled from the air in the heat of the moment. Not at all. It gave him time to bring his troops over. And if it had stopped there I might've been more confident about the outcome. Calum Bishop had his own agenda – no doubt about that. In the long run it would come down to him or me, winner takes all. But him putting his thumb on the scale in the Giordanos' favour was bad news. Maybe we'd have the edge in numbers, maybe not, but it was a bloody big city to cover. By the time I knew for certain, it wouldn't matter.

As for my old pal Bridie O'Shea in Kilburn – not hearing from her told me everything I needed, a cautionary reminder of who I could depend on; at the end of the day a very short list of only one name: George Ritchie.

Although my sisters had been spawned in the same gene pool, they were very different from each other. Except, in one regard, they were the same, living on their own terms, refusing to compromise. It was a brave man who'd go against them, yet I had. Keeping them prisoner, albeit for their own good, was as unpopular as a garlic milkshake and I expected both of them to come down on me for pulling rank. It didn't happen.

Charley was alone in the lounge, sitting on the couch with her hands in her lap. As soon as I walked in I sensed something wrong. Since the morning when she'd waltzed, larger than life, through the door of the King Pot and into my life I hadn't seen her less than perfectly turned out – the clothes, the hair, the make-up, every detail meticulously attended to. Always. Nothing fazed her and I'd come to expect it. That wasn't what was in front of me today.

Her clothes were so creased and crumpled she might have slept in them; her wild hair hadn't been combed and without make-up the face underneath was pale and puffy. She dabbed her eyes with a tissue and went into the apology she'd offered me at LBC. I hadn't needed it then and didn't need it now. I said, 'Listen, Charley, this isn't your fault.'

'How can you say that? Of course it's my fault. Who else is to blame? If I—'

'Stop beating yourself up. The Giordanos aren't the good guys here.'

'And what am I? What are we?'

'The not-as-bad-as-the-bad-guys guys.'

In spite of herself, she laughed. I'd won a battle, not the war. Her voice was a raw whisper. 'You're wrong, brother. My biggest mistake was thinking they'd let a thieving whore make a fool of them. That's on me. I should never have come to you.'

I put a hand on her shoulders and tilted her head. 'You're our sister, we're your family – where else was there? Tony Giordano's running his own agenda and it has nothing to do with Charley Glass.'

I wasn't getting through; she wasn't listening. Anger forced its way into the words. 'It's about them – those fuckers – all about them. I'm guessing their operation has been on the slide in New Orleans for a long time. Their best days are behind them and they know it. Tony wants war – it's how he can prove to the vultures hovering over the corpse that they're still a force to be reckoned with.'

Belief crept into my sister's eyes, flickered and faded; guilt took its place and I'd lost her again.

She said, 'Those two girls died. They died because of me. How do I forget that? We promised they'd be safe working for us. Well, they weren't. And that's only the beginning. The guys outside didn't sign on for this. I can stop it before more lives are lost.' She clasped my hand and bowed her head. 'Let me give myself up.'

It was the most courageous thing I'd ever heard. I unpicked her fingers, one by one, and closed mine round them. 'Not in a million years, Charley. Don't mention it again.'

'Please, Luke, please!'

'I'd rather kill you myself.'

She collapsed on the floor, her shoulders rising and falling, weeping like a child. Surviving these bastards had taken a toll; this was more. She was emotionally broken and I remembered how frightened she'd been in the office, about to tell me something when we were interrupted.

I hunkered down beside her. 'You said, "They burned". What did they burn? Was it the blackmail material? Is that why you don't have it?'

Her answer was spoken too quietly to make out. Before my eyes the sensual figure seemed to shrink, crushed under the weight of my questions.

'I can't hear you, Charley.'

'No.'

'Then, what? What did they burn?'

Anguished sobs wracked her body. From between them she whispered her awful truth and rocked my world. 'Our mother. They burned our mother.'

* * *

The warm sun on his face reminded Mura of New Orleans and for the first time since he'd done the hookers, he felt himself relax. The days of running errands for the Giordanos would soon be over. Tony was a fool and the old woman's belief that Silvestro, her dead husband, had been a great man, rather than an ignorant peasant who'd got lucky, revealed her own limitations; the enmity between grandson and grandmother never abated. Bruno would gladly have slit both their throats and let them continue their feud in hell.

He crossed Serpentine Road in the south-east corner of Hyde Park. From the Rose Garden, a string quintet played a Beethoven sonata that drifted on the air, while out on the lake, under a blue sky, people in pedalo boats giggled and laughed, unaware of what was about to go down in their capital. Mura felt the green plastic carrier bag with the signature gold Harrods logo bounce against his leg and allowed himself a smile. Calum Bishop had done well: it held exactly what the legend he was on his way to see had requested. Bruno knew who 'La Réponse' was by reputation, but hadn't met her. He wasn't alone; very few had. Unless they wanted an enemy eliminated and were prepared to pay a small fortune to make it happen, they never would.

Mura speculated what the female assassin would look like, imagining a hard-faced, tight-mouthed, lesbian bitch he wouldn't fuck if she was the last female on the planet. The Sardinian liked his women young and slutty – young enough to do what he ordered them to do, slutty enough to understand why. In New

Orleans, Charlene hadn't fitted the criteria but, for her, he would've made an exception. The wheezing, obese Beppe had hung her on his arm like a Christmas tree decoration, promenading on Royal and Dauphine, smirking at the barely concealed glances of envious males. The fat bastard had been kidding himself; he couldn't hope to satisfy such a sensuous creature. Trying had killed him.

Mura navigated his way through the traffic on Knightsbridge Road. At the impressive entrance on the other side, two concierges dressed in red three-quarter-length coats and black top hats followed his progress and nodded as though he were an old friend. He ignored them and strode up the stone steps to the lift that would take him into the august presence of the most successful assassin since Ilich Ramirez Sánchez, better known as The Jackal.

Roberta Romano opened the door and whatever the Sardinian had pictured, it wasn't this: she was tall and slim and beautiful. Her dark eyes assessed him coldly, without interest. Mura held out the bag and spoke to her in French. *'J'ai un cadeau pour toi.'*

She answered in English, unimpressed. 'Who from?'

'Tony Giordano.'

Roberta walked to the centre of the room and waited for him to follow, toying with the belt of the Prussian blue satin robe that ended mid-thigh. Mura saw the tanned legs and guessed that under it she was naked. She read his mind. 'Forget it, I'm not your type.'

'I'll be the judge of that.'

'No, you won't. Put the bag on the table and get out.'

Bruno was being dismissed. 'Tony's asking about the plan. He'd like to know.'

Roberta tossed her hair over her shoulder and Mura saw the scar on her cheek. Whoever had wielded the knife had committed a crime against perfection. She said, 'Your boss has paid for a result and he'll get it.'

'So, what shall I tell him?'

'Tell him to go fuck himself.'

Mura laughed. 'I've got a better idea.'

* * *

Roberta Romano had no opinion on Tony Giordano, one way or the other. And when this was over, she still wouldn't. Getting a contact for her had required persistence, she'd give him that. It had taken all of two minutes to understand why: his request was outrageous, the timescale dangerously unworkable; taking on a job without rigorous preparation was beyond foolish and her gut instinct had been to turn it down flat. The money the gangster offered had changed her mind.

She'd made an early decision she was never going back to where she'd come from. Romano lived in New Orleans because the cultural melting pot appealed to her artistic soul and because she could afford to. She was aware of the Giordano family – it would've been impossible not to be – but they operated in a different universe. When Tony told her the target, he'd expected a reaction – she hadn't given him the satisfaction. On the other end of the line the anxiety in his voice had been unmissable. 'Can you do it?'

Roberta had started as she meant to go on. 'It'll save time if you ask the right questions.'

'Okay, what should I be asking?'

'*Will* I do it.'

'And will you?'

'Have the cash in my account in twenty-four hours and get me everything I want. All of it or it's off.'

'Consider it done.'

'I haven't said what I want.'

'Fucking details. All that matters is a positive outcome. Tell me where to send the money. I'll book your flight to London.'

'First-class non-stop return.'

'Naturally.'

'And a junior suite at the Mandarin Oriental Hyde Park.'

Tony Giordano's appreciative whistle had been like a high wind blowing through the rafters of a derelict building. 'Is that it?'

'Not even close. You got a pen handy?'

* * *

There were five items in the Harrods bag: a Beretta 92A1 – the twin of the one she normally used, a long matt-black aluminium suppressor, three seventeen-round magazines of Parabellum cartridges, half a dozen orange-coloured rubber discs called wipes, and a tube of water-based gel. Roberta gave a satisfied nod; Giordano had done well. Her fingers caressed the shortened barrel and the grip, all that would stand between success or failure. Shooting from a distance was every hitman's preferred option and the best chance of escape. Failing that meant close quarters with a suppressor. Hollywood had a lot to answer for when it came to guns. In movies, the bad guy ominously screwed on the silencer and started putt-putt-putting away. Roberta Romano smiled – if only it were that simple. She was a pro, and pros understood the difference, even if directors and screenwriters didn't: the initial shot was always the loudest; a silencer provided a bigger space for the gases to expand. Using a wipe significantly muted 'first round pop'. Coating the inside of the barrel with water or gel – firing 'wet' – further reduced the mini-shockwave produced by the release of hot gases, making what she'd agreed to do possible.

Roberta trusted the science and remembered Giordano's money sitting in her bank account. This would be her last kill.

28

With the dying sun lengthening the shadows, the green expanse of Hyde Park rolled into the distance towards the grey water of the Serpentine, tranquil and inviting. A beautiful evening, though it held little for the eighty-one-year-old Madeline Giordano; she wanted this to end so she could go home. Across the room, Bruno Mura cleaned his nails with his knife – the blade he'd used to brutally murder the two hookers. The Sardinian was ten times savvier than her grandson and smart enough to keep it to himself but he couldn't deny his nature. Silvestro used to say, 'Even if they let you pet them, never forget a wild animal is always a wild animal.'

Calum Bishop was due to arrive. Madeline said, 'All right, where are we with everything?'

Mura answered. 'Our men are in the city waiting for instructions.'

'And the guns?'

He glanced at Tony. Madeline caught the dumb insolence in the hesitation and rounded on him. 'I asked you a question, boy.

Don't look at him and don't dare disrespect me. Where are the weapons?'

'Delivered this morning. As soon as we know where Glass is hiding the thief we'll strike.'

Tony poured himself a whisky and faced Madeline and Mura. 'Let's understand each other. Bishop is expecting to show up, collect his money, and fuck off.'

Madeline eyed her grandson. 'Naturally, he got the guns and he wants paid.'

'You think he's on our side? You're being naïve. Bishop has an agenda. And it isn't the same as ours. Luke Glass is all that's standing between him and control of three quarters of this city and he knows it. I'd bet he lies in bed at night thinking about it. With the family no longer a threat he'll be the new king of London. All thanks to us. We'll have done the work for him.'

'None of this is news. What's your point? Or are you just enjoying the sound of your own voice?'

Tony let the slight pass; he wouldn't have to listen to the old bitch much longer. 'You talk as though all Bishop has to do is take his money and go, when the reality is far from that. True, he got the weapons for us. But without a target they have no value. Why would we need them?'

The struggle for supremacy between the grandmother and the grandson was old. Mura was tired of listening to it. He'd happily spit on both their graves.

Madeline asked, 'And you're saying... what, exactly?'

'When this guy gets here, I do the talking, okay?'

She threw her head back and laughed out loud. 'In your dreams. If it wasn't so sad it would be funny. It seems to have slipped your mind that you're the clown who got us into this mess. You and your father. Dumb and fucking Dumber. I wouldn't trust you to run to the store for a carton of milk. Sit down and behave yourself.'

'We need him to find the thief. The job isn't done until he does.'

Madeline saw where this was heading and gripped the arm of her chair with her bony fingers. 'Don't cross him, Antoine, you'll regret it. One enemy at a time is enough. This isn't New Orleans.'

'On the contrary, I'm inviting him in. Payment for the guns is small potatoes given what's on offer. He's greedy. I'm sharpening his appetite. Bishop won't be unhappy if it comes to war.'

Madeline shook her head. 'Now who's being naïve? War fits his agenda *only* if he wins. Unless Glass has been completely destroyed Bishop would be a dead man walking. Maybe he's thought about that.'

Tony emptied his whisky and sneered. 'Would you rather go back to Louisiana with our tails between our legs? Because I wouldn't. We came here to get a result we could show the world. I'm not giving up on that. Bishop produces Charlene or he doesn't get a dime.'

A knock on the door interrupted the conversation. Mura answered it and Calum Bishop came into the room. He looked the two men up and down and nodded to Madeline: the atmosphere was like a bad smell and he sensed the hostility wasn't only directed at him – these people detested each other. The old woman was the best of them, a formidable character worthy of respect – somebody he could do business with. The others were weak; under any circumstances he would've despised them.

He said, 'Have your men arrived?'

Giordano answered. 'Yes.'

'Then you're ready. I got what you wanted. Give me my money.'

'You said you'd find the Glass woman.'

'No, that wasn't the deal. I said I'd try.'

'And?'

'And nothing. Her brother's hidden her deep. My people are still on it.'

Giordano lowered his voice. 'Come on, Bishop, are you seriously asking me to believe that with all your connections in this city you've discovered nothing? In case you've forgotten, you stand to substantially benefit from your association with our family. In a couple of days, Glass could be dead and you could be running this town.'

Calum fought down his anger. 'That'll fucking happen with or without you. We had a deal. You're moving the goalposts again, and I don't appreciate it.' He turned to Madeline. 'Can I ask what the plan is if your thief doesn't surface? For all we know her brother may have sent her out of the country.'

Tony jumped in. 'We hit them and keep hitting, starting with the club. We—'

Talking big was a smokescreen to cover the fact he had no idea what to do next, except start a shooting war on the streets of London. Bishop cut him off. 'I'm speaking to your grandmother.'

Madeline said, 'For once I agree with my grandson. Glass will hand her to us – eventually – or lose it all. He'll have no choice.'

'With respect, Madame Giordano, there's something you don't understand about Luke Glass.'

'What?'

'Family is everything to him. Nothing is more important. To have an outside chance would require more resources than you have. Glass would strike back. A lot of people would die.'

'And if you came in with us, Mr Bishop? What would that give us?'

Calum Bishop shrugged the notion away as though it hadn't occurred to him. 'You'd have a much better chance.'

'How much better?'

'Against Luke Glass? Better than even.'

'Well, then, why are we wasting time haggling about money? Antoine, pay our new partner.'

* * *

George Ritchie cut the engine and let the BMW roll to a halt at the kerb behind a white Transit with COLLINGWOOD CONSTRUCTION written on the side. The company and the phone number that went with it were as fake as a six-pound note but gave the impression of work in progress to cover the coming and going of strangers. He studied the house in the quiet residential area where moderately successful businessmen, accountants and ambitious junior executives made love to their wives and watched Super Sunday football on Sky TV with their young sons. Charley and Nina were being kept here for their own safety. They wouldn't be happy and Ritchie expected to be hearing about it. Tough titty. The sisters could complain as much as they wanted; their reaction wasn't important – their brother was the boss. End of story. In a few days, this would be over and they could argue the toss with whoever was left standing.

If they could find anybody.

The detached property in a quarter of an acre of land, surrounded by a six-foot-high wall and a thick hedge on the inside, had been sold on only three occasions in its one-hundred-and-fifty-year history, the last time to an anonymous buyer. Nina had chosen it because it had privacy without looking like a fortress. CCTV cameras and barbed wire attracted attention. It was 'safe' because it was ordinary. The potted plants on either side of the front door hadn't made it through winter; metal scaffolding, still to be erected, and a pile of dust sheets lay under a tarp on the lush ankle-deep grass.

The Americans had shown the finesse of schoolboys, though

surely even an incompetent clown like Tony Giordano would be smart enough to have eyes on them. Ritchie had taken a circuitous route to get here – from the City of London to Finsbury, skirting Clerkenwell and the Barnbury Estate, before joining York Way and Camden Park Road. Not an unusual practice for the cautious Geordie; he'd done something like it every night for twenty-five years – one of the reasons he'd survived: an extreme reaction to the dangerous world he moved in. Time-consuming and tedious? Absolutely. Though, if inconvenience was the difference between staying alive and choking on your own blood, it was no contest.

A light shone from a downstairs window, apart from that there was little sign of habitation. Ritchie scanned the avenue to make sure he was alone. The gate was open – a bloody bad start. When he was halfway down the path, he heard the quiet crunch of boots on gravel and knew they were behind him. Two of them, over-confident fools who believed guns gave them an advantage. Against anybody but George Ritchie, they'd be right.

He slowed imperceptibly until they were close, then threw himself backwards. Caught off-balance, they bumped into each other, cursing; one of them dropped his weapon. Before he could pick it up, it was in Ritchie's hand, the black muzzle pointing ominously at the would-be attacker. 'Bang bang! You're dead.'

When the front door opened he pushed the men inside and barked at a guy in paint-stained overalls. 'Is this really the fucking best we can do? They're bloody lucky it was me, otherwise you'd be sharpening your shovels and digging a hole in the New Forest.'

'Sorry, George. They're from Liverpool. I expected them to be better but...'

'I'm not interested in excuses. Why is the gate open?'

'It's always been like that. It doesn't lock properly.'

'Then wake up and get it fixed! Put somebody out there who

knows what the hell they're doing and send those morons back to Merseyside.'

'You said we needed them.'

'No, we need pros who understand what they're about. These wankers will get themselves killed and us with them. Anything isn't better than nothing. All they're fit for is mutt work. Get rid of them.'

'Okay. Any news?'

Ritchie sensed the man's fear and mellowed. Waiting for the hammer to fall while adrenaline charged through your body like electricity was hard; doing drugs without the high was how George remembered it. And when it was finally over and you hadn't died, the sleepless nights and the crushing awareness of your own mortality. Everybody processed it in their own way.

Some lost themselves in booze, phoned their mother, or went to confession.

Others fucked the first woman they met without asking her name.

And the one after that.

It didn't change anything: they'd been reminded they were probably going to die violently and they were scared.

Ritchie clapped the guard on the shoulder. 'As for on the news front, you'll be the first to know.'

He got the joke and smiled. 'Is that a promise?'

'That's a promise. Where're the girls?'

* * *

Nina heard the drone of voices in the lounge and ducked under the bedclothes. She was exhausted – worn out and depressed. She'd avoided Luke once already; it wouldn't happen again and she prayed it wasn't him. She'd snorted the last of her stash in the middle of the night, eventually falling asleep only to wake from a nightmare so vivid it had taken every atom of her sanity to accept it hadn't been real. This was the downside. Nina had suffered it before. That didn't make it easier. And while cocaine withdrawal wasn't as physically intense as heroin or alcohol and lacked the visible symptoms of shaking and vomiting, psychologically it was a bastard. Aches and pains were nothing compared to the over-whelming feeling of despair and the suicidal thoughts that kept on coming. The pizza ruse had worked the first time; it wouldn't again. Nina lay curled against herself, wracked by anxiety. Her dealer would know what to do.

But Stevie D wasn't answering his phone.

29

George Ritchie had never married. Never even considered it. The right lady hadn't come along. Even if she had, he'd instinctively understood that, in his line of work, marriage wasn't viable. When he needed a woman he paid for one, an arrangement that avoided commitment and the disappointment of broken promises that would inevitably follow. Too late now but if he'd met Charley Glass twenty years ago he might have had to reconsider.

She was standing in the middle of the room, arms folded across her chest, chin tilted defiantly – signs Ritchie recognised only too well. The Glass sisters were magnificently flawed creatures who'd caused him more trouble than most of the villains in London. That said, there was something fierce and untamed – noble even – about them. On the table he saw paper and a pen and wondered who she was writing to.

Her welcome was surprisingly friendly given the circumstances. Charley said, 'George, thank God, it's you. I thought Luke had come back. I need you to help me.'

'Help you, how?'

'I have to get out of here.'

'Not until it's safe.'

'Safe?' She forced disbelief into her voice. 'When the hell will that be?'

The question was easy to answer. 'When they're dead, Charley. When the Americans are dead.'

The answer fell short of the mark; she pounced on it. 'Don't patronise me, George. Don't treat me like a fool. You say when but, really, you mean if.'

He saw the anger rise in her pale cheeks and walked towards her. Charley's eyes didn't leave his face. 'No, I mean when. One way or the other it'll happen. It has to.'

She stepped away from him. 'Give me your best guess. How many people will have lost their lives? How many fathers and sons and brothers?'

'I don't know.'

'Yes, you do. Of course you fucking do. Don't be a coward. Go on, spit it out!'

'As many as it takes.'

She sighed. 'Ah, at last, he speaks the truth.'

Her shoulders sagged as though an invisible weight she was carrying had suddenly become too heavy. Charley stared at the floor, talking to an audience of one: herself. 'It's me the Giordanos want. If I give myself up, this all goes away.'

She raised her head to look at him. 'Two girls have already died because of me. I can't let that happen to anybody else.'

'Your sacrifice won't make any difference.'

'Yes, it will. It's me they want, me they've always wanted. I'll tell them I'll give myself up on one condition – that it ends.'

Ritchie felt his mouth go dry. 'Do you have the slightest notion what they'd do to you? The unbearable agony Giordano's mongrel would inflict and grin while he was doing it? You think you understand people like them. You don't. They murdered the girls from the club for fun. For fun, Charley, remember that. Will I describe how they looked with their guts trailing out of their bellies?'

'No. No.'

'And it wouldn't be over. No matter what they said.'

'They'd have no reason—'

The conversation was pointless. Ritchie didn't want to discuss it any more. 'For fuck's sake grow up, will you? We couldn't save those girls. What chance do you imagine we'd have storming the fucking Dorchester?'

As soon as the words were out of his mouth Ritchie knew he'd made a mistake and spoke quickly to cover his error. 'Tony Giordano doesn't want to end anything. Shooting it out on the streets of London makes a statement to his rivals in New Orleans. Throwing out a challenge to people lurking in the shadows for a chance to strike at him on his own turf. He's saying: this is what we do to those who cross us. No matter how far they go or how long it takes, we'll hunt them down and destroy anybody who gets in the way. Your sacrifice would be for nothing, Charley. Because it isn't about you or money or blackmail stuff – it's about them. Their egos. Their family.'

Ritchie sat on the edge of an armchair, breathed in and exhaled slowly. 'So, as for helping you to give yourself up – apart from the fact your brother would put a bullet in my brain? Forget it.'

She waited until he was done. 'Unfortunately, George, you're the one who doesn't understand. When Beppe collapsed I did nothing. I watched and I enjoyed the show. He was an animal and I wanted him to suffer. Then, I emptied the safe.'

Ritchie answered impatiently. 'Okay, you're a thief. So what?'

'I robbed a dead man. A corpse.'

'Again, so what? Soldiers on the battlefield have done that since the beginning of time. None of us are perfect, Charley. We all do things we regret. Somehow, we find a way to live with them and go on.'

'Maybe you can.'

'No, not just me. Everybody. The first time I killed a man was like falling down a deep dark hole. Violence was one thing. Actually taking a life was something else. The guy had raped the sister of a friend of mine, a girl in Newcastle. Beaten her, broken her jaw and left her unconscious in an alley. When I called him out, he laughed.' The memory of his original sin darkened Ritchie's brow as he confessed. 'I strangled him with my bare hands. Only meant to teach him a lesson, but the laugh, the smug expression that said he wasn't sorry and would do it again – I couldn't stand it. And there was no road back. Not from that. Not for me.'

'He deserved what he got.'

'That's what I told myself to justify becoming the bastard's judge, jury and executioner. You got caught up in something bigger than you. Let it go.'

She repeated the words like a child copying an adult. 'Let it go.'

'Make a decision. It's that simple, Charley.'

'So, when does it start to get better? When does it come out even?'

Ritchie's reaction was bitter. 'Even? Never. Why would it?'

* * *

Charley was afraid but there were no regrets. Luke and Nina had taken her in and given her a home. Repaying their trust by bringing destruction to their door, as she'd done to their mother, would be truly shameful.

This was the right thing. The only thing.

She tiptoed along the hall to Nina's room at the back of the house, slowly turned the door handle and slipped inside. Nina hadn't made an appearance since yesterday – the isolation of the addict on full display. The drug was killing her. In the dark, Charley sat on the edge of the bed and listened to her sister breathing. She squeezed her clammy hand. Nina stirred but didn't waken. The scribbled note was inadequate; there was so much more she'd wanted to say. Luke would read it, be confronted with the harsh reality that Nina was a junkie and get her the professional help she so desperately needed.

Losing one sister would be hard for him, losing two unimaginable.

Gently, afraid she might wake her, Charley drew Nina's hair aside and kissed her cheek. They'd had so little time together and now it was too late.

The wooden frame was a survivor of the original building, crumbling and old. Charley freed the lock and opened the window as quietly as she could, praying none of the guards would hear her. She straddled the sill and took a last look at the pathetic figure in the bed. The rasp of a car with a dodgy exhaust and the thump-thump-thump of a boombox carried in the night. George Ritchie had been a revelation; she'd witnessed a side of him she hadn't known existed. There was no doubt he'd been telling the truth. Dropping his mask to share an incident in his past had been an extraordinary act, a selfless attempt to persuade her to forgive herself for what had happened in St Charles Avenue. Knowing him, knowing what he was capable of, it had been difficult to imagine the Geordie had ever had a soul, far less searching it over the death of a brutal rapist, or any death for that matter.

Ritchie had reached an accommodation with himself over what he'd done. Charley couldn't. As for his take on the Giordano's motives, she wasn't so sure.

Bruno Mura was a reptile – no argument there – and Tony, well, who but an idiot would've come to the club when the easier option was right in front of him? Maybe he'd still wanted her. Beppe had been bad enough – the thought of Tony made her sick. The biggest obstacle would be his grandmother: for all her advanced years the future of the family was Madeline. She hadn't hidden her hatred for Beppe's mistress. Exacting a slow revenge on the woman who'd brought on her son's fatal heart attack would be something to be savoured.

Yet, honour would be satisfied without either side suffering casualties. It made sense.

Charley lowered herself over the edge onto the ground, conscious of the cold air against her skin. She dropped to her knees and crawled on the overgrown grass towards the fence separating the property from next door. There would be men in the bushes. Any noise and it would be over; they'd catch her and take her back. Ritchie would double the guard and the war would begin. But they were expecting people to break in, not out.

At one-thirty in the morning, the tree-lined street was deserted, every light in every house extinguished as the good people of Kentish Town slept the sleep of the just. Thirty yards on a couple came towards her, the boy with his arm round the girl, their heads bent close together, unaware of the rest of the world. Charley darted down the stairs of a garden flat. They stopped to kiss; she heard him whisper he loved her and envied their ordinary lives. Lives unsullied by a London they didn't realise existed all around them.

When they'd moved on she climbed the stairs, crossed the road and quickened her step. Mayfair was a good five miles away. Too far to walk – she'd catch a taxi when she'd put some distance between herself and the house.

A shadow moved inside a white BMW parked further along. As Charley drew level with the car the door opened and a man stepped onto the pavement barring her path. With the street light behind him she couldn't see his face and suddenly realised how foolish she'd been. Her heart raced, terror overwhelmed her, she wanted to run but her legs were too weak. On the edge of panic, she frantically looked for someone to save her. The young lovers had disappeared; she was alone.

George Ritchie said, 'Nice try, Charley, nice try.'

* * *

Stevie D emptied the beer can, aimed it at the bare light bulb hanging from the lock-up's whitewashed ceiling and missed. Life was good and about to get better. Calum Bishop had been impressed with his information about Nina Glass. More or less promised him a job. Santa Claus settings, he'd said, and Santa Claus settings it was turning out to be. He was reaching for another can when his mobile vibrated in his pocket. Stevie read the caller ID and put the phone back in his jacket unanswered. In the last three hours the Glass woman had tried to contact him two dozen times. Not his concern; not any more. Even if he cared about the pain she was in – which he mostly certainly fucking did not– he was out of the drug business.

* * *

Ritchie sunk his hard fingers into her arm deeply enough to bruise the flesh, not bothered whether or not he was hurting her. Charley gritted her teeth but didn't complain, thankful it had been him waiting rather than Tony Giordano. George Ritchie rarely lost his temper, though she guessed the Geordie was close to it now. Back in the house he drew one of the guards aside, poking him in the chest, a fist clenched at his side. The man didn't attempt to defend what had happened but over Ritchie's shoulder his eyes bored into her.

In the lounge, Charley said, 'The guards aren't to blame. It isn't their fault.'

Ritchie had a different view. 'Really? Not to blame? Then who is?'

'Me.'

'Wrong. You didn't choose to be here. They did. The minute they signed on, their job became protecting the family, not smoking cigarettes and telling dirty jokes. If a woman can get past them, what hope do we have? I'll tell you. None. None at all. When this is behind us somebody's going to explain to me what went on here tonight and it better be convincing. So stop making excuses and stay in your lane. Nothing you have to contribute is relevant, Charley.' He pointed to his chest. 'I decide what is and what isn't good enough from the people working for us. That's what your brother pays me for.'

'They couldn't know I'd run away. They weren't expecting—'

'Do yourself a favour – no disrespect intended – shut the fuck up! And for Christ's sake stop being a martyr. Heaven already has more than its share. Go to bed, get some sleep, and don't try anything else. I'm too old to be chasing women.'

He fired an order at the nearest guard. 'See Miss Glass to her room. Stay outside. Anything happens to her you'll answer to me, understood?'

Ritchie's outburst had been a performance to force her to come to terms with the past.

It was what it was. Why had ceased to matter. Tony Giordano – a week ago George hadn't even heard of the bastard – was in London and determined to have his moment in the sun. Reasoning with him had never been an option. All that left was wiping him and whoever stood with him from the face of the earth.

Tomorrow was the last day. After that they could expect every pub, every betting shop, every street-corner dealer – any business associated with the Glass family – to be hit. LBC had to be top of the list – a prime target almost impossible to defend. An attack on it would be front-page news from London to Louisiana: exactly what Giordano was looking for and exactly what George Ritchie was determined wouldn't happen.

Ritchie went to the table and picked up the note Charley had left for Luke to find. The writing was spidery, almost illegible, a heartfelt message of regret from a sister to her brother not meant for other eyes. Towards the end Nina's name jumped off the page. George cursed and put it in his pocket. The next forty-eight-hours would be tough enough without Sister No 2 making them tougher.

When the time was right – if it ever was – he'd give the note to Luke.

Until then, he'd deal with it.

30

THE THIRD DAY

Felix Corrigan had been asleep when Ritchie called. George had spoken quietly, terse, even from a man of few words. 'Kentish Town. One hour.'

Corrigan had thrown the bedclothes off and sat upright. 'Is it the Giordanos?'

The question went unanswered. 'One hour, Felix.'

At the house, the guards let him in. Felix had worked with most of them. They couldn't look at him and he realised something was very wrong. In the lounge, Ritchie was waiting, his expression devoid of emotion. His first sentence revealed the depth of his anger. 'I should put a bullet in your head and dump you in a lime-pit in the New Forest, you bloody idiot.'

'George—'

Ritchie held up his hand. 'Don't push it, Felix. And don't insult me by lying. I deserve better than that. You knew Nina was using and covered for her, didn't you?'

'Yes.'

Ritchie hammered the arm of the chair with his fist. 'Why, for Christ's sake?'

'She was hurting. I was sure she'd pull it together. When this is over I was going to help her.'

Ritchie shook his head. 'That kind of secret is too dirty; it can't be kept. Lucky for you it was me.'

'She needs time, George.'

Ritchie was tired. He said, 'You're disappointing me, Felix. I expect better. In case you aren't getting it, you're in big trouble. If Luke can't trust me, then I'm no good to him. If I can't trust you... you see where I'm going with this?'

'You can, of course you can. When have I let you down?'

'A couple of nights ago for a start. Explain it to me. I want to understand before I decide what to do with you.'

Felix was shocked. 'What to do with me? You... you're serious.'

Ritchie's reply chilled him. 'Deadly serious. Tell me.'

'You asked me to go round and check she was okay, remember? When I got there she was on the floor unconscious. At first I thought she was dead.'

'Why didn't you contact me?'

'You called me just as she was coming round. I panicked and made a stupid decision.'

'"A stupid decision". You mean you lied?'

'I mean I lied, yeah.'

'I remember some crap about taking her to A & E.'

'Sorry, George.'

'All right. You were doing her a favour. After that why didn't you bring her here?'

Felix pinched his eyes with his fingers. 'It's complicated.'

'It usually is.'

'Okay. This... this is the truth: Nina's a junkie. Not just using. Cocaine's got a grip of her. She's at the stage where she'll do anything to get it. I thought I had the situation under control. I was wrong – somehow she'd scored. When I got back she was as high as the moon. Where is she?'

'In her room climbing the walls, poor cow.'

'Can I see her?'

'Not a chance.'

'What about Luke?'

'This isn't the time to tell him. I'll handle Nina.'

'Let me help, George.'

'I think you've helped enough, Felix, don't you?'

* * *

This is what I know: how many times had I said that to myself? Sometimes with certainty, at others to bolster a faltering belief things would work out. The phrase wasn't part of my vocabulary any more. Because I didn't know anything worth knowing.

Today was the third day since Tony Giordano spat his threat at me surrounded by a dozen loaded guns all pointing at him.

I'd wanted to laugh in the stupid bastard's face. I wasn't laughing now. The ground had shifted; Giordano had blustered like an out-manoeuvred fool giving me seventy-two hours to hand over my sister. Except, he hadn't given it to me, he'd given it to himself and bought the time to bring over a small army. But the blow we might not recover from was Ritchie's discovery that Calum Bishop had gone over to the dark side. And if that wasn't enough my brain was on fire with Charley's shocking revelation about our mother, mutilated and burned alive when she wouldn't give up her daughter.

I wanted to kill Tony Giordano so badly it was like a cancer eating me from the inside.

My eyes closed as I recalled the prison gates shutting behind me and the giddy sense of freedom that didn't last. Neither had my resolve to quit the life that had sent me to Wandsworth in the first place. The memory was vivid and fragmented: rain fell from an overcast sky; across the road a slim girl – in sunglasses, for Christ's sake – slouched against the bonnet of a Lexus. Nina: a wild, untameable handful yet, in the seven years since Lord Justice Peyton Richardson had delivered his guilty verdict, the only one I could lean on.

That had been the moment, the chance to sever ties with my brother and his 'Team Glass' bollocks. Nina was a free spirit who would've taken me anywhere. All I'd had to do was ask. But I hadn't asked and this was the result.

Footsteps echoing on marble snapped me back to the present. The club was closed and there were guards on the door; my sisters were in the safe house in Kentish Town and I wasn't seeing George Ritchie until later.

She stood inside the entrance leaning on an ebony cane, a tiny figure wearing sunglasses, hair tied in a bun, a shawl covering her shoulders, waiting for me to invite her in. When I saw her I got to my feet. Madeline marked my respect with a stiff nod and came towards me. I said, 'What can I do for you, Madame Giordano?'

She returned my formality with some of her own. 'You know the answer to that, Mr Glass. Tomorrow the world changes – my world as well as yours – unless cool heads prevail. May an old woman sit down?'

'Of course. Can I get you something to drink?'

'A little water would be appreciated, thank you.'

'Still or sparkling?'

'Still. Sparkling gives me gas.'

I went to the bar and returned with a bottle of Icelandic Glacial Natural Spring and a glass. She poured it slowly without looking at me and took a sip. 'Is it really from a glacier or is that just the marketing hype?'

'All I can tell you is our markup is 800 per cent.'

'For water?'

'For water.'

'And nobody complains?'

'In LBC there might be a lot to find fault with. What we charge isn't one of them. It would defeat the point of being a member.'

She took another sip and set the water down. So far it had been all very civilised but it couldn't go on. The matriarch realised it, raised her head and removed the shades. I glimpsed the younger Madeline in the deep-brown eyes assessing me. Her next statement was probably the only thing we would agree on. She said, 'My grandson is a fool. On behalf of the Giordanos I apologise for his behaviour.'

'Accepted.'

'But he isn't the only fool. Your sister took something from us.'

'I've already offered to repay the money. As for the rest... I'm sure that's been replaced.'

My simplistic response tested Madame Giordano's patience. 'I'm not referring to the money. The money is nothing. And you're right. With our resources the other thing was sorted in a month.' She laughed, a short dry laugh without humour. 'So long as men in power are corrupt and immoral, Mr Glass, our business will thrive.'

'Then, what else did she take?'

'The most important thing of all. The bedrock everything depends on. Your sister stole our reputation. An injury that cannot be allowed to stand.'

I studied the taut contours of her once-beautiful face. It had taken courage to come here and it occurred to me she might not know about the atrocity her grandson had sanctioned at the cabin in the woods. Even if she did, she wouldn't care. Tony hadn't got his twisted values from a rock; this old bastard was the wellspring. The polite persona, the old-world charm – all of it an act. Underneath breathed a ruthless matriarch fiercely committed to restoring the Giordano name in the eyes of their rivals in New Orleans.

Unfortunately, for both of us, she'd knocked on the wrong door.

The tremble in my voice was slight but it was there. I said, 'And you have a proposition?'

She turned away and whispered something I wasn't meant to hear. Hatred for her and her kind stirred like an animal inside me. Her sense of entitlement blinded her to the danger sitting across the table. Madeline played with my words. 'A proposition isn't how I'd describe it. No, what I've come with is a solution. You may wish it otherwise but the sister you care so much about is a thief who stole from the wrong people. By protecting her your family is flirting with extinction.'

I'd listened to enough; the dam broke and I shouted, 'Your reputation! Your fucking reputation! Is it really worth all this?'

Her eyes blazed with the fire of a zealot. 'Worth it and more.'

Her belief was absolute. Her dark eyes stayed on me as I got to my feet, conscious of the sweat that had broken out on my brow and a humming in my ears.

Madeline looked up at me like a hundred-year-old child. I said, 'Forget it! You're kidding yourself. As far as you're concerned London might as well be the other side of the moon. It's our town. We won't give it up. My advice is to realise you aren't getting what you want and go home.'

My reaction didn't surprise her; she was expecting it and had her little speech ready. 'I feel sorry for you, Mr Glass.' She waved a wrinkled arm around the club. 'Today you have everything. After tomorrow, nothing. The fall will be swift. I wonder how you'll cope with your new station in life.'

'Whatever happens, you won't live long enough to see it.'

She smiled, amused at the reference to her age, and used the ebony cane to lean forward, sharing a secret I already knew. Close up the years hung heavy on her; folds of skin gathered at her neck and above her eyes. 'And you think that matters to me? You actually think I care about that?' The smile disappeared, switched off as easily as a light, and pretence fell away.

She hissed, 'Listen up, you arrogant motherfucker. I came here to offer you a chance to save yourself from annihilation. The last chance you'll get.' She lost it and screamed, spraying an arc of saliva into the air. 'Because your sister's a thief this is where we are: for one family to survive another must perish! Give her to us and I'll call off Antoine. Otherwise...'

It took all I had to stop myself wringing her flabby Haitian neck and throwing her back into the gutter she'd crawled out of. She sensed she'd failed, struggled out of the chair, and pointed the stick at me. 'You've been warned, Glass. We won't meet again in this life.'

This creature was a force of nature, used to having the last word. Not this time.

I snarled, 'Save your breath, old woman. Soon, everything you've spent your life working to protect will belong to somebody else. When we're done the Giordanos will be a joke. Tell your grandson to bring it on. We're ready for him.'

* * *

Roberta looked round the lobby of The Dorchester from behind horn-rimmed glasses. The blonde wig, wide-brimmed hat and black three-quarter-length coat meant she was overdressed for the warm weather but unrecognisable from her real self. She ordered an espresso and waited for it to arrive. Further down The Promenade a couple with East European accents loudly discussed the selection of pastries on a three-tier stand as if they'd never seen a slice of fucking chocolate cake before. Russian peasants over to buy a property in Kensington or Chelsea and visit their ripped-off millions in a City bank. No wonder they called it Londongrad.

A good-looking waiter in his late twenties brought her coffee with the tiniest croissant she'd ever seen. She paid in cash, took a paperback from her bag and pretended to read. The cameras weren't obvious; for sure, they'd be there, hidden amongst the gilt mountings, the marble columns and chandeliers in the long green and gold room. If the police ran the footage from previous days they'd see an eccentric woman minding her own business and move on. A female would be the last person they'd consider for the hit. She felt herself relax. Getting in and out wouldn't be a problem – no one would know until room service discovered the bodies the following morning. By then, she'd be touching down at Louis Armstrong International in New Orleans.

And the page would close on who she'd been.

La Réponse would cease to exist.

31

Charley sat on the edge of the bed holding her sister's hand. She'd said she was sorry a dozen times and wanted to say it again. Nina lay on top of the covers, her eyes dull and empty, shaking uncontrollably, constantly sniffing as the constricted blood vessels in her nose expanded beyond their original size. Even the slightest movement was painful for her and her mood lurched between irrational irritability and a crushing lethargy that left her drained. She hadn't slept; that had been an act to avoid Luke.

Ritchie came in without bothering to knock. Behind him a guy in a checked jacket with patches at the elbows had a dark-brown leather satchel draped over his shoulder. George Ritchie was angry and it showed – somewhere in the city their enemies were gathering; he didn't need this shit. He addressed the ashen Nina without a shred of empathy in his voice. 'This man will supervise your recovery. Don't ask his name. As far as you're concerned he doesn't have one. Don't ask him anything, just do as he says and you'll get through this.'

The doctor took a blood-pressure testing kit and a heart-rate monitor from the bag, slipped the cuff round Nina's upper arm and clipped the monitor to her finger.

'Let's see where you are before we start, shall we?'

Nina stared across the room and let him get on with it. When he was finished he ignored her and spoke to George as though she wasn't there. 'Your sister's made a fair stab at messing herself up.'

'She's not my sister.'

'Oh, I thought...'

'You thought wrong.'

'All right. No harm done. As you'd expect, her blood pressure's low. I'll give her clonidine to help the physical symptoms. Cocaine addiction takes a toll on the body. Vitamin C, B and B12 to will help rebalance her system.'

'What about methadone?'

'If you want to kill her, absolutely. Tomorrow, we can start her on a low dose of haloperidol. Let's hope she doesn't need it. And make sure she drinks plenty of water.' He put the equipment back in the bag and got up to go. 'I'll be back in the morning. Call me if there's any deterioration.'

Ritchie blocked his path. 'I think there's been a misunderstanding. You're staying, Doctor. For as long as it takes you're staying right here.'

* * *

Late in the afternoon, the bar downstairs in the King of Mesopotamia was empty apart from a few florid-faced diehards who hadn't realised spending most of their waking hours in a pub had less to do with avoiding nagging wives and preferring their mates' company than the elephant in the room nobody talked about: their drinking problem. Across the desk, George Ritchie was ready to answer my questions. I wasn't ready to ask them. On the wall behind him, the clean lines of a rectangle marked the wall-paper where the photograph of the Queen had hung in Danny's day, and I wondered how my brother would've responded to what was going on. Of course, I knew – he'd have shot Tony Giordano through the heart the first time he laid eyes on him, fed his body to the fish off Bell Wharf Beach, and damn the consequences. There was definitely something to be said for it.

Ritchie set an unopened bottle of Glenfarclas single malt on the desk and poured two fingers. He caught me looking at my watch. 'Not too early, is it?'

'Not when you consider it might be the last whisky we'll ever drink.'

'Still, maybe you'd rather leave it out... a clear head and all that bollocks?'

'My head's already clear, unfortunately. Where do you think they'll hit first?'

He blew air though his teeth – not a good sign. 'Anybody's guess. As far as we know they haven't found where Charley is. We—'

Ritchie stopped, as though he'd been struck by lightning. 'Holy fucking Christ!'

'What, George?'

'I'll explain in a minute.' He pulled out his mobile, tapped a number, and spoke into it.

'Felix, where are you? Forget that. Who's Nina's supplier? Her supplier, who is it? Right, get yourself to Kentish Town. Now! Get the girls out. Take them to fucking Scotland if you have to. And make sure you're not followed. It's got to look like they're still there.'

And without him having to explain I understood what Charley had been trying to tell me. I'd looked at my sister and seen a woman emotionally devastated by the loss of the man she'd loved and assumed all she needed was a sympathetic ear and time to come to terms with it.

Wrong! So very wrong!

She'd been dying, buckling under the weight of her grief, slowly killing herself with drugs.

I jumped to my feet. 'This isn't a job for Felix. They're my sisters – it's my responsibility.'

Ritchie put himself between me and the door. I said, 'Don't do this, George. Get out of my way.'

'No, Luke. Felix will get them away but this changes things. If a fucking street-corner dealer knows where they are, we have to assume Calum Bishop knows, too.'

'And since he's in with the Americans...'

The sentence went unfinished.

I said, 'Forget the club, forget Glass Houses, forget everything. We need every man we have in Kentish Town.'

'What if we're wrong? What if we're spooking ourselves? It'll be the end. The family will be finished. Once Giordano's picked the bones clean he'll come after Charley and there will be nothing we can do to stop him.'

His hand went to my shoulder; the voice of reason, as so often in the past. He raised his clenched fist in front of my face. 'We don't give up an inch of ground to these bastards. We fight them in Margaret Street, in Bishopsgate, south of the river...'

'Do we have the numbers?'

'I fucking hope so. Our first priority is getting Nina and Charley to a safe place. They can go to my flat.'

For a guy who guarded his privacy as jealously as he did, it was a selfless gesture.

I said, 'Thanks, George. I appreciate it. I've got a better idea.'

* * *

We drank in silence, hypnotised by the amber in the bottom of the glass. I glanced at my watch for the second time in ten minutes. Ritchie said, 'It's too soon. Felix won't be there yet.'

'It's a reflex. In seven hours Tony Giordano's three days are up. Whatever happens, don't let them get her, George. Promise me. Felix has to shoot her. He has to shoot both of them. He'll be doing them a favour.'

'You have my word.'

The conversation had taken a turn for the worse: in the circumstances difficult to credit, but true. I emptied my glass; Ritchie refilled it before I could object, although I wouldn't have. Keeping to myself what these twisted bastards had done to our mother was an ache in my soul, a wrong I'd gladly spend the rest of my life avenging.

Maybe it was the booze but hearing myself unload surprised me. 'There's something... something I need to say.'

'What is it?'

'They murdered my mother, George. Not just murdered her, slaughtered her like a dog.'

'How do you know?'

'Charley told me. She was there.'

His reaction was vintage George. 'One more reason to send these fuckers back to hell.'

* * *

Tony poured a drink and held the liquid up to the light like a connoisseur with an appreciation of the finer things, instead of a jumped-up pimp fortunate to have been born into a powerful family. His grandmother marked the belly straining against the belt, the puffy cheeks and the dark clouds in the corners of his eyes. The issues that had sent his father to an early grave were already visible in the son; in ten years his body would betray him, irrevocably damaged by his lifestyle. It was only a matter of time before he ballooned into a grotesque caricature of the handsome younger man he'd been. Madeline didn't lie to herself: the meeting with Glass hadn't gone well. His strength was apparent, and his intelligence. Even as she'd screamed threats and promises of destruction she'd wished the future of the Giordanos rested with him rather than this excuse for a human being.

Bruno Mura sat by the window, again cleaning his fingernails with the serrated blade of his knife – a habit that revealed the uncouth peasant he'd never rise above – and answered a question that hadn't been asked. 'Our men are ready. Everything's in place.'

Tony asked, '*Everything?*'

'Except Bishop.'

Giordano sipped the cognac and slid a wet tongue over his lips. 'You worry too much. He'll be here. There's still time.'

'What if he's changed his mind?'

'In that case, he's a fool who let his golden moment pass him by; a coward who doesn't deserve to survive. The end of the Glass family is more significant for him than for anybody. With them weakened he can take over almost without firing a shot.' Tony laughed. 'He'll be a fucking king.'

The explanation didn't satisfy the Sardinian. Mura couldn't let it go. 'Bishop has us by the balls. He holds all the cards and he knows it. If he decides he doesn't want to be king, we're fucked. Starting a shooting war is high risk anywhere, but especially in a strange city. Glass won't stand still and let us just gun him down. He'll fight back. And what about getting away? Should we call a taxi to take us to the airport?'

He walked to the middle of the room, still holding the knife. 'It doesn't work without Bishop. Right now we need him more than he needs us and it's time we acknowledged that.'

Tony wasn't swayed. 'With or without him we'll hit the club a minute after midnight. Glass won't be able to claim Tony Giordano didn't give him his three days. Our men will systematically torch his businesses on the other side of the river. By morning, his soldiers will be dead and he'll be ruined.'

Madeline had listened to the exchange in silence. 'Your optimism is admirable, Antoine. I applaud it. Except, in your enthusiasm for war, you seem to have forgotten two important details – if Glass wouldn't give up the thief, he certainly won't surrender his empire without the mother and father of battles. And I give the orders, not you.'

'We've done the work. You prefer to sit in your hotel dreaming of the past. Your contribution so far has been zero. Or have I missed something?'

Madeline's wrinkled fingers gripped the head of her stick. 'This morning, while you were sleeping off your hangover, I talked with Glass.'

Tony shouted, 'You did what? Why?'

'To get what we came for without unnecessary bloodshed. Gunfights in the streets may be an everyday event in New Orleans. Not here. This is London, the capital of England. And I'm afraid I have to disappoint you. The man I spoke to isn't about to give up his sister or his crown.'

Tony sneered. 'I feel for you, I really do. It can't be easy being a frightened old woman, weary of living, scared of dying. Knowing your time has come and gone and the world has no use for you. What did you hope to achieve?'

'I asked myself what your grandfather would do.'

Tony mocked Madeline. 'So we're to be guided by a ghost, are we? All right. What was the phantom's advice?'

'To know my enemy. To understand who Luke Glass is.'

'And who is he?'

'A man who can't be broken. A man who will die rather than give in. A man like Silvestro.'

Tony fingered the pendant on his chest with his left hand and flicked ash from his cigarette onto the carpet. 'Voodoo horseshit. Keep it to yourself, I don't want to hear it. By this time tomorrow, Glass will be on his knees begging to give us the sister. With my boot on his neck he'll have no choice.'

Mura said, 'And what about Bishop?'

'I told you, Bruno, he'll be here. Whatever crap he peddles, trust me, he wants that crown.'

* * *

As evening turned to night, the light went out of the day, and traffic thinned on Park Lane. Downstairs, men wealthy enough to buy anything but their youth escorted expensively dressed females to the bar for a drink before taking their seats in the hotel's lavishly appointed restaurants. On the sixth floor the atmosphere was very different. Madeline's thoughts went back to Little Torch Key, remembering the thrill of knowing they'd left the hellhole of Haiti behind forever and were standing on American soil. Bruno Mura played with his ever-present knife, balancing the murderous tip on his finger; he was calm. Since his over-the-top outburst Tony Giordano had retreated into himself and avoided looking at the other two.

At five minutes past eight there was a knock on the door. Mura answered and Calum Bishop strode confidently into the room, ignored the others and poured himself a cognac. Mura saw his face and guessed what he was about to tell them.

'You've found her. Jesus Christ, you've found the bitch, haven't you?'

Calum stared at the alcohol in his glass and made them wait. 'Yes.'

'How?'

'That doesn't matter. What's important is how we get to her.'

Tony should've been pleased; instead, he was angry. 'We shoot our way in, that's how.'

Bishop emptied his drink in one gulp, wiped his mouth and spoke to Madeline. 'Charlene Glass is in north London, heavily guarded. I suggest we ignore John Wayne here and get real.'

'What would you do, Mr Bishop?'

'Again, thanks to your grandson, they're expecting us, which means surprise isn't possible. You hit them at dawn. Take the guards outside without announcing your arrival and go through every door and window at the same time. Grab the woman and get out as fast as you can. Some nosey neighbour with insomnia is bound to call the police. I reckon you'll have ten to twelve minutes before Kentish Town's swarming with coppers.'

Tony said, 'I'm hearing a lot about us – what we'll do – no mention of your contribution.'

Calum Bishop scanned the three Americans. Given their previous conversations it was a stupid question that could only have come from Tony Giordano.

'I told you at the start I wasn't prepared to let my guys go down for your cause. That hasn't changed. When you attack, we'll be behind you. But if there's dying to do – no offence – you're doing it, not us.' Calum ran a hand over his bald head. 'You've got a short memory, Tony. So far, I've supplied you with transport, information, and guns, *and* found where Glass is hiding his sister. I've kept my side of the arrangement. This is the last bit. I promised to get you in, and I will. After that...' he shrugged '... what happens doesn't concern me. My job is to get you away from London, and, in a week or so, out of the country.'

Tony wasn't impressed. 'And that's it? What about the club? What about the other businesses?'

Mura said, 'We'll have what we came for. Why put ourselves in harm's way?'

Giordano dismissed the Sardinian. 'Shut the fuck up, Bruno. My grandmother isn't usually right but she was right about you. You shouldn't even be in the room. You're not family. As to your question, the answer is simple: because it isn't enough. I want to erase them, rub them out like they've never existed.'

Bishop put the whisky on the table and turned to Madeline. 'You can have the woman and your honour, or you can have a war. You can't have both. Your call, Madame Giordano.'

32

Through the plate-glass windows London was a neon panorama stretching beyond the river into the distance. Felix Corrigan slumped on the dark-green leather Chesterfield, surrounded by chic furniture and artwork on the walls: this was how the other fucking half lived.

His gun lay on the coffee table beside his mobile phone. Felix didn't smoke and wished he did; waiting was killing him. On the journey to St John's Wood and the apartment on the ninth floor overlooking Lord's cricket ground he'd tried not to think about what was happening behind him in the back seat. Nina hadn't improved – if anything, she looked worse, her breathing shallow and laboured, her skin the colour of bread dough. When they'd arrived, the overweight concierge had been expecting them and had the keys ready. Now, the doctor was with her in the bedroom, constantly monitoring her vital signs, making sure she wasn't about to have a stroke or a heart attack while the drug was flushed from her system.

Felix was at an all-time low. Shielding Nina from the consequences of her addiction had backfired on him big time; he'd lost

George Ritchie's trust. Fighting the Americans would've been a pleasure if it meant regaining it. Next door a distraught Charley was on the guilt trip of the century, pacing up and down; the Glass sisters certainly knew how to punish themselves.

The doctor came out and closed the door behind him. Felix said, 'How is she?'

He spoke quietly but didn't sugar-coat his reply. 'Not great. Physically she's strong but she's having a hard time psychologically. It isn't pretty.'

Felix sat up straight, immediately concerned. 'She's going to be okay, isn't she?'

The reply didn't offer the reassurance he needed. 'Every addict's withdrawal experience is different. Normal doesn't exist. The process begins with intense cravings around the time they'd have the next dose so, if you use twice a day, you can expect cravings about twelve hours in. Nina was hammering it. As for the mental and emotional damage, it's too soon to come to any meaningful assessment.'

'Yeah, but you've seen withdrawal before, what do you think?'

'I'd really rather not speculate.'

Felix got to his feet. His guts were churning; he wanted to beat this man to a pulp. And the truth was clearer than it had ever been: he was in love with Nina Glass and always would be. 'I'm afraid I'm going to have to press you for that answer.'

The doctor nervously eyed the gun and sighed. 'Very well, I'll give you my opinion for what it's worth, which, at this stage, isn't much. She's young. She's healthy. And, from what I understand, successful. Clearly, it wasn't enough or we wouldn't be here. People don't just become addicts – it isn't a conscious choice – some inner demon drives them to seek escape. If I knew why, I'd be a very rich man. Only Nina can tell you. Maybe she will. Let's hope so. When you ask me if she'll be all right, quite frankly, the only answer I can give you is... it depends.'

'Depends on what?'

'If she wants to live or die.'

* * *

The barman dimmed the lights to signal the bar was closing, sending a noisy group of Asian businessmen partying on company expenses into a frenzy of last-minute orders. On another day Tony would casually toss a racial slur or two in their direction and go on with what he'd been saying. He let it pass and toyed with what was left of his drink, strangely at peace, not a state of mind he was famous for. Considering what was going down in the next six or seven hours, Bruno had expected him to be wired. At times like these his own thoughts invariably turned to sex. The cute chick waitressing at Café Du Monde seemed a lifetime ago; he wondered if she was still carrying trays of bitter coffee and sweet beignets, strutting her funky stuff under the green-and-white awning, 100 per cent aware of what she had. He'd soon be finding out.

They'd travelled far from the night Hurricane Martha blew through New Orleans leaving a trail of destruction downtown and Beppe Giordano dead on the floor in St Charles Avenue. The storm wasn't to blame. Another force of nature had done for him; her name was Charlene. Until the night in LBC the closest they'd got to her was the cabin in the snow.

Bruno had learned to be careful. Madeline needed no provocation. Her grandson could strike like a cottonmouth and frequently did: it was who he was. Who all the Giordanos were.

He ran a finger along the rim of his glass, choosing his words. 'You took a lot of heat for showing up at the club. It made you look stupid, but it wasn't a mistake, was it, Tony?'

'No.'

'You understood what you were doing, didn't you?'

Giordano's fingers closed round the chunk of amber at his chest. He leaned back in his seat and frowned at the Asian guys, still making too much noise. 'Lifting the thief would've been easy and it could've been over on the first night. But, at the end of the day, what would it prove, eh? Our standing had fallen in Bourbon Street and out on the bayous. My father fucked everything that moved, including us. It needed something more than a mutilated tart to redress the balance.'

'It needed a statement of intent.'

'Correct. "A statement of intent", exactly. If she'd only taken money, I doubt I would even have bothered going after her.'

'Except she didn't, you did, and we're here.'

'Yeah, we're here, Bruno.'

'Will you say a last goodbye to your grandmother?'

Tony finished his drink, set the empty glass on the table, and spat on the floor.

'No. Fuck her!'

* * *

According to my Rolex, a present from my brother for my twenty-first birthday, there were exactly forty-one minutes left of the three days Tony Giordano had given me to surrender Charley to him and avoid whatever came next. Turning him down had been the easiest decision I'd ever made; I didn't regret it. But how we'd got involved with these bastards, how it had to come to this, still didn't feel real. Except, it was.

On my way out of LBC I rubbed my hand across the alabaster base of Fortuna, the goddess of luck, appreciating the reassuring warmth of the smooth stone against my fingertips. I needed every little bit the lady could spare and wasn't too proud to ask for it under my breath.

Kentish Town was less than four miles away. The last time I'd driven there I'd taken a tour of north London, glancing in my mirrors every few minutes to see if I was being followed. This was different: if the Americans hadn't already been told, I wanted to lead them to the prize.

It had started to rain, a scattering of drops hitting the windscreen that quickly became a steady drizzle. I slipped across Euston Road into Albany Street to the slurping of the wipers beating a steady tempo, travelling slowly enough for even a stranger in the city to keep up with me. As I was passing the legendary Dublin Castle music venue in Parkway a red Seat estate flashed its lights, blasted the horn, and cut in front. My overreaction was a clue to what was really going on with me; I screamed at him and cursed Charley for getting us involved in this.

The Giordanos had been in my life forever, or so it seemed.

Tonight, one way or another, it would end.

My family was a mess, some of it my fault. I'd been too busy fucking about with the hoi polloi to see what was in front of me. Nina had been hurt more than I'd realised and gone over an invisible line into addiction. Her grubby secret was out and I wasn't confident we could help her, but we'd bloody well try.

That still left a lot of sorting out to do but we'd do it. Together.

* * *

On the sixth floor of The Dorchester, Madeline Giordano lay back in an armchair thinking about the early days at Silvestro's side when she'd washed his bloodied wounds, fed him cane spirit and bootleg absinthe, and cheered as he vanquished rival gangs from Canal Street to Esplanade Avenue, establishing himself at the head of a new order in the French Quarter. He'd been a man among men – brave and kind yet capable of great cruelty. Under him the family had stood for something, not just in New Orleans, but in Louisiana: a golden era that ended when he passed and Beppe took his place.

They said: 'a fish rots from the head' and it was true. Antoine had all his father's weaknesses and none of his grandfather's strengths, a womaniser and a fool who kept company with a rabid Sardinian fox.

In the darkness, the old woman cried out to her dead husband. 'Tell me what to do, Silvestro! Tell me!'

There was no answer. She didn't need one. Madeline already knew.

The Giordano name would die with her. It was how it had to be.

* * *

It was ten minutes to midnight: George Ritchie had been in Kentish Town since his meeting with Luke to satisfy himself everything was as it should be. A few of the men had come up against him when he was Arthur Anderson's enforcer and were mightily glad that tonight he was on their side. George was aware of being watched as he moved from one group to the other, spending a few minutes talking to them like a general with his troops. As a student of history he understood battles had been won or lost in these hours. Ritchie kept it light. Telling them not to be afraid would've been foolish; an insult. Of course, they were afraid – anything else would be unnatural, even dangerous. His job was to drop a quiet word in anxious ears and keep them focused on defeating the enemy.

Raindrops streaked the windowpanes and raced to the bottom. Let it pour. Anything that made it unpleasant to be out there was good news.

A guy with a heavy East-End accent asked, 'Where's Felix? Ain't he coming?'

George answered him. 'He's taking care of a bit of business in another part of town. He sends his regards, by the way.'

'I bet he does, lucky bastard. Where are the—?'

Ritchie put a finger to his lips. 'No questions, it isn't the time, just do what you're supposed to and tomorrow you'll be propping up the bar in the King Pot with a fat bonus on your hip.'

The lounge where Charley had tried to convince him she was to blame was unaltered and he remembered the note to her brother, still in his pocket.

Somebody stuck their head round the door. 'Luke's car's outside. The boys were starting to think he wasn't going to show up.'

Ritchie grabbed him by the lapels, hauled him into the room, and slammed him against the wall. 'Listen, Luke Glass is worth ten of you any day of the week.' He shook him like a rag doll. 'Any fucking day! Got it?'

* * *

Roberta Romano ran her painted fingers through the blonde wig and studied her reflection in the mirror; she'd preferred the other disguise, though the coat and the navy-blue beret gave her the result she was after. Unless they saw the scar on her cheek, no one would guess it was the same woman. Dinner had been a room-service omelette and a green salad washed down with two glasses of Evian water – she didn't do drugs and when she was on a job anything that might slow her reactions was out. Roberta had paid her bill in cash an hour ago and assured the smiling girl on Reception she'd enjoyed her stay and, yes, she'd visit them again.

On the bed where she'd had sex with the stranger from the bar a small suitcase was packed next to the clothes she'd change into before leaving for Heathrow Airport and her mid-morning return flight to New Orleans. But there was still work to do. Always the professional, she checked the action of the weapon Tony Giordano's man had given her one last time, screwed the silencer onto the barrel, and stuck it in the waistband of her skirt underneath the coat.

In Park Lane light rain fell from a black sky and the city air smelled fresh; Roberta walked briskly towards the hotel. At The Dorchester, the staff on the main desk were too busy to notice her enter the lift; she rode to the sixth floor, got out and listened. Nothing. Not a sound. This was the heart of London, one of the most exciting capitals in the world; most of the guests would be enjoying a last drink in the bar or still be out on the town.

But not the guest she was there for.

Roberta's hand closed round the butt of the gun. She knocked on the door and waited for it to open.

33

The new day began over east London as a faint glow behind the clouds that slowly melted the darkness. For some people it would be their last day on this earth. I watched from a window on the top floor, taking comfort in the knowledge that, whatever happened, Charley wouldn't be one of them.

In the King of Mesopotamia the idea of a small-time drug-dealing nonentity being savvy enough to put two and two together and come up with Luke Glass' sister seemed not only reasonable but exactly how it had played out. Now, doubt gnawed at me and I wasn't sure I hadn't let wishful thinking influence the decision to go for broke in Kentish Town. Travelling on my own opinion had taken me far, except this time the consequences of being wrong would be fatal: an attack on the club would be a massacre; innocent people would die; all over the south side businesses would go up in flames. When he didn't find what he was looking for Giordano's vengeance would be unleashed like never before: my family wouldn't survive.

George Ritchie tapped me on the shoulder. 'Nothing anywhere. We haven't been hit.'

'Which means?'

'We were right. They know about here.'

'How are our guys doing?'

'Nervous. Better than the alternative. In a situation like this over-confidence will get you dead. We've got every door and window covered and there's a couple on the roof. Now we need something to shoot at.'

I held out my hand; he took it. 'Thanks, George.'

'What the hell for? I haven't done anything.'

Not true. 'Yeah, you have.'

He smiled and looked away. 'You offered me a job and saved my life. Retirement would've fucking finished me. Wouldn't have lasted twelve months.'

'And here you are with punters you've never even met getting ready to do you in. The bad news is, it's too late to change your mind.'

'Hadn't occurred to me. Thought I'd told you – I'm an eccentric millionaire. This is my dream.'

It was a strange moment to be laughing, a sign of the pressure we were under. I said, 'Do something for me, will you? When this is over, for Christ's sake tell me where you live.'

'No chance, because then I'd have to kill you.'

* * *

'I want Charlene. No matter what it costs I want her, do you hear me, Bruno?'

Mura read between the lines. 'No matter what' meant no matter how many died. Giordano had left a man to perish in the snow when he'd broken his leg. Valoir, who'd been with the family for fifteen years, had a nice wife, two young kids, and a brick house with a shingle roof in Oak Ridge Park. Abandoned to freeze to death in a fucking wilderness. With luck he was already a corpse when night fell and the wolves sniffed him on the air. Loyalty had counted for nothing then and counted for nothing now. Tony was prepared to sacrifice everybody except himself. Ruthless, even by Bruno's standards; the man didn't deserve to live.

'Speak to the men. Make sure they understand that this is it. Our last chance.'

'They get it, Tony.'

'They better, Bruno. Go, I'm right behind you.'

* * *

The iron gate was seven feet high. I watched a figure dressed from head to foot in black climb it in seconds, lower himself down the other side, and slip into the bushes. Two more, agile bastards, made it look easy and once more I realised what the hell we were up against. Tony Giordano had proved he wasn't the sharpest tool in the shed but his determination to get what he'd flown across an ocean for couldn't be underestimated. All around the property armed men would be scaling the wall, regrouping in the rhododendrons, waiting for the signal to attack. If, as we believed, Calum Bishop's contribution to the party was still to come, we were in trouble.

I drew my gun and ran downstairs. Ritchie met me at the bottom.

'We're on, George.'

He slid a magazine into the Sig Sauer in the palm of his hand. 'Then let's give them a good old south London welcome.' Ritchie turned on the outside light and threw the front door open. 'See how brave these guys really are.'

'Brave? Don't you mean stupid?'

'Brave. Stupid. Same thing.'

The first shot shattered the picture window in the lounge and brought a response from our guys. Silencers dumbed the cracks but they were still audible in the early morning air. The sound of running feet meant some of them had abandoned the bushes and were closing in. Ritchie caressed the barrel of the gun and whispered to himself. 'Come on, bonnie lads. Don't be shy.'

On cue, two men charged through the door firing indiscriminately, not close to hitting anything. George glanced across at me. 'Told you. Brave. Stupid. No difference.'

We both shot at the same time and they dropped to the ground never to get back up. The quiet after that seemed to go on forever. In reality, it could only have been seconds. Then, all hell broke loose. One of our guys fell from the roof and lay still on the grass, eyes staring, seeing nothing. He wouldn't be the last.

I should've sorted Giordano when I'd had the chance. A bit late to think about that. The way to end this was to find him and put him out of his misery. The rest were mercenaries. Guns for hire. For them it wasn't personal: with their paymaster gone they wouldn't fancy it.

* * *

Bruno Mura dropped over the wall at the back of the house, hunkered down and drew the thick stems of the nearest bush apart. His sharp eyes caught the movement of a curtain on the top floor and his mouth spread in a grin – the fool thought he was invisible. He took aim and fired; the window exploded and a man cried out. One less to worry about. When Bishop's troops weighed-in the outcome would be beyond doubt. It occurred to him the north London gang boss would have second thoughts and dismissed it. Calum Bishop had more to gain from Glass' downfall than anybody.

Mura hadn't seen Tony since they'd split up at the car; he was probably hiding until it was over. Giordano was too much of a coward to put himself in harm's way. Other poor bastards did the dying for him. He didn't care how many men lost their lives to satisfy his need to re-establish the family's power in New Orleans. The old woman, on the other hand, was a warrior and, though she publicly insulted him, Mura could respect what she'd done in the past.

He edged his way forward towards the back door. The thief was the prize. With a gun biting into the soft flesh of her throat her brother would call off his dogs.

* * *

I crept through the house, staying low to avoid catching a stray bullet, white smoke and the choking smell of cordite heavy in the air around me. The two heroes who'd gone to an early grave inside the open front door had grown to five. George was everywhere, guns in both hands, blasting away like the final scene from *The Alamo* – in the lounge one minute, the next upstairs firing down on men in the garden. There was no fear in him; he was actually enjoying himself.

He crawled across to where I was, pressed his back against the wall, and gave me a progress report I hadn't asked for. 'Nine dead, two of them ours.'

'So, we're winning?'

He reloaded and pushed himself to his feet ready to go again. 'Not how I'd describe it. We can't keep this up forever. Sooner or later we'll run out of ammo or the police will arrive. More cars have just pulled up out front.'

'Fuck you, Bishop!'

George shrugged. 'He was always going to move on us. Might as well get him off our backs now.'

'Any sign of Giordano?'

'No. And there won't be. This is too hot for him.'

'I'm going after the bastard.'

He grabbed hold of me. 'Don't, Luke, he isn't worth it.'

I didn't disagree. 'It has to be done, George. Or this never ends.'

* * *

Moments ago I'd witnessed George Ritchie walk towards the guns, an inspiration and an example to the troops, unlike Tony Giordano, a lowlife whose time was almost up. I'd relish putting a bullet in his brain. But his sidekick was the animal who'd taken a blade to our girls in Limehouse, and mercilessly tortured a defenceless old woman. I wanted him so bad I could taste it.

Charley's confession about our mother had soured in my gut like bad food. At night when I closed my eyes, I saw blood and flames and vowed to kill the fucker who'd made her suffer.

I edged the back door open and listened: the firing had stopped, an unnatural silence screamed in my ears, and I wondered if Calum Bishop's men were lined up waiting to gun down anyone foolish enough to try to shoot their way out. A bullet clipped a brick inches above my head. Another pinged the wall. I raced to the bushes and dived into the foliage. As I was getting to my feet something hard and heavy struck me on the temple and the lights went out.

When I came to, one of Giordano's men towered over me, the gun in his hand pointing directly at my face. Up close the muzzle looked as big as the entrance to Blackwall Tunnel. Any second, a kinetic piece of tooled metal would exit the chamber faster than the speed of sound, faster than I could duck or yell, and rip through my brain.

Bullets beat bone. Every time.

My only consolation was I'd never know. It would be the easy way out.

'Mr G wonderin' where y'at.'

His accent was deep and brown – distant thunder rumbling in his throat.

'On yo' feet.'

A shaft of regret lanced through me; Charley and Nina were safe – Giordano couldn't get to them. But there would be no one to avenge Frances Glass. As head of the family, that was my job. I'd been looking forward to it and wasn't ready to give it up.

He stepped back to let me get up, sweat glistening on his forehead; he wasn't as confident as he sounded. Or maybe that was what I wanted to believe. My fingers trailed the earth still damp from last night's rain, frantically searching for something to use against him. Dark eyes guessed what I was doing; he flashed two rows of perfectly white tombstone teeth, amused. 'Suit yo'self. He wants you alive. I ain't p'ticular. Either way's fine with me.'

A twig snapped, breaking his concentration for a vital second, presenting me with the opportunity I needed. He turned to see what it was and I lashed out, kicking him in the groin. He doubled in pain and dropped the gun. I grabbed it and shot him twice in the face, at close range not pretty.

In the morning light, Tony Giordano raced down the drive towards the road away from the battle his lust for power had caused. Catching him wasn't a goer; I was still groggy from the blow on the head. With little hope of hitting him I let go two rounds, both well off the mark. The third, more by luck than anything, grazed his arm; he stumbled but went on.

Gunfire was still coming from the house. I pressed myself to the wall and took as much air into my lungs as I could, trying to figure what to do when the decision was taken from me: Calum Bishop swept away a rhododendron branch and stepped out of the bushes holding a Beretta. The twig had been him. His eyes were hard and unblinking; he raised the gun and I saw tomorrow without me. He fired. Over my shoulder a man groaned and fell to the ground, a crimson jet spouting from the hole in his throat like a burst drain.

Calum Bishop said, 'Strike one for our team.'

My reaction should've been gratitude – he'd saved my life – instead, it was anger. 'Your fucking team? Christ Almighty! I thought it was me you were shooting at.'

His lips pressed in a thin line and I knew he'd considered it. Bishop said, 'Don't tempt me. Giordano's getting away. Somebody should go after him.'

I was too stunned to move. 'You mean, you're not—'

'I'm telling you he's getting away.'

'Yeah, but it's the other one I want.'

'Mura? We've got him.'

'Why're you doing this?'

He looked up at the sky and back to me. 'We should get going, the police will be here any minute and I don't fancy explaining all this, do you?'

'Help me understand. Why?'

'Listen, don't read too much into it, Glass – you don't owe me or any of that bollocks. Let's just say I prefer people who stick to the deal.'

'You might be sorry you said that.'

'No, I won't. You've had a good run. One day it'll end.'

'And you'll be there.'

'And I'll be there.'

34

Giordano opened the car door and threw himself inside, frantically shouting orders to the man behind the wheel. 'Go! Fucking go!'

He didn't register it was the same guy who'd picked him and Mura up outside the club and taken them to Limehouse. The driver put his foot to the floor and took off at speed with a terrified Giordano peering anxiously out of the back window to see if anybody was coming after them. On Kentish Town Road two police vehicles, sirens wailing, blue lights flashing, raced past in the opposite direction: it had all gone horribly wrong and the priority now was to get as far away as he could. The driver observed him, white-faced and sweating in the rear-view, a shadow of the arrogant bastard who'd stood by while his friend brutally murdered the hookers in the lane off Narrow Street; he wasn't so sure of himself now.

'Where're we going?'

Giordano barked his reply. 'The Dorchester. Move it!'

He felt a stinging sensation above his elbow and fingered the cloth. He'd been lucky: the material was frayed where the bullet had ripped a hole in the sleeve of his Armani jacket and gone straight through. In seconds, his arm was on fire, hurting like a bitch.

When they stopped at traffic lights at the bottom of Hampstead Road, he said, 'Give me your jacket.'

The driver didn't understand. 'What?'

Giordano held up his gun. 'Don't argue, your fucking jacket, give it to me.'

The man reluctantly handed it over. Giordano took it and tried to relax; panic was the enemy. He was packed; all he had to do was collect his case and get on the first plane from Heathrow out of this goddamned country.

They turned left into Park Lane. At the hotel entrance, Giordano folded the borrowed jacket over his bloodied arm and started to get out. He said, 'Wait. I'll be back in five minutes. You can take me to the airport.'

The man behind the wheel didn't acknowledge him. Giordano roared at him. 'Are you hearing me or do I have to blow your fucking head off?'

'I hear you.'

The driver watched his passenger disappear inside, engaged the gears, and pulled away. Under his breath, he whispered, 'Fuck you, mister.'

In his room Tony Giordano lifted his case off the bed and took the stairs to the sixth floor. It would be over; the old witch would be dead, but he couldn't resist spitting on her corpse.

Giordano opened the door with his key card and went inside; the curtains were drawn, it was dark, and as his eyes adjusted he saw the outline of a figure and assumed it was Madeline. His fingers searched the wall for the light and switched it on: Roberta Romano gazed at him over the muzzle of a gun that, until a moment ago, had been pointed at his grandmother in the other chair. Giordano ignored the old woman and spoke angrily to the assassin.

'Why isn't it done? Why is she still alive?'

Roberta was unfazed: the reaction was expected. She casually brushed a strand of blonde hair away from her face, revealing the scar on her cheek. 'We've been waiting for you.'

'That wasn't what we agreed.'

'You're right, it wasn't. Don't you have anything to say to your grandmother? No final words?'

Giordano took a step forward. 'I paid you to kill this bitch. Do it or give the gun to me and I'll do it myself.'

Madeline listened to them discuss her death and wasn't afraid. They didn't get it. How could they? The years without Silvestro had been empty, as first Beppe and then Antoine had presided over the decline of what he'd built. Ending her life would be a mercy. Her grandson had arranged this – maybe even before they'd left New Orleans. If he'd had the chance Beppe would've done the same, cried crocodile tears at her funeral and, later, drunk champagne from a whore's shoe.

These people could do whatever they liked. It didn't matter; she was ready to die, and she'd been ready for a long time.

Roberta raised the gun. 'Don't worry, Mr Giordano, you'll get your money's worth.'

The bullet exploded in Madeline's chest; she was dead before the second shot left the chamber. Giordano nodded. 'All right. Good. But if you want to work for me again, next time follow instructions.'

Roberta trained the barrel on him, a manicured fingernail tightening on the trigger.

'I am following instructions. Bruno Mura sends his regards.'

* * *

In line with the rest of the flat, the sofa Felix Corrigan had bunked down on in St John's Wood was bigger and more comfortable than his own bed, yet he hadn't been able to sleep for worrying about Nina and what was happening in Kentish Town. In the old days, when Danny was head of the family and Albert Anderson was the enemy, he'd been a foot soldier in the thick of the action. No denying he'd come a fair way from there to running the East End. But this new role, albeit only until Nina was clean, didn't sit well with him. Although the men Luke trusted to protect his sisters could be counted on one hand, Felix saw it as a punishment. Once the sisters were safe he should've been shoulder to shoulder with him at the house. Because he was pissed, George had reduced him to a glorified babysitter. The Geordie had a long memory; crossing him wasn't wise, as the very few who had would confirm – if they were still breathing. But Felix wasn't a fool. He also realised George Ritchie had done him a favour – with his mind on Nina instead of the Americans, in a shooting war he'd be a bloody liability.

The doctor came out of the room carrying his bag. Felix got up, immediately anxious.

'Is she all right?'

'She's fine. Whether she stays fine is really up to her.'

He walked to the door. Felix blocked his path. 'Sorry, you can't leave, not until Luke or George say so.'

The doctor sighed. 'What more do you want me to tell you? Her heart rate's normal, her blood pressure is 124 over 84. Remarkable considering what she'd been through. There's nothing more for me to do here. People need me. Sick people.'

A noise made Felix turn round. Nina stood in the bedroom door, pale, clearly weakened by her ordeal but with a fire in her eyes he'd seen more often than he could recall. Her lips were chapped, the voice coming from them hoarse. 'For Christ's sake, stop being an old woman and let him go. I'm okay. We have to talk.'

Felix closed the door behind the doctor and sat next to her to the sofa. Nina said, 'I owe you an apology. More than one, actually. The way I've behaved is inexcusable. If you can't forgive me, I'll understand.'

'That was the drugs, that wasn't you.'

She smiled a sad smile and gently took his face in her hands. 'You're sweet, Felix, do you know that? But excuses won't work any more. Unless I'm completely honest with myself I'll slip back into the abyss.'

'No, I won't let you.'

'You won't be able to stop me. Nobody will. Pinning the blame for who I am on drugs is too easy. They've played a part, sure, but it isn't the whole story.'

'Then tell me what is.'

'I was fucked up before I started messing with that stuff. I've always been fucked up. Danny couldn't handle me.' She laughed out loud. 'Imagine that. South London's psycho-in-chief, Danny Glass, couldn't cope with a teenage girl. He was scared of me. Mark Douglas was the only man I'd ever met who could stop me wanting to destroy myself. Because, believe me, without knowing it, that's what I'd been doing. All my life.'

Felix took her hand in his. 'You don't have to explain. Maybe—'

'Except I do, Felix. I need to hear it more than anybody else. Will you let me tell it my way?'

'Of course.'

Nina took a deep breath. 'I remember that morning as clearly as if it was yesterday. Luke woke me up. His eyes were wet. He'd been crying. Danny was in the kitchen cooking breakfast; his shirt sleeves were rolled back; he'd been crying, too. And I realised that while I'd been asleep something bad had happened to our family. When Danny sat me down and told me Frances – our mother – had left us, I didn't cry. But from that moment there was an empty space in me I couldn't fill no matter how hard I tried. And I did try. With boys and men and drink and drugs. Over the years, all kinds of embarrassing "rebel" shit.' She paused and stared at her hands. 'Or maybe that's just how I see it now. Maybe I was always going to make everybody around me unhappy. Then, I found Mark. I trusted him, trusted him with my life, and I was wrong. Completely, absolutely, terribly wrong, Felix. Suddenly, I was back at the start, a little kid who'd woken up to discover she'd been betrayed. Again. Except, this time I did cry and kept on crying.'

Felix didn't interrupt. Telling her story out loud was the first step on the road back. Nina needed a friend she could depend on not to let her down. He'd be that friend. Perhaps... He cut the thought short but it didn't die. It whispered to him. Maybe some day.

* * *

Of all the things I'd inherited from my brother – and I'd inherited a few – Fulton Street was the one I hated most. I'd been in Wandsworth prison serving seven years for helping Albert Anderson off the forty-third storey of a building in Bishopsgate when Danny bought the freehold. On the days when he wasn't being a paranoid psycho he could be a shrewd businessman. The building was derelict, the slate roof caved in long since, the brick-work rotted and crumbling. His original intention had been to demolish it and hold onto the land long enough to see a respectable profit on his investment. Somewhere along the way he'd found another use for it as his own private abattoir.

Fulton Street was a London underworld legend: a place of execution you wanted at all costs to avoid. For 170 years the Victorian factory south of the river had witnessed man's inhumanity to his fellow man: women and children had been cruelly exploited for coin and, when they were broken and no longer fit to earn their masters' money, left to starve in the gutter. To the best of my knowledge, Danny hadn't starved anybody but he'd added his singular brand of retribution to the list of atrocities.

So had I. And I was about to again.

Limehouse had been the work of a madman and our guys had taken their revenge for Aisha and Zia: Bruno Mura was naked, his right eye swollen shut, and his head lolling on a body the colour of wax covered in purple bruises. They dragged him through the rusted iron door, his shoeless feet trailing on the flagstone slabs, and dropped him on a wooden pallet. He didn't get up: he couldn't. Knowing what this nightmare of a human being had done to my mother, it was impossible to feel anything other than revulsion.

When Charley arrived from nowhere claiming to be our long-lost sibling we'd been suspicious. George Ritchie, especially, hadn't been convinced. Neither had I, but in the end I'd believed because I'd wanted to believe, and I let Charley spin half-truths into a selective history that had kept the awful reality hidden.

I wasn't angry; I pitied her for the pain she'd endured alone and fantasised about what I'd do to the sick bastard who'd so brutally murdered our mother.

That time had come.

Ritchie gave the order to tie Mura to the wood; somebody – I couldn't say who – handed me his knife. I ran the tip of my finger over the serrated edge, imagining the damage it had done in the hands of this sadist, until light from the hole in the caved-in roof flashed off the blade and broke the spell.

As the ropes tightened on his wrists and ankles, Mura moaned. This man had mutilated the woman who'd given birth to me, and roasted her alive. Now, I had him where I wanted him: I should've been satisfied. Instead, I felt a crushing sadness for the people whose lives he'd so callously ended. I knew of three – there were countless others.

Slicing pieces off him while his screams echoed in the rafters, startling roosting birds into flight, wouldn't change anything: that ship had sailed the night a pregnant Frances abandoned her kids and ran away. And it would make me the same as him.

I couldn't live like that – what was coming was revenge enough.

The knife slipped from my fingers to the floor. Ritchie took it as a sign and nodded to his men to go to the cars. They returned with petrol – fourteen cans, more than enough – and poured it from the entrance to the back of the building, then in a zigzag line from one side to the other all the way to the pallet balanced on its edge at an angle against the wall.

I needed him to be aware, like she'd been aware, of what was happening and feel the pain he'd caused her. Bruno Mura would have the best seat in the house as an agonising death raced across the concrete floor, coming for him. And maybe in the final seconds before he was consumed he'd remember a sick old woman in a cabin nine miles from the Canadian border.

The men threw cold water on him and slapped his face to bring him round. He stirred and smelled the fuel; his one good eye opened and he screamed. When they doused him, Mura struggled like a drowning man, spluttering and crying and fighting the ropes in vain as petrol fumes rose off him like a dawn mist over the Channel.

There was no escape. His sins had caught up with him.

George laid a hand on my shoulder. 'Sure about this, Luke?'

'Absolutely.'

'Okay.'

Mura's mouth was set in a rictus of terror, white balls of spittle gathered in the corners, his teeth clamped shut against the pain he was already enduring. I hunkered down and whispered in his ear.

'This doesn't begin to even the score, but it'll make me feel a whole lot better.'

From the open door I heard Ritchie call to me. 'Ready when you are.'

A chrome lighter appeared in his hand, the blue and orange flame that would reduce Fulton Street to a blackened shell flickered and I savoured the moment, the last of its kind. Whatever the future held for my family, this hellhole of human misery would play no part in it.

George Ritchie was where he always was: at my side.

I said, 'Fire it up, George. Fire the bastard place up.'

EPILOGUE

Stevie D put his Rock Rebel boots up on the workbench and tried to relax. He felt uneasy without knowing why. Except, that wasn't true – he did know. Calum Bishop wasn't answering his calls. Strange, because he'd seemed pleased, delighted even, when he'd told him about supplying the Glass woman and given him something to hold over her brother. How Bishop used the information was his business but having a junkie for a sister didn't fit with the south London gangster's new-found respectability.

Stevie had finished with the Yamaha: it was looking good and ready to go. He'd lost interest: his dream of opening a bike repair shop had faded. It didn't excite him as much it had; there were bigger dreams than spending his life up to his elbows in motor oil. The coffee he'd made when he arrived had gone cold. Or was that yesterday? He drank it anyway, rolled his first joint in years, and considered giving Bishop's number another go.

The newspaper, smeared with axle grease, was days old. Buying it had been a right waste of money. Normally, Stevie didn't bother with them – all bollocks, in his opinion. He'd got this one from a stand in King's Cross, drawn by the headline.

GUN BATTLE IN NORTH LONDON

The report underneath was short on detail and long on specu-
lation. Vague phrases like, 'A number of bodies have been found
at a house in Kentish Town after neighbours reported what
sounded like gunshots.' Or put another way: *we haven't a fucking
Scooby so this will have to do you until we find out.* Stevie D didn't
know either, though he'd bet money it was connected to what
he'd told Bishop.

Somebody hammered on the corrugated shutter door. Kids,
probably, making a bloody nuisance of themselves, thinking they
were funny. Well, they'd picked the wrong day, hadn't they? He
threw a spanner that clattered off the metal. 'Get out of it before I
kick your arse!'

The banging came again, echoing in the lock-up. The mechanic
took his feet off the bench and started out of his chair. 'You... D'you
hear me, you little bastards? If I have to run after you...'

'Open up, Stevie! It's Calum Bishop! Let me in!'

Wanting to speak to Bishop and wanting him to come looking
for you were different things and Stevie suddenly felt nervous.

Bishop wasn't alone – when was he ever? Pockmark, the
shadow who followed him everywhere, was behind him along with
two guys he hadn't seen before crowding into the space. Calum ran
a finger over the Yamaha's gleaming silver chassis and inspected
the tip of it for dust. 'So this is what you do when you aren't selling
to vulnerable women?'

Vulnerable? Had he actually said that?

'Don't know what you mean, Mr Bishop.'

'Yeah, you do, Stevie. I mean Luke Glass' sister?'

'She was in a bad way. I could've turned her down, instead I
helped her out. What should I have done?'

Bishop's bald head shone under the strip light. He lifted a

torque wrench and slapped it into his palm. 'Retire gracefully like we agreed. You decided to keep operating. That was naughty.'

Stevie guessed where this was going and blurted out his defence. 'It was a one-off, honest, Calum.'

Pockmark growled, 'Mr Bishop to you.'

Stevie apologised. 'Sorry. Yeah, it was a one-time thing. Just that time. She was hurting; I did her a turn. If she'd gone to some wide boy they could've palmed her off with baking soda or laundry detergent. All kinds of crap that would've sent her straight into withdrawal.'

Bishop sat on the edge of the bench, still holding the wrench. 'Let me get this right. You helped her out, yeah?'

'Yeah.'

'One time. Is that what you're telling me?'

Stevie sensed danger. He'd backed himself into a corner: it had been more than once and they both knew it.

Pockmark played to his boss. 'Mr Bishop's asking you a question. Answer him.'

'I meant it was just her. Nobody else. That was how I twigged where the woman was. You were pleased.'

'True, Stevie, but weren't you told in Dollis Hill that you were out of business? No exceptions. I thought I'd made myself clear. Am I right or am I right?'

Bishop raised an eyebrow and waited for a reply. This wasn't what Stevie had expected. Nothing like. He'd found fucking Nina Glass, hadn't he? Calum Bishop should've been shaking his hand, praising him, maybe even slipping some coin his way for a job well done. He said, 'You're right. It won't happen again.'

Calum slowly clapped his hands. 'At last we agree on something. But here's the thing – the junkie you fed was my new partner's sister, which kind of puts me in an awkward position.' He saw the expression on Stevie's face and qualified the remark. 'Well, not exactly my partner. Still, stranger things and all that, eh? But you can see where I'm coming from?'

'What're you saying? What're you saying, Mr Bishop? I thought—'

'I'm saying it is what it is, Stevie. Don't take it personally.'

The two men who'd been silent grabbed him and held his arms. Bishop brought the wrench down hard on his nose, shattering it so badly shards of broken bone broke the skin. Stevie fell to the floor howling. Blood gushed into his eyes, blinding him; he swallowed and tasted copper. Bishop beat him with the metal tool, again and again, until he stopped moaning. The grunts carried him unconscious to the rusted meat hook embedded in the wall and looked to their boss for approval. Calum Bishop nodded. Pockmark helped raise the dealer up and ram his body against the brick. It took three attempts before the hook entered Stevie D's back and pierced a lung. His mangled head bobbed in a macabre dance as crimson air bubbles gurgled and popped on his lips.

Luke Glass hadn't demanded the dealer's death but he wouldn't be unhappy to hear about it. And that would make two favours Calum was owed.

No rush. He'd collect them in his own sweet time.

At the door, he glanced at the Yamaha Stevie had spent so many hours restoring and spoke to Pockmark. 'Get the keys of this thing and bring it with you. I need a hobby.'

* * *

The FedEx logo was an impressive piece of design that had won over forty awards. It was easy to see why – the arrow hidden between the purple and orange fonts was genius. More interesting was why anybody would be sending anything to me.

George Ritchie read my mind. 'You've got a secret admirer.'

'I hope not. Life's complicated enough.'

He watched me rip the cardboard open and spill the contents into my palm. We'd both seen the amber nugget on the heavy gold chain before; Tony Giordano had worn it round his neck when he'd come to the club. He wouldn't be needing it but whoever had put a bullet in him had taken a souvenir. Nice of them to think of me. I dangled the stone between my fingers so Ritchie had a better view. I said, 'Is it real?'

Ritchie turned it in his hand, studying the air bubbles that had been imprisoned millions of years ago. 'A jeweller would tell you in ten seconds, I'd guess yes, though it's probably meant to be symbolic.'

'Symbolic of what?'

George shook his head. 'Who knows? Is there anything else?'

'No.'

'Obviously, it meant something to Giordano, otherwise why wear it? Charley might be able to tell you. Ask her.'

'I will if I ever see her long enough. She's with Eamon Brannagan in his flat in St John's Wood. He's found a reason to grow up and doesn't want to let her out of his sight.'

'Give her a call.'

'No, after what she's been through she deserves a break.'

It was the conversation of winners but I had something to say. I'd waited for the right moment: this was it. 'How did you and Felix know?'

A shadow crossed behind his eyes. I wasn't the only one who'd been waiting. He bought himself a couple of seconds with a question of his own; it wouldn't change anything.

'How did we know what?'

'That Nina had a dealer.'

Ritchie wanted to deny it and save his friend. Fortunately, for all of us, he didn't and our relationship could go on: to lie now would've ended it. He said, 'Luke, listen to me. By accident Felix discovered how far off the rails Nina had gone and tried to deal with it himself. He made a mistake.' He glanced apologetically down at his hands. 'We both did.'

'You're telling me Felix kept Nina's addiction from you, then you kept it from me.'

'Yes.'

I breathed deep and exhaled slow; it helped. 'You should've come to me, George. I'm disappointed.'

The force of his reply took me by surprise. 'No, I shouldn't. You had enough on your plate with the Giordanos. I decided to handle it. And I'd do the same again. So, if you need to blame somebody, blame me.'

'It isn't about blame. Just don't make a habit of keeping me in the dark or we're going to fall out, okay? As for Felix and Nina, anything to know?'

'Only that he's the best friend she'll ever have.'

'And you and her?'

Ritchie didn't commit himself one way or the other. 'That depends.'

'On what?

'On which Nina comes out of the rabbit hole. I promise you'll be the first to know.' He looked at his watch. 'When's Bishop due?'

'One o'clock.'

'It's almost that now. I'm off. And a word to the wise. Don't believe anything he says. He's north, we're south, and that's how it works best. His uncle Kenny was a reptile. His nephew is a chip off the same block. Get into bed with him on anything and we'll regret it.' He stood and made the sign of the cross. 'Here endeth today's lesson.'

I laughed. 'You're not wrong, George. We're resetting the lines.

Calum's a greedy bastard. A lucky greedy bastard. He's got where he is because of his uncle. His ultimate ambition is to have it all.'

'And why not?'

'Why not, indeed, but he's going to have to go through you and me to get there.'

'And Felix.'

'Yeah, and Felix.'

* * *

Calum Bishop didn't arrive at one. Or even two. It was ten minutes to three before he made an appearance. The tan leather jacket had been swapped for a three-quarter-length coat in the same material and he was riding a metallic-silver Yamaha. Clearly, he had a thing about leather and I made a mental note to google the deeper meaning. When he took off the crash helmet I realised the new image included his head: rather than wait for what little hair he had left to fall out, he'd shaved it. If he liked it, fine. I couldn't have cared less – but fair dos, he'd done all right in Kentish Town. If he'd thrown in with the Americans it might've been a different result.

Bishop scratched his chin. 'Your sister, how is she?'

'Which one? I've got two.'

The conversation had been going for thirty seconds and already it was heading in the wrong direction. If he said 'the junkie' I'd beat his egg head to a pulp.

Bishop was smarter than that. 'Nina, isn't it?'

'She's okay. Thanks for asking.'

'The guy who was dealing to her is... not in that business any more.'

'Again, thanks.'

'Don't mention it. Maybe some day you can return the favours?'

Plural. It didn't escape me. I didn't rise to it.

'Is there something you wanted to discuss?'

'Discuss? No. There's nothing to discuss but if some foreign fuckers come around, feel free to give me a shout.'

'Good to know.'

'That's what neighbours are for, or am I wrong?'

I'd had enough of his horseshit to last me till Christmas, though there was one thing maybe he could answer. 'You supplied the firepower, which makes you better placed than most to know.'

'Know what?'

'Who shot the Giordanos?'

He shrugged. 'For sure, the old woman was Tony. Had to be Mura who did for him. Set up a hit he didn't see coming.'

'The man who would be king.'

Bishop yawned; he wasn't interested. 'Not any more he isn't. The bodies are still at the mortuary with tags on the toes. Nobody's claimed them.'

'Nobody left to claim them. The Giordanos have ceased to exist.'

for one family to survive another must perish

He said, 'Good news for some back in the Big Easy. If they can stop killing each other long enough to realise the city's on a plate for them. Lucky bastards.'

Another pop that didn't escape me; Calum couldn't help himself. There wasn't much anybody could tell this guy about lucky bastards: he was one of them. Bishop ploughed on unburdened by insight, personal or otherwise. He smiled. 'I'm assuming that psycho's no longer with us. Bet that was sweet.'

He'd never know how sweet.

Bishop got up. At the door he said, 'Is this the best job in the world or is that just me?'

Two minutes after he left, Ritchie reappeared. I said, 'Thought you'd gone, George.'

'While that snake is slithering around, no chance.'

'In case you've forgotten, "that snake" pulled our nuts out of the fire. Unfortunately, he knows it. Imagines it'll count for something next time we cross paths.'

'Not with me it won't.'

He took a folded piece of paper from his inside pocket and passed it to me. 'Meant to give you this.'

'What is it?'

'Charley wrote it for you before it all kicked off. But it's ancient history. We've had a result, your sisters are safe. I'd tear it up and put it in the bin if I were you.'

I read the first line and understood what I held in my hand.

'Except, here's the thing: you're not me, George.'

* * *

I hadn't seen Charley since Kentish Town. She was avoiding me and that was okay; she'd come when she was ready. Until then, the Irish actor was exactly the distraction she could use. When I'd called Eamon Brannagan and told him I needed somewhere for her to hide, he'd agreed to let us have his flat without asking questions. But I missed the energy of the foxy lady, brassy and full of light, who'd arrived in my life claiming she was my sister and had a birth certificate to prove it.

The clack-clack-clack of high heels on the concrete stairs told me the wait was over.

The first time we'd met she'd come through the door of the office like a tornado. This was a different Charley: she'd lost weight and her inner light was dimmer than it had been. The note Ritchie had given me was on my desk. She clocked it immediately and bowed her head so I couldn't see her face and what it would reveal.

'So George gave it to you? Thought he would. I'm more trouble than I'm worth, aren't I?'

'Yes, but don't sweat it, everybody is.'

'Yeah, but...'

'Everybody is, Charley.'

'I've been a bloody fool.'

'There's a lot of it about. I'm your brother. No more secrets.'

She didn't respond and I asked again. 'Do you hear what I'm saying, Charley?'

Her eyes strayed to the crumpled paper and the spidery scrawl. 'Yes. No more secrets. I'll tell you anything, anything you want to know. About me. About the past. All of it.'

'That's good because I have a question. Think carefully before you reply. And I need a straight answer.'

'Okay.'

'When are you coming back to work? Asking for a friend.'

* * *

The maître d's smile was warm and welcoming, honed by years of practice. This was my first visit to the restaurant and it felt like coming home. His accent was French; he probably spoke two or three languages fluently and could get by in another couple. His fingers, like everything about him, were elegant – long and tapered. He steepled them, glanced at the Manila envelope in my hand, and got ready to enquire if I had a reservation. I didn't. And it wouldn't matter a damn. Because for all his polish and professionalism he was a guy with a life to finance, maybe a young wife to keep sweet, and kids to feed. When I slipped a fifty into the breast pocket of his cream jacket he stood aside and let me pass. The great ones in his profession anticipated their customers' needs and accommodated them. He'd certainly done that.

Being here reminded me of my doomed lunch with the oily Jocelyn Church – an experience I'd no intention of repeating, today or any day. The air hummed with the drone of conversation as I scanned the dining room. Rupert Neville's jaw fell when he saw me. He was alarmed and he should be – together with his chum he'd set me up for a murder I'd refused to commit, an act that was about to be answered for. They'd both get what was coming to them – Church already had. Neville was the next name on a very short list. But he wasn't the only name, although I struggled to pronounce the others.

It had taken a couple of days to figure out how best to use the information Ritchie had unearthed. The Skytrain was as ambitious as anything proposed for London in decades. To make the project a reality took money – a shedload of money. Neville and Church were no more than window dressing. Unimaginative establishment dolts. Thanks to George, I knew who was financing it and if their identities were suddenly plastered across the front page of *The Telegraph* or the *Mail*, public opinion would make certain it died on the drawing board.

That might happen anyway without my help. In case it didn't, what I had in mind would redress the balance and then some.

There were five seats and four people – Rupert Neville and three strangers: men who'd been born old. Too much vodka had thickened their necks, and when they looked at me their eyes were dead. The empty chair was reserved for Jocelyn Church. He wouldn't be needing it.

I started to sit down. One of the Russians planted his chubby palm on the seat. 'It's taken.'

I threatened him with a smile. 'You're right, it is. Taken by me.'

Neville took a stab at asserting himself. What a prick! He said, 'I suggest you make yourself scarce, Glass, before you embarrass both of us even more than you did in Yorkshire.'

Fucking rich coming from him: the last time I'd seen him a seven-stone hooker had been propping him up and he couldn't have strung two words together if his life had depended on it.

The idiot had forgotten, assuming he could flex his upper-class privilege whenever he felt like it. Not with me. I said, 'Good to see you, too, Rupert. Tell your sister I'm sorry about turning her offer down, but I make a point of not fucking any woman who's had the Household Cavalry between her legs.'

His cheeks reddened. If he'd had a riding crop handy I would've felt it on my plebeian back. 'You're a disrespectful bastard not fit for decent company.'

'A lot of people say that.'

'Why're you here?'

'I came to tell you that approximately fifty-five minutes ago, Jocelyn Church was on his way to Charing Cross police station and by this afternoon will be helping the police with their enquiries.'

'Ridiculous; what's he done?'

I leaned my elbows on the pristine white table cover, poured a glass of Far Niente Chardonnay from the bottle chilling in the ice bucket beside me, and shot a look at the po-faced Ruskies. 'Done? Nothing yet. This is still England, our very own green and pleasant land, not some fucking police state. Surely you mean what's he suspected of doing? Innocent until proven guilty and all that bollocks. Although, the kiddie porn on his computer and the coke upstairs in the bedroom will make a pretty compelling argument. Under the Child Protection Act of 1978, even saving an indecent image to a hard drive is considered to be making the image, did you realise that?' I drew away as though he suddenly smelled bad. 'Come to think of it, of course you did.'

I lowered my voice to a whisper. 'The bit I really don't get is the anonymous caller who tipped off the police. How could he know old Joss was living a double life? I mean, you're his oppo – and by the by, sincere apologies for that comment about Daphne. Below the belt. Then everything is with her, isn't it? Did you suss Church was a perv? Makes you think, doesn't it? Strange how all the people you thought were odd turn out to be... odd.'

Whatever he'd taken had made him brave; he sneered his contempt. 'Since when does a fucking gangster have the moral high ground?'

'It's a fair question, Rupert, give you that much. Let's see if this answers it.' I emptied the envelope and spread the photographs on the table so his companions could have a good look at what His Lordship got up to in his spare time.

The girls were Asian. All very young. All very naked. All three of them.

Neville shook his aristocratic head. 'I won't be blackmailed, so you can forget it, Glass.'

'You're right, you won't be. Copies are being sent to the newspapers as we speak. Buying your way out isn't an option this time. Your old girlfriend, Madam Chang, keeps a diary. Apparently, she has stories about you going back thirty years. The tabloids will be falling over themselves to cross her palm with silver. My advice would be to wait for the book deal.'

'She's a dried-up old Chinese tart.'

'Yeah, and you're finished, Lord Holland.'

One of the Russians had heard all he was prepared to listen to. He reached out and gripped my arm. 'Okay, we've seen the show. What do you want, Mr Glass?'

'Simple. I want a seat at this table. I want in.'

He translated for his associates; their fat lips parted, their broad peasant shoulders rocking with laughter. When he came back to me he was grinning. 'You British.' He wagged an admonishing finger. 'Have you even the slightest idea what you're asking? How much a seat like that is worth?'

'What it's worth now, no. What it's worth after the press are told who's really behind the Skytrain, I'd guess marginally more than fuck all.'

I held out my hand. 'Do we have a deal?'

* * *

This is what I know: for most of my life it had been Danny and Luke and Nina. Now, it was Luke and Nina and Charley: the children Frances and Daniel John Glass had brought into the world. Shitty parents, though I didn't judge them; a mismatched couple playing a losing hand from the start and, in the tradition of these things, tainting their kids with their own weaknesses. They would've succeeded, too, if my brother hadn't imagined a different future and gone for it. Who we were was because of him. Not because of me. Fighting our way out of the dysfunction we'd been born into had left us flawed, fucked-up people, yet Danny's ambition, as ruthless as it had been, had lit a fire that wouldn't be denied.

And I was a believer, the vow written on my heart.

Family first. Family last. The Glass family always.

Cross us at your own risk. Go on, I dare you!

POSTSCRIPT

Madeline and Tony Giordano were buried in a public health funeral at Mill Hill cemetery. In the months following their deaths, New Orleans was gripped by unprecedented scenes of violence as rival gangs battled for control of the city.

Roberta Romano lives quietly, cooking and playing piano at her home in the Garden District. No information is available about the assassin known as La Réponse.

After four weeks in the Priory, Nina Glass joined Narcotics Anonymous and Alcoholics Anonymous. She attends meetings twice a week and hasn't had a drink or taken drugs in 162 days. No one suspects the quiet, plainly dressed woman who makes the tea and sits at the back of the room is a member of London's most powerful crime family.

Charley Glass ended her relationship with Eamon Brannagan after he had an affair with his co-star. She is currently unattached and managing LBC.

Luke Glass has returned to actively running his businesses. Asked in an interview by *City Insider Magazine* if he planned to retire, he answered 'God no, I'd only get into trouble.'

George Ritchie sold his basement flat in Moscow Road, Bayswater. His new address is unknown.

One month after the scandal hit the newspapers, Rupert Neville – Lord Holland – suffered a massive stroke at his home in Yorkshire. He never regained consciousness and died. His estate is in the process of being sold to cover death duties and debts, estimated at five million pounds.

Jocelyn Church was found guilty at the Old Bailey of possessing a Class A substance and of making child pornography. He was sentenced to six years in prison and is currently an inmate of HMP Whatton in Nottinghamshire where he continues to maintain his innocence.

Sadiq Khan, the Mayor of London, published an update to his bold 2018 strategy for the future of transportation in the capital, restating the commitment over the next two decades to record investment, improved capacity, a West London Orbital rail line, and a specific proposal for the Sutton Tram extension. A Skytrain isn't part of the vision.

ACKNOWLEDGMENTS

It would be natural to assume the process of writing gets easier with time, that once an author has been doing it for a while and happens on a strong idea, the rest – plot, characters, dialogue, place and pace – flow readily. In my case at least, the truth is far from that. Fortunately, I'm not in it by myself. A host of talented people have added their skills to this book beginning with the team at my publisher Boldwood Books. As always, Sarah Ritherdon is due a special mention for believing in me when others didn't, as well as Sue Smith and Candida Bradford, whose editorial input makes me look better than I am. My sincere thanks to each and every one of you.

And through it all, my wonderfully gifted wife, Christine, helping to shape every aspect of the story, reassuring me it was going to work when I was convinced it wouldn't, dredging her seemingly bottomless imagination in search of a fiendish twist or turn, pausing only to correct my dodgy grammar.

Without her, *Thief* wouldn't exist.

MORE FROM OWEN MULLEN

We hope you enjoyed reading *Thief*. If you did, please leave a review.

If you'd like to gift a copy, this book is also available as an ebook, digital audio download and audiobook CD.

Sign up to Owen Mullen's mailing list for news, competitions, updates and receive an exclusive free short story from Owen Mullen.

https://bit.ly/OwenMullenNewsletter

ALSO BY OWEN MULLEN

ABOUT THE AUTHOR

Owen Mullen is a highly regarded crime author who splits his time between Scotland and the island of Crete. In his earlier life he lived in London and worked as a musician and session singer.

Follow Owen on social media:

 twitter.com/OwenMullen6

 bookbub.com/authors/owen-mullen

 facebook.com/OwenMullenAuthor

Boldwood

Boldwood Books is an award-winning fiction publishing company seeking out the best stories from around the world.

Find out more at www.boldwoodbooks.com

Join our reader community for brilliant books, competitions and offers!

Follow us
@BoldwoodBooks
@BookandTonic

Sign up to our weekly deals newsletter

https://bit.ly/BoldwoodBNewsletter